Mrs Hudson & Sherlock Holmes: Book 1

A HOUSE
OF
MIRRORS

LIZ HEDGECOCK

WHITE
RHINO
BOOKS

ISBN-13: 979-8754424760

For Stephen,
my first and best reader

CHAPTER 1

221B Baker Street, 4th January 1881

When would he come?

I checked my watch for perhaps the fourth time in five minutes. Ten past two. I risked a peek at the street outside, buzzing with life on the crisp winter day; carriages rattling past, costermongers shouting their wares, nannies with perambulators, and couples arm-in-arm.

Don't be silly, Helen, I scolded myself. A grown woman of twenty-eight, behaving like a little girl on her birthday morning! I knew full well that between two and half past was the agreed time. I picked up a novel, *Edwin Drood*, to occupy myself, but my eyes kept straying from its pages to the window and the world beyond.

The doorbell pealed as though the person ringing it was annoyed at being kept waiting.

It was a quarter past two precisely. Billy ran down the stairs, and the front door creaked.

I rose, straightened my skirts, and glanced in the looking glass. All was in order except my expression, which was altogether too excited for a landlady-in-waiting. I breathed deeply to calm my racing heart, but the effort was wasted as I heard Billy's light steps in the passageway.

'Come!' I called.

Billy entered, grinning. 'He's here, ma'am. The man to see the rooms. Name of Holmes. Shall I show him in?'

'Yes please, Billy.'

***

Mr Holmes was a tall, spare young man, well-dressed in a frock-coat and top hat. Despite his height, he reminded me of an intelligent bird as his eyes darted around the room. He took my hand in a firm but delicate grip. 'Mrs Hudson, I am sorry for the circumstances which have led you to take in a lodger.' His hand was slim and long-fingered, but mottled with stains and little scars. Mr Holmes saw me examining his hand, and gently withdrew it.

I looked down at my black-trimmed dress. 'Thank you, Mr Holmes.' My voice remained steady, but my emotions were fighting to break free. There was excitement at what I was about to do, misgiving that it might be too early, curiosity about my visitor, and fear that this might not be what Jack would have wanted. But excitement and curiosity were winning the race. 'Would you like to see the rooms?'

He inclined his head. 'I would.'

***

I had expected Mr Holmes to ask questions as I showed him the suite of rooms which were to let, but he was quiet. I found myself babbling about breakfast preferences and domestic matters. 'There are two bedrooms, both opening off the sitting room…'

'Two bedrooms?' Mr Holmes raised his eyebrows. 'I was not aware of that.'

'Oh yes,' I said. 'I am sorry, I thought you had been informed.'

'No, Lestrade didn't mention it...' He wandered round the first bedroom, looking outside, opening drawers and cupboards, inspecting the washstand and the mirror. 'The room would suit me admirably, though. A good view of the street outside, excellent natural light, plenty of space for clothes...' He walked back into the sitting room, and I followed. 'How much do you propose to let the rooms for?'

I should say four guineas a week. That was what Inspector Lestrade said the agent had advised. 'Three pounds ten shillings?'

Mr Holmes let out a low whistle. 'That is more than I can afford at present, Mrs Hudson. I am in the process of establishing my practice, which is an expensive business, and my income is not steady as yet. The sitting room would be an excellent consulting room, though, and the address most respectable.'

'What is your profession, Mr Holmes?' I looked at him afresh, to deduce what sort of work he might do. Nothing manual, judging from his hands – but what of the stains and scars on them? Could he be a surgeon? But then he would not need a consulting room. That ruled out a scientist, too. He might be a sculptor, or another sort of artist, but then he would require a studio...

A low laugh shook me out of my speculations. 'You are trying to work me out, Mrs Hudson!' Mr Holmes looked at me from under his eyebrows. 'You won't guess, though. As far as I know, I am the only one of my kind. Your best clue is my connection to Inspector Lestrade.'

'Ah.' That explained the inspector's ready acquiescence when I had proposed taking a lodger, and his recommendation of the gentleman standing before me. 'You don't look like a policeman.' I tried to smile, but my mouth refused to obey. Jack was in the sitting room with me, striding in with a smell of London fog and smoke and outside about him. He would pull off his gloves, fling himself into the basket-chair and launch into a detailed account of the day's investigations. Perhaps another woman would have been bored, but I loved every minute of it, just as I loved Jack.

'Mrs Hudson, are you quite well? You looked a little...'

I waved a hand. 'I am quite all right, Mr Holmes. Just a – well, a memory.'

'Good, good.' He seemed a little distracted too, as if debating something with himself. 'Mrs Hudson, I shall be frank with you. I am setting up as a consulting detective. That is why I am seeking rooms, and I have seen none that would suit me so well as those you offer. I take it that you do not mind callers? Frequent callers?'

Now I was back on safe ground. 'No, not at all. I am likely to receive more visitors myself soon.' I indicated my half-mourning.

'And your staff would provide meals, and clean the rooms? Is that included in the price?'

I nodded.

'Then it is settled. I shall attempt to find a partner in these rooms, and contact you if I am successful.' Mr Holmes rose.

'If you can find someone to share the cost, I might be able to reduce the price to three guineas a week.' The words shot out of my mouth, and I blushed.

'Mrs Hudson, that would be extremely kind of you. I shall begin my enquiries immediately.'

I rang for Billy to show Mr Holmes out. Then I sank back onto the settee and clapped my hands to my burning cheeks. Soon I would become a landlady to two complete strangers, an occupation I knew nothing of. Soon I would be able to start my life again, and Mr Holmes had no idea that he was a key part of my plans.

CHAPTER 2

5 St James's Terrace, Clerkenwell, 13th September 1878

Helen Hudson is my third name. I was born Helen Marsden, though everyone called me Nelly. When I married Jack I became Nell Villiers. And now I am Mrs Helen Hudson, for my own safety.

The day that Jack disappeared began like any other. We breakfasted early. I was still in my dressing gown but Jack was fully dressed; not in uniform, but in what he called an 'unremarkable suit', designed not to attract attention.

'Which case is it today, Jack?' I poured him a cup of tea and took another piece of toast.

'Opium den in Limehouse, Nell. Today's the day we crack it open.' Jack smacked his fist into his palm.

'You haven't mentioned it before.'

'That's because it's one of Napper's cases. He's invited me along.' Jack crossed to the bureau and took his gun from the top drawer. He emptied the cartridges out of the barrel onto the table, and held it up to the light.

'Do you have to do that here?' I got up to clear the

breakfast plates.

'I'm going straight to Limehouse, Nell, and I can't afford a misfire.' Jack cocked the gun and smiled in satisfaction at the click.

'I'm sorry, Jack,' I said, as he reloaded the gun. 'Please be careful.'

'Don't worry, Napper and I will look out for each other, and we've got back-up.' He holstered the gun. 'Oh, that reminds me!' Jack put on his overcoat and rummaged in the pocket, bringing out a flattened roll of papers tied with string. 'The inspector asked me to give you this. I completely forgot last night, 'cos you were asleep when I got home.'

'What is it?' I took the bundle and worked on the string. 'Statements?'

'Yes, from the robbery in Bow. Lestrade asked if you would go through them and write him a short report. There's a map at the back. Now, I must be off.' Jack took the last slice of toast from the rack and kissed me on the cheek. The stubble he had missed that morning scraped at me.

'Will you be late tonight?'

He paused at the door. 'No, this should be a quick one. Expect me home for six; seven at latest.' He clapped his hat on his head and pulled the brim down. 'Goodbye, Nell.'

I fetched a notebook and pen, poured myself another cup of tea and pulled the papers towards me. There were at least fifty pages to work through. I marked the jeweller's shop on the map, and turned to his statement. After a few minutes I placed a hand on the tiny flutters in my stomach. I had meant to tell Jack the night before, but by the time he got home I had already fallen asleep. Then I had resolved that I would tell him this morning, but the gun on the table had put me off. *I'll tell him tonight*, I thought. *I'll cook him a steak, and I'll tell him tonight.*

6

By midday I had read the statements, marked the locations, plotted witnesses' movements, and listed contradictions and confirmations. I was ready to untangle the knotted snarl of the various accounts and weave them into a report. But my eyes ached from poring over the handwritten pages, my lower back twinged from sitting still so long, and I was starving. I ate a cheese sandwich then made another, even though the cheese tasted a little sour. Little Jack or little Helen was having a strange effect on my appetite. The cake tin was empty, which perhaps a good thing. Then I remembered the steak I was planning to cook that night. A walk to the butcher's shop would do me good.

'Mrs Villiers!' The butcher twinkled at me from behind his counter. The smells of sawdust, blood and meat mingled to make me quite faint, and I sat down hurriedly.

'Could I have two beefsteaks please, Mr Jones?'

'On a Friday, ma'am? Of course!' The butcher selected a piece of beef. 'A big one and a small one?'

'Could I have two the same, please?'

He raised his eyebrows, and selected a knife. 'I'll put these on your account, Mrs Villiers. Will you take them now?'

'I shall, thank you.'

At the greengrocer I purchased tomatoes and runner beans, and on my walk back home I bought two chocolate éclairs at the bakery. The shopgirl laid them side by side in a white cardboard box, and tied it with a blue ribbon. I wondered whether that meant I was carrying a boy, and almost laughed aloud at my silliness.

I climbed the few steps to the front door with a sense of relief that I was home; even the shortest journey was becoming a chore. The time was ripe to tell Jack the good news, before he could guess. I had enjoyed having my own little secret, though.

I put my purchases away, stirred the fire back into life, and settled to write my report, stopping only for tea and biscuits. By four o'clock I was making a fair copy. At a quarter to five I blotted the last sheet and placed my report in an envelope, ready for Jack to deliver to Inspector Lestrade. My right index finger was ink-stained, and my hair was coming down on one side. I smiled as I imagined delivering my news to Jack in such a state, and went to tidy myself and change my dress. I turned this way and that in front of the glass to see if I looked any different. Despite my near-constant hunger, I could still tight-lace. I took my hair down and brushed it out, and redid it into its bun on top of my head. Perhaps, if Jack was in the humour, he would unpin it for me later... I sat down in the basket-chair and picked up the *Illustrated London News* to try and distract myself from the vivid picture forming in my mind.

I started as the clock struck six, and looked down guiltily at the magazine, open at page five. I had dozed off again. At least Jack hadn't come home and caught me asleep. I walked into the kitchen and saw the parcel of steaks. Perhaps I should undo it – or I could wait, and unwrap it as a surprise for Jack, before my big surprise. I poked the fire, which had burned low, resumed my seat, and took up the magazine again.

A quarter past six. He would be home soon. He had said so.

Half past six. Jack had said between six and seven o'clock.

Twenty to seven. *He said he'd be home on time!*

At five minutes to seven I was pacing up and down. It would serve him right if I cooked the steaks and left his to grow cold. I wondered if he had talked Napper into a pint of ale at the Ship and Shovell, to celebrate their success. After all, Jack didn't know I had an announcement to make. I poked the fire and sat down. The last thing I wanted was to seem like

8

a nag, or a clinging vine. Once Jack knew about the baby, he would be home on time every night.

Or would he? We had never really spoken about children, beyond agreeing that we would like to have them. Not too many: no more than four, or perhaps five. I had been the oldest girl in a family of nine, and I recalled how tired my mother had always looked as she tried to get us bigger ones to do our share, encouraging us to turn the mangle or make the beds while she darned and knitted and nursed the latest addition to the family. I loved the peace of my life with Jack, the freedom to read and chat and take walks in the park without a thousand tiny hands pulling at us...

Where was Jack? The clock said ten past seven. That was more than enough time to have a drink with Napper and walk home.

By half past seven I had given up any pretence and sat by the window. An omnibus rattled past. A gang of boys ran by. And then a cab, a hansom cab slowing to a stop outside our house. Jack hardly ever took cabs; he said that they were an extravagance.

The door of the cab opened, and Inspector Lestrade stepped down. My heart fell to the ground and shattered. He saw me at the window and bowed his head.

'I'm so sorry, Mrs Villiers,' he said, standing at the door with his hat off. 'I have bad news.'

CHAPTER 3

221B Baker Street, 5th January 1881

'Telegram for you, ma'am,' said Billy.

I frowned as I pulled the flimsy paper from the envelope. Who would send me a telegram? I read: *Partner found viewing 221B 1pm today wire if inconvenient Holmes.*

'Any answer, ma'am? The boy's waiting.'

'No, Billy, no answer.' I slid the telegram into its envelope. 'Would you mind polishing the knocker on the front door? Mr Holmes is bringing someone to view the rooms.'

'Yes, ma'am!' Billy would be glad to have more people in the house, I reflected. He liked to be busy, and I had taken to devising little errands to keep him occupied.

At exactly one o'clock the bell rang and Billy ran to answer the door. I walked into the hallway and prepared to welcome my second prospective lodger. On the steps stood the tall figure of Mr Holmes, and next to him a thin, tanned man. Both men appeared excited, and composed themselves with difficulty as I advanced towards them.

'Mrs Hudson, may I introduce Dr Watson? He has expressed an interest in sharing the rooms with me.'

'Delighted,' I said, extending a hand to Dr Watson, who shook it with enthusiasm.

'Would you mind if we go up?' asked Mr Holmes.

'Not at all,' I said, and followed them upstairs.

As it turned out I could have saved my effort, as Mr Holmes showed Dr Watson round the rooms expertly, praising the views, the furnishings, and the cost in a proprietorial way. Dr Watson followed Mr Holmes around the rooms slowly, putting an occasional 'Quite so' or 'Indeed' into Mr Holmes's monologue. I wondered how they knew each other, and what Dr Watson had been doing abroad to get so brown.

'It is settled then!' Mr Holmes's cry broke in on my thoughts. 'We shall take the rooms, Mrs Hudson.'

'Well, that is good news,' I said, although now that the moment had come, I was less sure. 'When would you like to move in, gentlemen?'

'Now seems as good a time as any,' said Mr Holmes. 'I have some work to finish off at the laboratory, then I shall pack up my things for tomorrow morning. Watson, how about you?'

'I shall be glad to leave the hotel,' said Dr Watson, smiling. 'My belongings will pack into a couple of suitcases. I can move in tonight. Do you have anything in for supper, Mrs Hudson?'

'Well, now,' I said. 'Do you like lamb cutlets, Dr Watson?' I had planned them for our dinner, but I could make do with an omelette.

'I do!' he said. 'Holmes, will you join me?'

'I am afraid not, Watson,' said Mr Holmes. 'My lab work will keep me until late, and then I shall have to pack.'

'Supper for one, then, Mrs Hudson,' said Dr Watson, with the air of someone used to giving orders.

'Very well,' I said, feeling ridiculous. But the two men

11

took little notice of me as they walked round the room again, trying the chairs and discussing where they would hang their pictures. Billy had taken the dust sheets off the rooms not two days before, and they were already in someone else's possession. I noted again how bright the sitting room was compared to mine upstairs.

Dr Watson was true to his word, arriving in a cab just after six. He asked if Billy could assist him with his suitcases, and I saw that he held his left arm a little bent, as if it had been in a sling for a long time and had grown used to its confinement. I left him to put his things away, and brought supper up to him at nine, as requested. Already the sitting room looked different. A pipe-rack had appeared, along with some copies of *The Lancet*, and a pair of silver-framed photographs on the sideboard.

'Thank you, Mrs Hudson, that looks tasty.' He picked up the napkin and cutlery.

'I hope you like it,' I said.

He coughed, and I realised that he was waiting for me to go. 'Will that be all for tonight, Dr Watson?'

'Oh, I should think so,' he replied. 'Good night, Mrs Hudson.'

I went to bed early that night. I had not realised how much, over the past year and more, I had grown used to my own company. I shall not say, to doing as I pleased. I would never have chosen the cloistered, shuttered life I had lived for so many months. Waiting on Mr Holmes and Dr Watson would be a small sacrifice for the new freedoms which their presence in the house would allow.

CHAPTER 4

Unknown, September 1878

I woke up in a strange bed. My head felt thick and muzzy, yet light as well, and I was wearing a starched nightgown which wasn't mine. Carbolic soap and beeswax mingled in the air, and the sunshine hurt my eyes.

I focused with difficulty on the woman sitting at the end of the bed. She was wearing a nurse's uniform. 'I'm glad you're awake. You've been asleep a long time, Mrs Hudson.'

Who was Mrs Hudson? 'There must be some mistake,' I said. I tried to pull myself into a sitting position, but the effort was too much, and my head swam. I sank back onto my pillows. 'I'm not Mrs Hudson.'

'Yes you are.' The nurse thrust a piece of paper under my nose. On it was scrawled: *Mrs Hudson – complete bed rest until further notice. Laudanum p.r.n.* The note was signed by Dr Hayward, MD, Bart's Hospital.

'I'm not Mrs Hudson, even if the doctor says I am! Why am I here? What has happened?'

The nurse straightened the bedspread, then came to check my pulse. 'You must stay calm, dear. You don't remember why you're here?'

I shook my head. 'There's nothing wrong with me. I am never ill. Is this a hospital?' I only knew hospitals from the outside.

She pursed her lips. 'This is a nursing home. The doctor will answer your questions when he comes. I must go and attend to another patient.' The nurse patted my bedspread and bustled out of the room.

I craned my neck to see if the view from the barred window gave any clue to where I might be, but there was nothing but fields and trees. Why wasn't I in London? Bart's Hospital was in London, not far from my home, and surely I would have been taken there... How many days had I been away? And where was Jack? Something slipped out of reach in my brain, like a little boy running round a corner to hide, laughing at me. I shook my head to clear the fog inside. It must be the laudanum...

Laudanum was an addictive pain-killer and sleep-inducer, I recalled, from a book on drugs which I kept for reference. They could have kept me under for days. But that was dangerous. Dr Hayward must be an invention! But why? Why would anyone take me from London and put me to sleep? What else had the book said?

Laudanum, a tincture of opium, is a powerful analgesic—
Opium.
Opium den.

The inspector, standing in my parlour. 'Jack is missing.' He did not need to say more; his expression told it all. But I still pressed him for information, hoping beyond hope that there was a chance Jack might be safe.

Inspector Lestrade told me that the small back-up team, concealed in the streets around the opium den, had grown uneasy when there was no signal within the agreed time.

Eventually they stormed the den, coming in at every door and window. They searched each room, finding nothing but men lying in stupor, dead to the world. At the top of the building they broke open a locked door to find Napper bound, hooded and unconscious. He had been beaten to within an inch of his life. The open window led only to the river below. There was no sign of Jack, either in the building or the surrounding streets.

The door flew open and the nurse rushed in, followed by a man in a white coat bearing a bowl. 'Mrs Hudson!' he thundered. 'Stop that screaming at once!' He put the bowl aside and held me down in the bed by my arms. 'You will do yourself an injury with this hysteria! Calm yourself, or I shall calm you by force.'

There was no use in struggling against him, and I did my best to breathe deeply and compose myself. He released me, and I rubbed my sore arms. 'I don't understand why I'm here,' I said. 'Please could you tell me?'

The man in the white coat glanced at the nurse, and they conferred in the corner of the room. Then they walked back to my bedside. 'Mrs Hudson, will you promise to remain calm?'

I swallowed, and nodded.

The nurse crouched by my bed, and laid her hand on mine. 'Did you know you were pregnant, dear?' she said, and her eyes were full of kindness.

I turned my face away as the tears poured down.

'Never mind, Mrs Hudson,' the white-coated man said, 'perhaps you can try again.' The nurse flung him an angry look.

'I can never try again! I have lost everything!' I cried, and beat the bed with my fists, until he pressed the pad from the bowl over my nose and mouth, and my sobs drifted away.

CHAPTER 5

221B Baker Street, 6th January 1881

I hurried down to a key in the door at just after nine in the morning. Mr Holmes was laden with bags, which he deposited in the hallway just as the cabman came through the door with a large, square black box in his arms. 'Where shall I put this, sir?'

'Leave it in the corner, if you would. Carefully, now!' Mr Holmes went back outside. 'Can you give me a hand upstairs with this?' he called.

The cabman left, and a minute later his back reappeared followed by an enormous brown leather trunk, with Mr Holmes on the other end. They progressed jerkily up the stairs, and the trunk bumped down overhead. Mr Holmes gave the cabman half a crown, for which he tipped his hat. 'Good day to you, sir.'

'You're sure you haven't left anything behind, Holmes?' said Dr Watson, smiling.

Mr Holmes frowned. 'I hope not. This is my professional equipment.'

The rest of the morning and most of the afternoon was full

of scraping from the rooms below as the gentlemen moved the furniture about. I popped in to offer tea and luncheon, but they dismissed me over their shoulders, and took their lunch at a restaurant.

I peeped into their rooms, which reeked of tobacco, when they were out. Dr Watson's was quite plain, and apart from necessities the only ornament was a painting of a landscape over the mantel. Mr Holmes's room was overstuffed with belongings; a violin case, some half-assembled chemical equipment, neckties strewn on the bed. I had not expected him to be a dandy in the matter of clothes. In the sitting room the bookcase was filled with new volumes; apart from a few medical textbooks, a Bible, and a complete Shakespeare, all were penny dreadfuls. I opened the silver card case which lay on top of the bookshelf. *Sherlock Holmes, Consulting Detective. 221B Baker Street.* The card was a thick cream pasteboard, the black lettering deeply engraved. Mr Holmes had lost no time in getting established.

Over the next few days we settled into a routine. Mr Holmes would ring for hot water at seven, followed by breakfast at half past seven, while Dr Watson was close to two hours later in his habits. Neither required lunch as a rule, but both were usually in to dinner at half past six, followed by a light supper at half past nine. Mr Holmes's movements were unpredictable; he might go to the laboratory, or for a long walk, or lie on the settee scraping at his violin, my least favourite of his occupations. Dr Watson generally stayed at home in the mornings and took a walk to his club at midday, returning in the afternoon to read until dinner. At least, that was what I could gather, as both men were polite but sparing in their communications towards me.

One morning Mr Holmes was in a lethargic mood. He breakfasted at the same time as Dr Watson, and when I collected the breakfast things he was curled on the settee, staring into the fire, while Dr Watson was writing a letter at the bureau.

'Not going to the lab today, Mr Holmes?' I had to ask the question twice.

He flapped a hand at me. 'No, Mrs Hudson. I am thinking. Please do not disturb me.'

I raised an eyebrow at Dr Watson, who appeared oblivious to this exchange, and left the room laden with dirty crockery. As I carried the tray down I heard a low exclamation. 'What a busybody!'

The phlegmatic tones of Dr Watson replied, 'She's a childless widow, of course she's going to fuss.'

I thumped down the stairs resolving that I would engage a maid-of-all-work as soon as I could. Housekeeping for two rude, thoughtless gentlemen was a poor substitute for the analytical work I had done in the past, and now that I had two paying lodgers the expense was more than justified. I set Billy to wash the plates, and retired upstairs to compose an advertisement.

Before I sat down at the desk, though, I stood before the glass. I saw a woman in a plain purple dress, with her hair scraped back from her face. *A busybody, a childless widow.* I turned my back on her and took up my pen. The quicker I could get domestic help, the less time I would have to spend waiting on the ungrateful pair downstairs.

I had never written an advertisement before and the task was harder than I had imagined. I sat chewing the end of my pen, wondering what experience I should ask for, and how much I should expect to pay. I was roused by the sound of the front door closing. I glanced at my watch: a quarter to twelve. That would be Dr Watson going out, and I had wasted most of the morning. I decided to investigate what was in the larder.

Billy was sitting in the scullery, polishing a pair of brown boots. On the floor next to his chair were three more pairs. I found the remains of a joint of beef in the meat safe and carved off a slice for myself. 'Billy, would you like a roast-beef sandwich?'

'Yes please, ma'am.' Billy's eyes gleamed. I made two thick sandwiches and set one before him. He regarded the boots critically and put them down on a piece of newspaper. Of course! The newspaper would have a list of situations vacant, and I could base my advertisement on one of those.

'Billy, is the rest of that newspaper still in the house?'

The sandwich stopped halfway to his mouth. 'That's the last of it. It's a couple of days old, anyway. The gentlemen upstairs might still have today's, if they haven't burnt it.'

'Thank you, Billy.' I ate my sandwich with undue haste and wiped my mouth. 'I shall go and see.' I would combine the errand with an enquiry as to the best time to clean the rooms, as there was already a film of dust shrouding the mantelpiece.

I tapped lightly at the sitting-room door, but there was no response. Perhaps Mr Holmes had slipped out when I was upstairs. He was catlike in the lightness of his tread. I opened the door and walked in. The room was empty, and I spied a folded newspaper lying on the settee. I walked in and picked it up, and as I did so a little sound, like a sharp intake of breath, came from Mr Holmes's room.

'Mr Holmes, are you all right?' I called.

'Yes, quite all right, thank you.' His voice sounded high and nervous.

'I'm just borrowing yesterday's newspaper, if I may…'

'Yes, yes, that is perfectly all right.' Perhaps he was still thinking.

I advanced towards the sitting-room door, and a rustle from

Mr Holmes's room made me turn my head. The door was half open, and my eye was caught by the looking glass in the corner. It reflected a frightened-looking elderly vicar standing motionless against the near wall. Underneath the grey hair, bushy whiskers, and dog collar, Mr Holmes was just visible.

'What on earth!' I exclaimed.

'It is I, Mrs Hudson!' said the vicar, in Mr Holmes's voice. His head peeped round the door, and I am afraid I giggled, which made him scowl. 'It's a disguise,' he snapped.

I walked to his bedroom door and glimpsed the large trunk, standing open. It was packed with clothes, and a drawer full of wigs was pulled out. 'I had guessed as much, but why are you dressed as a clergyman?'

Mr Holmes adjusted his dog collar. 'I am shadowing the wife of a known criminal in the hope that she will reveal his whereabouts. Respectable old vicars tend to pass unnoticed.'

'I see.' Jack had rarely bothered with disguises, relying on a set of workman's clothes only when absolutely necessary.

'I shall try not to surprise you too often, Mrs Hudson. It is part of the job, though.' He grinned at me and the effect was so comical that I had to bite my lip to keep from laughing.

'That's quite all right, Mr Holmes. I am going for a short walk, so if you need anything, Billy will wait on you.'

I ran downstairs, dropped the gentlemen's newspaper on the hall table, and rammed my bonnet on my head. 'I am going to the park, Billy,' I called, and hurried down the road. I do not know how many people that afternoon saw me laughing as I walked the frosty paths. I did not care what they thought, either. I had not laughed for so long that I had forgotten what it felt like.

CHAPTER 6

Unknown, September 1878

I am not sure how many days I spent alone in that room, kept in a perpetual half-life by laudanum. When I woke I remembered Jack and my baby, both lost, and wailed for the nurse to help me sleep again.

She brought my meals on a tray: first thin gruel, then dry toast and beef tea, then a piece of steamed cod in white sauce. I pushed most of it around my plate and the nurse scolded me. 'You need to get your strength back, Mrs Hudson.'

'I'm not Mrs Hudson. Why do you keep calling me that?'

'That's the name you came in with.'

I ate another mouthful of cold fish. 'When can I leave?'

'When you're strong enough, and you're allowed. Now finish that plateful, dear.' She whisked out of the room, and I ate as much of the fish as I could stomach before drifting back into sleep.

I was woken by the clatter of curtains being drawn, and shielded my eyes from the bright light. 'Rise and shine! Hurry up now, you have a visitor waiting.'

I blinked and sat up. 'A visitor?' A list of possibilities ran through my head. My best friend Lottie? My sister Susan? One of my parents?

'Yes.' The nurse unhooked a dressing gown from the door and threw it onto the bed. 'Inspector Lestrade is outside, waiting for you to make yourself decent. Your slippers are by your bed, and there's hot water here.'

I wrapped myself in the dressing gown and slid my feet into the slippers. Both were at least two sizes too large for me. 'Do you have a comb?' My hair felt dirty and matted, and I wondered how long I had been confined to bed.

'That's better. I'll go and find one.'

The few steps to the washstand were the longest journey I had made since my arrival. I washed my face and hands, and braved the glass.

I barely recognised the woman peering back at me. She was pale and exhausted-looking, with red-rimmed eyes. Her lank hair hung down each side of her face as if it would pull her to the floor, and threads of grey showed among the brown. But this was no time to feel sorry for myself. I must get ready for the inspector, and hope that he would explain it all.

The nurse returned with a comb and helped me to plait my hair. 'There,' she said, 'you look like a Christian now. I'll show the inspector in.'

Jack and I had often joked that Inspector Lestrade looked more like a criminal than most criminals. He was a slight man with sloping shoulders, and his black eyes darted about like a rat looking for food. They darted now, taking in the room, the window, and me, and he quickly covered his dismay with a smile. 'Good morning, Mrs, er, Hudson. I am sorry to call so early, but it is the only time I have free.' He sat down in the easy chair and I perched on the bed, as there was nowhere else.

'Why do you call me that?' My voice rose. What was the

point of this Mrs Hudson business? I was Nell Villiers, and always would be.

He looked into my eyes with an expression I couldn't quite work out. 'Mrs Hudson is your name here, and for the foreseeable future.'

'Why? What is going on?'

The inspector moved to sit beside me on the bed. 'Do you recall that I visited you at home on the night when—'

'When Jack went missing?' I grabbed his arm. 'Do you have news of Jack? Have you found him?'

He released my grip gently, taking my hand. 'I am sorry, Nell. We searched the area several times, we interrogated everyone in the opium den, and we offered rewards. But no trace of Jack has been found.'

'So he could be alive?'

He looked down. 'It is almost impossible.'

'But not completely impossible!' The inspector was silent. 'You will keep looking?'

'We shall. We are still investigating the case.' He was looking at the door as he spoke, and I sensed that it was to avoid meeting my eyes.

'Is this what "Mrs Hudson" is about?'

He nodded. 'It is best for your safety that you live retired for a while.'

I frowned as I tried to understand what Inspector Lestrade was saying. 'Do you mean that I am in danger?'

'Perhaps. It is too early to tell. But if they know or find out that you have been involved in police work…'

'Who?' The inspector shook his head, and I pulled my hand away. 'What does this mean for me? What am I to do?'

'The doctor says you are well enough to leave here.' He rubbed his jaw and sighed. 'We have made arrangements for you to live as Mrs Hudson, a widow in deep mourning, at a house in a different neighbourhood. You will not contact your family, friends, or acquaintances without my permission.' His speech was measured, as though he had rehearsed it.

'How long will I have to do this for? When can I return home?'

He looked at the floor. 'Until we have found Jack, or until he is presumed dead.'

'But that could be seven years!' I imagined myself sitting alone by a fire in widow's weeds, withering away like a rotting apple.

'There's no alternative!' he cried, half-rising from his seat, then sitting back heavily. I had never seen him look so defeated. 'I cannot say how sorry I am, Nell, but I must protect you. One man missing, one left for dead...' He cleared his throat. 'I hope this arrangement will be brief. We will tell your family and friends that you are well, and not to worry.' He checked his watch. 'I have another appointment. But first you must promise to follow exactly the path that I have set out for you.'

'What if I do not?'

His eyes were hard and black as jet. 'Then you will stay in this room, under conditions which ensure that you cannot leave.' He put a hand on my arm, which I shook off. 'I cannot risk putting you in danger, Nell.'

I looked around the room at the bed, the washstand, the chamber-pot, and the barred window, and I recalled the laudanum haze of the past few days. 'Then I give you my word, Inspector.'

'Thank you.' He stood and held out his hand, and I rose too and shook it. 'Goodbye, Nell. We cannot meet for a while, but I shall work my hardest to ensure this business is at an end as quickly as possible.' The strange expression was on his face again. 'Be brave, Nell.' And he was gone.

I crossed the room to the mirror and looked again at Mrs Hudson, serving her sentence as a friendless widow in an unknown place. I thought I had lost everything when I learnt that my husband was missing and my baby was gone; I had not realised how much more there was to lose. Then I understood that the expression on Inspector Lestrade's face was pity. I felt sorry for him; but not half as sorry as I did for myself.

CHAPTER 7

221B Baker Street, 11th January 1881

I awoke early with a slight feeling of unease, though I had slept well. I lay in bed for a few minutes trying to work out the cause. Then my eye fell on the notepad on the table, full of scribbles and crossings-out. The advertisement for a maid! I had worked on it until ten o'clock in the evening, and had given it up as a bad job. But now it occurred to me that I should probably ask Inspector Lestrade's permission first. Over time the inspector had relaxed the restrictions placed on me, and I did not want him to tighten them again.

I took a sheet of notepaper and wrote:

Dear Inspector Lestrade,

I write to offer my thanks for your recommendation of your acquaintance Mr Holmes in respect of 221B. There is a matter I would like to discuss regarding domestic arrangements, and if you are ever in the vicinity I would welcome a visit.

Yours sincerely,

H. Hudson (Mrs)

I looked at my small, plain signature and remembered how excited I had been to practise writing 'Helen Villiers', 'Nell Villiers', 'Mrs H Villiers', 'Mr and Mrs J Villiers', covering sheet after sheet of paper with swirls and flourishes, not caring how much Susan teased me. I wrote the name again. This time the signature was larger, the capital letters more elaborate, and the upright of the 'd' in Hudson curved back instead of pointing straight upwards. I took a fresh sheet of paper, copied the letter and found a stamp.

I heard Billy's feet on the stairs. Soon the fire would be lit and the day would start in earnest, with all its demands of hot water, breakfast, laundry, and shopping. I sat down at the dressing table, undid my plait and, as I parted my hair in the centre, the gentlemen's words of the day before rang in my ears. I put down the comb, and reached for yesterday's newspaper. An advertisement on the front page had a drawing of a fashionable young woman. Her hair was done in a high bun, with a wavy fringe. I took out my nail scissors, took a deep breath, and snipped a piece of my front hair to half its length. It sprang upwards. I snipped again, and again, until I wore a fringe something like the one in the picture. The high bun took a couple of attempts, as I had grown so used to making a bun at the nape of my neck. But when I had finished, the woman who smiled back from the mirror seemed a little younger and less careworn than she had twenty minutes before.

I started guiltily at Billy's voice outside. 'Hot water, ma'am!'

'Thank you, Billy.' I waited until his footsteps died away before opening my door and bringing in the jug.

I selected a lilac dress, the palest I had, and looked at myself critically. A necklace would set the dress off, but I did not want to weigh it down with the heavy jet which was all the jewellery I now possessed, save my wedding band. I would have to do as I was.

Mr Holmes's bell sounded downstairs; he would be ringing for hot water, which meant I should begin cooking his breakfast. I put on an apron and hurried downstairs.

Billy came into the kitchen as I was putting the kettle on to boil. 'Compliments of Mr Holmes, ma'am, and he would like an extra boiled egg – oh!'

'What is it, Billy?'

'Nothing, ma'am.' He grinned.

I put up Mr Holmes's breakfast tray for Billy to take upstairs. 'After that, Billy, please could you post a letter for me? It is on the hall table.'

'Yes, ma'am,' said Billy, balancing the tray and opening the kitchen door.

I wondered what Inspector Lestrade would think when he read my note. Surely he would not object to some extra domestic help? After all, I was supposed to be a landlady, not a maid. I reflected that perhaps I was growing lazy; but then again, keeping house for two in a Clerkenwell terrace was a world away from maintaining a household of paying guests in Marylebone. The front door closed behind Billy and I refilled the kettle. I might have an extra boiled egg too.

I prepared my own tray and climbed the stairs. As I reached the first landing the gentlemen's door opened and Mr Holmes appeared. 'Mrs Hudson, I shall not require dinner today—' He stared at me.

'Will you be in to supper, Mr Holmes?'

'Er, yes, probably.' Mr Holmes's face reddened. 'I do apologise, Mrs Hudson.' He looked down for a moment. 'You look – different. Very nice, I mean.'

'Thank you, Mr Holmes. If you don't mind, I shall take my

breakfast now, while it is hot.' I walked upstairs with my tray, closing the door firmly behind me. My heart was thumping. I hoped I had managed to seem calm in front of Mr Holmes. I sat down and poured myself a cup of tea. What was wrong with me?

I took a spoon to the first boiled egg, and watched the steam rise. I hadn't minded Billy staring; he was just a lad. But being looked at by Mr Holmes, being seen not as a widow, not as a glorified servant, not as an object of pity, but as a woman – it had been a long, long time since someone had looked at me in that way. I had grown so used to people's eyes sliding over me that I was quite unsettled by Mr Holmes's gaze. I chided myself. Here I was, planning to resume useful work, and one look from a man was enough to make me doubt myself! I had definitely been cloistered for too long. I thought of all the arguments I would place in front of Inspector Lestrade, and by the time I got round to eating my egg, it was stone cold.

CHAPTER 8

Unknown, September 1878

Inspector Lestrade made his arrangements quickly. Later that morning the nurse showed in a fussy little woman in grey flounces, who expressed her condolences then bustled about me with a tape measure. I had put on the only dress I had with me: the pale-blue cotton dress I had been wearing when the inspector had delivered his news. 'Would you raise your arms now, ma'am?' I did, wincing a little, and stood in silence as she pursed her lips and wrote numbers in a little book. 'Well, you're in luck, ma'am. We have a full outfit in stock, just your size, which I can send round today. You'll feel much better when you're properly dressed.'

'But how can I pay you?' Until now I had not considered how I would manage about money, or even whether I would have access to any.

The little woman waved a hand. 'Your uncle has opened an account for you, and will settle the bill. Isn't that kind.'

'Yes, it is.' I doubted my various uncles even remembered who I was.

'Well, I must be getting on.' She rummaged in her bag and

gave me a card. 'If you choose to lighten your mourning when the time comes, I do hope you will think of us.'

Soon after the dressmaker left, my nurse reappeared with the white-coated man who had treated me so roughly when I had awoken a few short days ago. After a cursory examination he pronounced me fit to leave, so long as I did not exert myself too much. The nurse helped me to wash and dry my hair. 'Could you put it up for me, please?' I asked. 'I can't reach behind quite yet.'

'Of course I can, dear.' As she set to work with brush, comb and pins, I remembered the sensation of Jack undoing my hair, spreading it over my shoulders, and drawing me towards him, and I shivered. It would never happen again.

'There you are, nice and tidy.' My hair was pulled back into a low, tight bun, stuck full of hairpins. 'Just in time for lunch.' She left the room and returned with a plate of pale food. 'Boiled chicken and mashed potatoes. And there's arrowroot pudding for after, too.' I picked my way through the tasteless meal, and resolved that once I had left this place I would not eat anything white for a long time.

I looked out of the window at the flat green field until the nurse bustled in. 'A big package has arrived for you, Mrs Hudson. I'll get it brought in.' She hurried out, and returned with a delivery man carrying a large flat box. He set it down on the bed and left, and the nurse and I looked at each other. 'Go on, dear,' she said.

I lifted the lid and removed a layer of tissue paper. Underneath was a black bonnet with a white border, and a thick veil. I looked at it for some time. 'Please could you unpack the rest for me? I am having some difficulty in bending.' The truth was that I didn't want to touch the stiff black things.

The nurse assented, and put the bonnet on the bed. Next

came two mourning caps, with long black streamers. Underneath were two heavy black dresses, two black petticoats, and a dense black cloak. The nurse reached into the bottom of the box and handed me several boxes and parcels: a pair of black suede gloves, a package of black stockings, a set of black-edged handkerchiefs.

The last item was a black morocco box. 'Go on, open it,' she urged. Inside I found a pair of dangling jet earrings, a matching necklace, and a large carved brooch. 'Isn't that lovely,' she said, pointing to the necklace. Then she looked at my face. 'You're still not used to it, are you, dear?'

'No!' The word came out strangled by the huge lump in my throat. *Jack, where are you?*

She patted my shoulder. 'Shall I help you dress?'

I gulped. 'I can't wear it. Any of it.' If I put it on, that meant Jack was gone for ever.

'I know, dear. I felt just the same when my husband passed, although the clothes weren't half as nice as yours.'

I said nothing, and the nurse took my hands. 'You've had a big shock, dear, but you've got to wear these things. The inspector said you couldn't leave without them.'

I sighed. 'I don't have a choice, do I?' I let the nurse dress me like a doll, enveloping me in heavy, puffy black drapery. Her hand hovered between cap and bonnet for a moment; she selected the bonnet, and tied the ribbons under my chin. She fastened on the jet earrings, and pinned the brooch at the neck of the cloak. 'Now you're ready.'

Bowed down by the weight of the clothes, I walked to the looking glass. Only my top half was visible, but that was enough. The unrelieved black washed out my face, and the swinging jet drops accentuated how still and sad I looked.

'You'll get used to it, dear. And you can put your veil to the back in three months. I'll go and tell the coachman that

32

you're ready, and pack up the rest of these things for you.'

'Where am I going?'

The nurse paused at the door. 'I couldn't say, I'm sure. But you will be well looked after.'

I sat down on the bed, fear flooding my heart. The nurse returned with a suitcase. 'The carriage will be here in a few minutes,' she said cheerily, and began folding my spare mourning into the case.

'What about my blue dress?' It lay crumpled on the floor.

She glanced up. 'Now, what's the use in taking that? You can't wear it, and it will be out of fashion by the time you can.' She snapped down the clasps on the case. 'If you need anything else, it will be arranged for at the other end.'

'Shall I ever see you again?' Now that I was on the brink of going, I realised what a comfort the nurse had been, and how kindly she had put up with my moods.

'Oh, I doubt it.' She smoothed the bed. 'I don't get out much.'

'Could you at least tell me your name?'

'Your carriage will be outside now, dear. Put down your veil, and I'll show you the way.'

I followed the nurse down a short passageway with many doors, all closed. At the end was a stout oak door. The nurse produced a key from around her neck and unlocked it, and as she opened it I savoured the fresh air even through my thick veil.

A plain black brougham was waiting, drawn by a fine-looking horse. The coachman helped me into the carriage, and it was only when he closed the door that I realised the window blinds were down. I tried to raise them, but they would not move. Apart from a chink of light at the bottom, the carriage was pitch black. A bolt snicked, and my heart raced.

'Goodbye, dear!' called the nurse.

'Goodbye,' I called back.

'Hup!' cried the coachman, and we set off at speed. I found a leather strap in the darkness, and hung on for my life as the carriage rushed along. This continued for around five minutes, and then the horse slowed to a canter. After a while the noises outside grew louder, and the carriage jolted on cobbles. *We must be going through a town*, I thought.

The noise increased, the pace slowed again, and the carriage made several turns before coming to a stop. The coachman jumped down and I blinked as the door opened. 'Here you are, ma'am.' In front of me was a tall brown-brick townhouse. The door was open – the knocker had been muffled in crape – and a lanky youth in brass buttons stood framed in the light.

'Delivery for yer,' said the coachman, jerking a thumb towards me. 'Name of Mrs Hudson.'

The youth stepped aside. 'Won't you come in, ma'am.'

I looked about me, and everywhere was hustle and bustle. This must be a city or a large town, and a well-to-do one, judging by the smart people passing.

'Thank you.' I ascended the steps, wondering when I would next be able to go outside. 'Could you tell me where I am, please?'

The lad's eyebrows shot up. 'Don't you know?' He waved an arm at the scene. 'This is London, and you're in Baker Street.'

CHAPTER 9

221B Baker Street, 11th January 1881

'There's a letter for you, ma'am, hand-delivered. The boy's waiting.'

I took the letter from Billy and opened it. Inside was a single sheet of paper: *Glad your lodger is working out. Am passing between 3 and 4 this afternoon and will call. L.*

'There's no answer, Billy.' I took up my bag from the table and found a penny. 'Can you give this to the boy for me?' He clattered downstairs.

My new hairstyle had produced a great effect on my spirits; I fairly danced upstairs with Dr Watson's breakfast tray. 'Thank you, Mrs Hudson,' he said from behind the newspaper. I went to my room smiling, my pale frock at odds with the grey sleet falling outside. I would plan next week's menus, then indulge myself and read a novel. Yet as the day wore on, and the front door closed behind Dr Watson, my mood became less positive. I had not expected the inspector's reply, or his visit, to be so prompt, and I began to wonder whether I had made a mistake.

The doorbell sounded at five minutes past three and I

fidgeted for Billy to answer it, anxious to know my fate. I heard the inspector's low voice in the hall and ran downstairs.

'Mrs Hudson.' He looked me up and down. 'Billy informs me that Mr Holmes is out at present, but I should be glad of a brief conversation with you.'

'Of course, Inspector,' I said, wondering why he persisted in the pretence that we were strangers. I asked Billy to bring tea, and led the way to my sitting room.

'I did not expect you to call so soon, Inspector Lestrade.' He visited perhaps twice a year, and the visits followed a common pattern. Inspector Lestrade would arrive without warning in the late evening, heavily muffled. He would enquire after my health, and I would reply that I was quite well. I would ask whether there was news of Jack, to which the response was always no. Then I would ask if I must still live under the same conditions, to which the response was always yes.

'I was in the area,' he said. 'Besides, I had intended to call on your lodger, as I have some business with him.'

'What sort of business?'

He frowned. 'Detective work. Now, Mrs Hudson, what was the domestic matter you wished to discuss with me?'

'Well, Inspector...' How should I begin? 'Now that I have two lodgers, I would like to engage a maid-of-all-work. The gentlemen's rent will more than cover the cost.'

'Why?' he asked, eyebrows raised. 'I thought that having two lodgers to look after would be a pleasant diversion for you.'

'Inspector, would you change places with your maid?' I asked.

'I see your point, Mrs Hudson,' he said, slowly. 'However, I would need to find someone suitable.'

I decided not to mention my idea of advertising in the

newspaper. 'There would be another advantage to the arrangement, Inspector.'

'Would there?' He sat back in his chair and made his fingers into a steeple.

'Yes,' I said, feeling absurd. 'Now that you can visit more freely, having a maid would also enable me to resume the police work I was engaged in before—'

There was a knock at the door. 'That will be Billy with the tea,' I said weakly. The inspector was staring at me with a horrified expression on his face, which he composed as the door opened. He glared at Billy, who put the tea tray down and made a hasty exit.

The inspector waited until Billy had reached the next landing, then turned to me. 'I am sorry, Mrs Hudson, but you will not be able to undertake work for us again.'

'Why is that, Inspector?' I tried to keep my voice calm, but there was an edge to it that I could not suppress. 'You were more than happy with my work before.'

'Things are different now.' The inspector rose. 'With Jack gone, I am responsible for your safety, and I cannot risk someone tracking you down for the sake of a few reports!'

'Inspector Lestrade, I have been shut away for two years, not knowing whether I am wife or widow. You cannot blame me for wishing to resume a useful occupation.' I wanted to say more, but I knew that to do so would not be in my interests.

He wiped his brow with a handkerchief, sighed, and sat down again. 'If Jack were here I would gladly offer you work, but he is not. I shall make inquiries for a maid for you, but you must content yourself with such diversions as you can practise at home. We cannot run the risk of someone connecting Mrs Hudson with Mrs Villiers.' It was the first time he had spoken my true name since the night of Jack's disappearance. 'Perhaps a hobby would help? Embroidery, perhaps, or watercolour painting. Something to keep you occupied.'

'Perhaps it would,' I said, automatically.

'Can you tell Mr Holmes that I called, please.' He rose. 'I shall wire him from the Yard.'

'Of course, Inspector.'

He put on his gloves. 'Good day, Mrs Hudson.' He opened his mouth as if to say something else, then closed it again and left.

I cried quietly, so that Billy would not hear. I had won the battle of securing domestic help, but my hopes of returning to police work had been dashed. I was sick of the restrictions hemming me in on all sides, and I determined that I would find a way to break through them, and take my chance with the consequences.

CHAPTER 10

Flat 2, 24 Wayland Street, Clerkenwell, 1876

When I first encountered Inspector Lestrade, I would have given a sovereign never to hear the word 'police' spoken again. I had spent almost every evening in the past year tutoring Jack for his sergeant's examination: testing his knowledge of law, setting him questions, and marking his answers.

Jack would invariably rub his eyes at eleven o'clock, declare himself thoroughly fagged, and retire, while I kept the lamp burning setting the next day's work. Often I was startled by the church clock chiming midnight, and guiltily stole another ten minutes of preparation time. Then I made my way to bed, away from the dirty dishes in the sink and the muddy boots by the door, resolving that tomorrow I would rise an hour early and tidy our flat before I left for school. I climbed into bed and inched as close as I could to Jack without waking him, to warm up my shivering bones. In the morning Jack would shake me awake and chide me for staying up, and I would stagger to make breakfast, generally burning it because I was in such a daze. I daresay that on some days I taught rather muddled lessons.

'I can't do it, Nell,' Jack said as I brushed his coat. 'I'm not ready.' He was sweating even though the room was cold. 'I feel ill.'

'Jack, it's just nerves.' I laid the brush down and helped him on with his coat. 'Do your best, and I shall be happy.'

'Oh, Nell!' He pulled me to him, and under the smell of wool and polish and soap there he was, the man I loved and would do anything for, and my heart swelled with happiness. 'You have done so much for me, and I don't deserve it.'

'Of course you do!'

He kissed my forehead and gently released me. 'I must leave now, or I will be late.'

'Good luck!'

He looked back from the doorway. 'Thank you, Nell.' He looked more grown-up than I had ever seen him before.

That evening I put away the books and papers which had strewn the table for the last month, dusted and swept, and scrubbed the stove until it shone. It was good to restore the rooms to order, and for once I enjoyed the mindless house-work. I had bent over books so long that I feared I was developing a stoop.

Eight o'clock. Jack should have been home an hour before. I had suggested that we could go out for supper to celebrate. 'Capital idea, Nell!' he cried, gathering me in his arms. 'We could meet Napper, perhaps.'

Napper Jenkins was Jack's boyhood friend, and they had joined the police force together. They made a comical pair to look at: Jack was tall, dark and well-set, and he wore his thoughts on his face. Napper was slight, fair, of middle height, and entirely unremarkable save for his eyes, which were a little prominent and the brightest blue imaginable. He was a quiet man who took in everything going on around him, and

40

while he was remarking on the weather, or the quality of the beer at the local pub, his brain would be working it all out. Jack had nicknamed him Napper after joking that his eyes were never closed, and the name had stuck fast.

I took off my apron and tidied my hair, and as I pinned it back up I became aware of raucous laughter and a scraping sound in the stairwell. My heart sank, even as I tried to convince myself it must be something to do with Mr and Mrs Jones upstairs.

The scraping was right outside now, and after a few moments' silence there was a thump on the door.

I sighed, and opened the door to find Jack and Napper, or, more accurately, Napper holding Jack up. The smell of whisky had come up the stairs with them. A button was gone from Jack's tunic.

'I'm sorry, Nell,' said Napper. I stood aside to let them in. Napper half-dragged Jack across the room and sat him on the bed, where he fell backwards.

'You went for a drink, then,' I snapped, then checked myself. It wasn't Napper's fault that Jack was in this state. I took a deep breath. 'What happened?'

'He thinks he's failed.' Napper flopped down in the nearest chair, and I realised what a hard evening he must have had. 'I was sitting near him in the examination hall, and every so often I'd look over. By the end he was staring at the ceiling. He grabbed me as soon as the papers were collected. 'I've ploughed it, Napper,' he said. 'Let's go and celebrate.' And, well, you can guess the rest. I know how hard you worked, Nell...' His blue eyes were full of sympathy. In the background, Jack began to snore.

'Was it a stiff paper?' I asked, as if we were making small talk.

Napper crossed his legs and considered. 'Not really. I

41

mean, it was much harder than the entrance examination, but I was expecting that. It was a fair test.'

That was probably why Jack had got drunk; he knew he should have passed.

'I'm sure you'll be fine, Napper; Jack tells me how hard you work.'

'No harder than you, Nell.' Napper's eyes rested on me and as usual, I couldn't tell what he was thinking.

My stomach growled. 'Have you eaten?'

Napper blushed. 'I meant to.'

'I don't have much in; we'd planned to go out for dinner.' I looked in the tiny pantry. 'There's bread and cheese.'

We ate at the kitchen table, talking quietly, though a thunderstorm would not have roused Jack. 'I was trying to look after him,' he said.

'I know, Napper. Thank you.' I put my hand on his.

He gave me an odd look. 'I must go. More criminals to catch in the morning.' He rose. 'Take care, Nell. Sleep well.'

Jack was spread across the whole bed, so I put my dressing gown over my nightdress and lay down on the settee. *Not quite the evening I had planned*, I thought, dashing tears away as soon as they formed. In that moment I decided that this was the end of examinations. There was no shame in being a police constable, no shame at all. The two of us could manage perfectly well in the flat, and my teaching probation would be complete in six months. If Mr Minchin chose to keep me on as a full teacher I would finally earn a proper wage for the hours of study I had put in, and given the school's late increase in pupils I presumed he would have no choice.

Jack was remorseful and woebegone the next morning. 'I'd let you down, Nell, and I couldn't bear it. I didn't want to come home and tell you.' I told him it didn't matter, that I had already forgotten it, and looked away from the charred specks of paper drifting up the chimney.

Jack stayed in bed on the morning the results were due. 'I'll face it tomorrow, Nell.' He sat up and pushed his hair back. Although he had shaved the day before, his stubble was already showing. 'I can't go in today. They'll be round the noticeboard, talking about who's in and who's not...' He turned his face away. I was distracted at school by unbidden visions of Jack torturing himself with might-have-beens, and I hurried home with a heavy heart.

As I walked up the stairs I heard the hum of voices. Perhaps Napper had called to ask after Jack, like the good man he was. I could trust him to be tactful, and break the news gently. I hunted for my latch-key and turned it in the lock.

'Nell!' Jack's voice was jubilant, his face wreathed in smiles. He was still unshaven, but dressed and sitting on the settee. Opposite him in the best chair sat a man I did not recognise, with the neatness of a policeman though he wore plain clothes. 'Guess what?' Jack leapt out of his chair.

'What?' I cried, laughing. Jack's good humour was infectious.

'I passed! I don't know how, but I passed!' He caught me up and whirled me round until, half-laughing, half-crying, I begged for mercy.

The stranger turned to me. 'It was a little closer than we might have wished, Mrs Villiers, but a pass all the same. The questions he did complete were exemplary, which I understand from Mr Villiers is your doing.' He bowed.

'I told Inspector Lestrade all about you, Nell.' Jack slung an arm round my shoulders and squeezed me to him.

'Indeed he did.' The inspector's mouth twitched as I pulled my skirts straight. 'It is a pleasure to meet you, Mrs Villiers, and I hope that you will continue to support, ah, Sergeant

Villiers in his new role. He will have much to learn, of which I am sure he is capable with your kind assistance.'

'I shall do my best, Inspector,' I said.

'Excellent.' The inspector picked up his hat and gloves. 'Now, I must be on my way. I expect you back at work tomorrow, Sergeant.' Jack blushed. 'Good day to you both. Mrs Villiers, I shall look forward to meeting you again.' He bowed, and I watched his small, tidy figure step carefully down the stairs.

'I'm a sergeant! I'm a bloody sergeant!' Jack caught me up again and we waltzed round the room.

'How did Napper get on?' I asked, catching my breath.

'Oh, he passed too,' said Jack. 'Now, get your best dress on! We're going out!' And we took another turn around the room.

CHAPTER 11

221B Baker Street, 11th January 1881

I kept to my room for the rest of the day, save to prepare and serve a simple dinner for Dr Watson. I changed out of my lilac dress before doing so; it no longer suited my mood.

Dr Watson was sitting in the armchair reading a medical textbook. 'A difficult case?' I asked, as I put the tray down.

'What? No, no.' He closed the book, marking the place with his finger. 'I am not in practice at present. I am merely reading up.' I had wondered about Dr Watson's occupation, since he was always either in his rooms or out at his club. However, he had paid his share of the rental for the rooms up front, without demur. Perhaps he had a private income. Then again, if he was reading a textbook during the evening he must be planning to resume his medical career in some capacity.

'Supper at the usual time?'

'Please.' He brought the book to the table with him, and stood until I had left the room. Though Dr Watson had been living in the house as long as Mr Holmes, I did not feel I knew him at all. He was not a man to give much away. Perhaps he came alive in Mr Holmes's company. I remembered how close Jack and Napper had been, and they were like chalk and cheese.

I fetched my own dinner, checked that Billy had got his, and left directions for the preparation of supper. Billy assented willingly, as he always did, but I was conscious that I had leaned heavily on him lately, and I did not wish to abuse my position. I had grown to like and to trust Billy, and I regarded him more as a friend than a servant.

In my own rooms I chewed over the problem facing me as I tackled my steak and kidney pudding. I could not return to police work under Inspector Lestrade; that much was clear. Unless . . . unless I could find out what had happened to Jack. Despite all the evidence I could not believe that he was dead, not while there was even a shred of a chance that he had survived. How could no one know what had become of my husband?

But where should I start? I quailed at the magnitude of the task before me. Jack had vanished over two years ago, and though I had asked the inspector about progress at every opportunity, he had never reported any, despite all his efforts on Jack's behalf. I would have given a year of my life for his true opinion of the case. The only thing I knew was that the inspector was bent on making sure that I lived incognito, which must mean there was still some doubt about the case. Inspector Lestrade was not a cruel man, I reminded myself, and had protected me. Another woman in my position could well have found herself with no money and no home.

Yet my friends and family would have helped me. In terms of money, I was dependent on the inspector. The bills for the house, for food and clothes, for Billy's wages, were paid without my having to ask, but I had no money of my own save a few pennies for tipping. I could only buy from shops where an account had been set up for me. Of course Jack had had an account at the bank, but I would not be able to touch that; the inspector would surely be informed if I so much as visited the premises. I thought sourly of the gentlemen downstairs, who could come and go as they pleased and spend money as they liked. They would never be hemmed in as I was. I had to ask the inspector for everything. Mr Holmes would—

Mr Holmes.

My mouth dropped open. I knew from the snippets of conversation I had overheard that Mr Holmes had the inspector's ear, and was privy to the detail of several cases. The inspector might even have informed him of my circumstances. A cold shiver ran down my back. I liked Mr Holmes; could I trust him? Was there a way that I could make use of his knowledge and his connections without divulging who I was? I resolved that I would make the load easier on Billy and spend more time waiting on the gentlemen. Perhaps the delay in securing a maid would work out in my favour after all.

But I could not rely solely on the leavings from Mr Holmes's table. I had to find someone I could trust with knowledge of the case. My mind flashed back to the inspector, sitting in the parlour in Clerkenwell, twisting his hat brim in his hands as he told me the bare facts of Jack's disappearance, to the point where they found Napper in the attic—

I half-rose from my chair. If anyone could shed light on what had happened, it was Napper. He was trustworthy; but what would he remember? How much had he seen or heard before he was beaten senseless? It might be that he had nothing more to tell me about that day in the opium den. Yet it would be a start. I would be doing something to try and unravel the mystery. Even if it turned out to be unsolvable, at least I would have found it out for myself, rather than waiting another four years only for my hopes to be dashed.

I must meet with Napper. And once I had that clear in my head, a plan fell into place so easily that I was shocked at myself.

The opportunity to put the plan into practice came the very next day. I waited on the gentlemen at breakfast, and discovered for my pains that Mr Holmes would be at the laboratory for the whole day, while Dr Watson would observe his usual routine. Both would be in to dinner. This posed difficulties, but they were not insurmountable.

I returned to the kitchen, where Billy was reading yesterday's newspaper. I had planned a stew for dinner, which would fit in admirably. 'It looks like a fine day, Billy,' I said. 'When I have finished my mending, I shall exchange my books at the library.'

'Yes, ma'am,' said Billy, not looking up from his newspaper.

I spent the morning engaged not in mending, but in writing a list of questions for Napper. The questions started like prompts for a statement, but as the list grew longer and longer I found myself asking how Jack had seemed that day; whether he had received any injury in Napper's presence; what his last words to Napper had been. My eyes filled with tears, but I dashed them away. Sentimentality would not help Jack.

After a simple lunch I walked to the library and returned my books, with a pang of regret for *The Trumpet-Major*, which was only half-read. 'Mr Rogers, please could you direct me to the books on hobbies and pastimes?'

'Of course.' Mild confusion crossed the librarian's beaming face like a cloud, since my staple reading was novels, but it was gone as quickly as it came. 'What would interest you, madam? Painting, embroidery, handicrafts, music...?'

I considered. As the oldest girl of a large family I could knit and crochet expertly; but the inspector would not know that. 'Handicrafts, I think.'

'Here we are!' He pulled out several large volumes – knitting, crochet, macramé – and placed them on a nearby table. 'Were you aware that the Institute hold classes?'

'Really?' I said. 'I had no idea.'

'Oh yes.' He dashed off and came back with a programme.

'Wonderful! Thank you so much.' I leafed through the programme, which contained many classes and demonstrations, then turned my attention to the books. A few minutes later I made my selection and thanked Mr Rogers for his help, remarking that I would be sure to attend some of the events which he had so kindly brought to my attention. I did not know whether the inspector monitored my library record; but it was best to leave nothing to chance.

I returned home all smiles and informed Billy of my exciting new hobby. 'Inspector Lestrade suggested that I should take up a pastime, and I believe he is right.' I waved the programme under Billy's nose. 'I shall attend today's knitting class at the Institute to learn the basics. It will mean that I am out at the gentlemen's dinner time, but I can prepare the meal in advance. I shall just dust their rooms first.' And I whisked out of the kitchen before Billy had a chance to reply.

As usual, Dr Watson's side of the sitting room was quite tidy, while the side which Mr Holmes favoured was strewn with papers and books. The cushions in the easy chair were askew, and a Persian slipper sat on the occasional table. I took it up, and a flake of tobacco floated out. I set as much to rights as I could, and proceeded to Dr Watson's bedroom, which was neat as a pin and required but a few minutes' work. Then I crossed to Mr Holmes's bedroom, the object of my quest. It was far tidier than the sitting room. I gave the room a brief dusting, listening for any sounds on the stairs, and approached the trunk. It was unlocked, and the brass catches clicked open.

I stuffed what I needed into my apron pocket, fastened the trunk, and listened again. In the gentlemen's sitting room I secured another aid, and retreated upstairs. I placed the booty under a dress in my ottoman, and hurried down to prepare dinner, humming as I went.

CHAPTER 12

Flat 2, 24 Wayland Street, Clerkenwell, 1876

The inspector had spoken the truth when he said that Jack would have much to learn; there were evenings when I despaired. Jack was a born policeman and his new constables loved him, but he had always said desk work was his weakness, and he put it off till there was no choice but for me to help him. Sometimes I thought at least one of Jack's stripes should belong to me; but I never said it.

My teaching probation came to an end, and Mr Minchin, with regret, took on two new trainees in my place. I told myself that the decision was about money, not competence. Yet in my heart I wondered whether the nights coaching Jack, and my occasional absent-mindedness the next day, had influenced the headmaster's decision. I learned from another teacher that the new trainees were both single women, and while I would not have changed my life with Jack for the world I wished I could have combined work and family life more successfully. I started to look for situations, but I was ineligible for so many that I lost heart. Jack's reports became an escape from the monotony of house-work, and I polished

51

them until they shone.

One night Jack came home with a peculiar expression on his face. He took his hat and coat off before greeting me. 'The inspector's asked if he can call round tomorrow evening.'

'Doesn't he see enough of you?' I laughed, but Jack didn't join in.

'Exactly.' I tried to work out what the subject of the inspector's visit might be, without success. It couldn't be about Jack's performance; the inspector had praised him lately.

Jack left early the next morning and I found it hard to settle to anything. I hovered around the flat picking things up and putting them down again, then went for a walk to clear my head. When I returned home I got all ready for our visitor, though it was a full two hours until he was expected.

Jack was home on time, and we ate our dinner in silence. His hand shook a little as he handled the salt-cellar, and my heart went out to him. I wanted to say 'Don't worry' or 'It will be all right', but they were empty words. I washed up the plates and we waited, while the rain pattered at the window.

The bell sounded at half past seven and Jack and I looked at each other. 'I'll go,' he said, and got to his feet. His tread was as measured as if he were on the beat. He returned with Inspector Lestrade, who bowed and accepted my offer of coffee. That must be a good sign. If it were bad news, surely he would deliver it and go.

The two men were sitting in awkward silence when I returned with the tray. I served the coffee and took my seat beside Jack, our knees touching on the small settee.

'Thank you, Mrs Villiers.' The inspector sipped his drink, then put the cup down. 'I'll come to the point. Over the last month I have been monitoring the work of our new intake of sergeants. I have noted a distinct improvement in the quality of Sergeant Villiers's administrative work.'

'Thank you, sir,' said Jack. But the inspector was looking at me as he retrieved a roll of paper from his inside pocket.

'I was particularly impressed with this report, Mrs Villiers.' He put it into my hand. I did not have to read it; I knew it almost by heart. 'Most intelligently reasoned.'

'I'm sure it is, Inspector.' I handed the document back, hoping that the inspector had not noticed how it quivered in my hand.

The inspector's dark eyes glinted. 'You are a much better writer than a bluffer, Mrs Villiers.' I began to stammer an apology, but he interrupted. 'The sergeant here tells me that you are currently out of a situation.'

I shot a look at Jack, who had a stricken expression as though waiting for the blow of an axe. 'Yes, sir. Jack's wage is all we have.' I bit my lip to keep myself from crying. 'I didn't mean to . . . to...'

'You were just helping your husband.' The inspector picked up his cup again. 'Well, it is time for Sergeant Villiers to stand on his own two feet.'

'Yes, sir. It won't ever happen again, Inspector,' I gabbled, looking at the floor.

'Oh, on the contrary, Mrs Villiers.' The inspector watched me over the rim of the coffee cup. 'I need good brains, and I do not particularly mind who owns them so long as they are reliable. Now, there is no place for a woman on the payroll of Scotland Yard—'

'No, of course not, I would not expect that.'

His eyes crinkled at the edges. 'At least, not on the official payroll. The work – desk work, of course – will not be regular. Police work never is. It will also be a private matter between the three of us. I propose that we nominate an initial salary of twelve shillings a week.'

I did a quick sum in my head. Twelve shillings a week was precisely what I would have earned as a qualified teacher. 'I accept!' I cried.

'Very well, it is settled.' The inspector shook my hand. 'You shall hear more from me in due course, via Sergeant Villiers.'

When the inspector left Jack walked to the window and stood looking outside for a while. I went to him and put my hand on his arm. 'Aren't you pleased, Jack?'

'Of course, Nell.' Gently he moved my hand away. 'I'm dog-tired, though; I'm heading for bed. Goodnight.'

I sat up and read for a while, but the words swam in front of my eyes and I gave up. When I went to bed Jack's breathing was regular as a sleeper's, but he held himself with a stiffness which gave him away.

CHAPTER 13

221B Baker Street, 12th January 1881

'I shall call in at the haberdasher's on the way to the Institute, Billy. I should be home by half past seven.'

'Hope you enjoy the class, ma'am.'

'Thank you, Billy.' Five minutes later I was ready and closing the door behind me. The policeman strolling down the road tipped his helmet to me as I walked by. After a quick stop at the haberdasher's I strolled towards the Institute. It was past four o'clock now, just at the point where the sky was darkening and the lamps not yet lit, and the streets were livening up as shoppers hurried home and workers left their offices.

I entered a Ladies' Room along with several other women and secured a cubicle. I put my basket down and set to work. On went the vicar's grey wig from Mr Holmes's trunk, its shortness concealed by a bonnet I had battered out of shape. I exchanged my light grey shawl for a large black woollen one, and studied the effect in my pocket-mirror. I had put on a darker dress that morning, and overall I looked nondescript enough. My face, though, was still the same, and I was not confident that a keen eye from my former life would not recognise me. However, in the basket were two twists of paper which would assist in disguising me further.

First I whitened my eyebrows with talcum powder, to better match the wig. Then I rubbed my eyes with a little talcum on my fingers, which made them water. I rubbed my nose to redden it, and from the second twist of paper took a pinch of snuff which made me sneeze five times in a row. Now that I appeared both pitiable and contagious, I felt that people would be more likely to keep their distance.

I repacked my basket and waited for more footsteps. Then, affecting a stoop, I shuffled through the knot of women to the washbasins at the far end, depositing a halfpenny for the attendant on the way. 'Thank you, mum,' she said drearily, without a second glance. I stole a sly peep at the looking-glass from under my bonnet, and I would hardly have known myself either. Off I crept, sneezing at intervals, towards the stop for the omnibus to Clerkenwell.

I kept my head down as I boarded the 'bus and paid my pennies, and spent the short journey looking out of the window. After a minute I had travelled further than I had since leaving the nursing home. I took in the sights greedily; the brightly lit windows of the different shops, the noise of street performers, even an argument outside a tavern was a welcome change from the square mile I had been confined to. Then I realised I was on the outskirts of Clerkenwell. I disembarked a stop early and shuffled along, taking another quick pinch of snuff to maintain my cold.

Napper had lived a few streets away from us, and I hoped with all my heart that he still did. Jack and Napper had always walked home together, talking over the day's business. Everything had changed since those days, and here I was relying on the maintenance of habits and customs! I had nothing else to cling to, though.

It had begun to rain, and the nearby archway of St John's Gate was as good a place as any to loiter. It was on Napper's way home, and dark. I checked my pocket watch: twenty minutes past five. If Napper left work at five o'clock and walked at his usual pace, he could be here within ten minutes. I hobbled under the arch and stopped, resting my hand against the stonework as if to catch my breath. People surged past, a tide of Londoners on their way home; busy people with parcels and bags, and families and lives to return to. A pair of girls without umbrellas ran laughing under the arch. I recognised one of them as Maisie Adams, whom I had known from a baby. Luckily my exclamation was lost in the bustle of the crowd. She walked close enough to touch, talking to her friend, before dashing for a shop doorway a few yards further on.

I turned to face the lane and scanned the crowds from under my bonnet, making a pretence of blowing my nose. But as more and more people passed I realised how unlikely it was that my plan would succeed. To have any hope of finding Napper he would need to be living in the same neighbourhood, walking home the same way, and keeping the same hours. If I did not find Napper this time I would have to invent more excuses to leave the house, steal Mr Holmes's property again, and run the risk of being recognised by an old acquaintance – or worse, caught by Inspector Lestrade. If that happened, I had no doubt that I would be locked up.

The rain was easing now, and with it the pace of those walking by. Now that the excitement had worn off, the cold was seeping into my bones. I began counting those who passed me, to take my mind from it. Ten, twenty, thirty . . . one hundred . . . two hundred . . . when I got to five hundred, I would look at my watch. Four hundred and ninety-five – wait!

In the distance I caught a glimpse of a slim, shortish man. Was that a policeman's helmet? I had seen at least fifty men who could have been Napper, and been disappointed as many times, but this man had a gait like Napper's, though there was a slight halt in it. I remembered the inspector's account of the beating he had received, and shivered.

It could be him. It could be. The man was heading towards the far side of the archway. I shuffled across the path and he sidestepped me without a glance. But I had seen enough.

''Ere, you sir!' Napper did not look back. I took a deep breath. 'Policeman Jenkins!'

He stopped and turned, looking about him.

'Mr Jenkins!' I called again, and made my way towards him as quickly as I could while still in character. 'You dropped something.'

'I don't think so.' He patted his pockets and frowned at me. 'Do I know you?'

'Yes, I've got it here,' I said, keeping my right hand closed as I advanced. He glanced around him, but stayed where he was. He held out a hand as I reached him. 'No lucky charms, now, madam.'

I grabbed his leather-gloved hand and placed my empty right hand on top of it. As he looked down at me in surprise, I whispered, 'Napper, it's me, Nell. Nell Villiers.' My name felt strange on my tongue.

'Good God!' He seized my arm and marched me to the nearest streetlight. He thrust my chin upwards and the light was so bright that I had to close my eyes. My heart was racing. Had I just made a terrible mistake?

'I thought so!' Napper cried. He let go of my chin, but his grip on my arm was as tight as before. 'I've warned you about this behaviour, madam, but you persist in it!' He pulled a set of handcuffs out of his pocket, and a group of bystanders let out a ragged cheer. He leaned down into my face. 'Now, will you come quietly to the police station, or do I have to cuff you?' And he winked, quick as lightning.

'I'll come quietly,' I quavered, and allowed myself to be led away, accompanied by the boos and whistles of a crowd I dared not look back at.

CHAPTER 14

221B Baker Street, September 1878

Dear Mrs Hudson,

Welcome to your new home. I am glad that you have recovered sufficiently to leave nursing care, and hope for further improvement on the next occasion that I visit. If you require anything in the meantime, please write a note and your servant Billy will ensure that it reaches me.

You will recall the promise you made to live quietly, with no attempts to contact anyone from your past. I have made arrangements which will enable you to do so with ease. Billy will tell you which shops you have an account with, and ensure that your orders are fulfilled. You may attend church on Sundays, and the Reverend Maltby at St Mary's has been informed that you will join the congregation.

As befits a newly widowed woman, you will not go into society for twelve months, nor make or receive calls. I have ordered that you be supplied with various periodicals and a selection of novels. Of course you will require exercise and fresh air. You may walk veiled in Regent's Park with Billy in attendance, or if you wish he will arrange for you to be driven out in a carriage.

As far as Billy is concerned, you are a widow under protection. He does not know your real name, or anything else about you, and will take you at face value. I urge you to behave in a manner which is consistent with your avowed status.

I apologise that I could not welcome you in person, but I shall visit as soon as I can. In the meantime, I ask you to keep within doors for the next two weeks to avoid rousing unwelcome interest. Do not disobey my instructions; they are made both to protect you and to ensure that our investigations are not hindered. To that end, I have instructed that the house be watched, and any deviation from the path I have set out will be noted and addressed.

Yours sincerely,
Inspector G Lestrade

PS This letter is for no one's eyes but your own. Once you have digested its contents, please destroy it.

I read the letter twice over, then cast it into the fire and jabbed at it with a poker, pushing it deep into the flames. Far from escaping captivity, my cage had merely been made larger. First I had been imprisoned by drugs and force; now the inspector was using law and convention to confine me.

There was a tap at the door, and another. 'Come in!' I called, perhaps a little more sharply than the occasion warranted.

Billy entered bearing a tea tray. His face wore the blank expression of a model servant, which I took to mean that he resented my tone. 'Your tea, ma'am. Shall I come straight in after knocking in future?'

'Yes, please do.' I sat down. 'I'm sorry, I'm not quite used to having – a new servant.' I had almost said 'having a servant,' before I remembered that my former life was off-limits.

Billy smiled. 'That's quite all right, ma'am. Would you like me to call you "ma'am", or "Mrs Hudson"?'

'I would prefer "ma'am", please.' I did not want to hear my new name more than I had to; moreover, I might forget to answer to it.

'Do you need help unpacking, ma'am?'

I thought of the suitcase sitting in the hall, holding all that I now owned. 'I shall be able to manage, Billy.'

'Very good, ma'am.'

I left the tea to brew while I explored my new sitting room. It was pleasant enough, warm and comfortably furnished, but with the strange absence of smell of a room long empty. There was a settee, a basket chair, a writing desk and a small table at which to take meals. By the window was a bookcase, and I knelt to examine the contents. A complete set of Dickens and Thackeray, several novels by Anthony Trollope and Mrs Oliphant, a few volumes by Mrs Gaskell and George Eliot, and Mr Hardy's *Under the Greenwood Tree*. I noted the absence of any works by the Brontë sisters, Wilkie Collins or Mrs Braddon. Perhaps the inspector had rejected them as too stimulating. The inspector had also included a Bible and a book of sermons. On top of the bookcase were some magazines: *The Graphic*, and the *Cornhill Magazine*. No newspapers, then.

Slowly I got to my feet again, sat down at the table, and drank a strong cup of tea. My earlier anger had been soothed a little by Billy's kindness, but I was uncertain quite what to think. I ate a biscuit and inspected the room further. The writing desk contained pen and ink and a few sheets of black-bordered paper and envelopes, but no stamps. I walked back to the windows and attempted to open one, but it had been fixed not to move more than an inch.

Two doors opened off the sitting room. One was locked, and peering through the keyhole revealed nothing, for all was shrouded in dust sheets. The second door opened into a bedroom furnished with the essentials. The bed was small, with a white counterpane. A silver brush, comb and mirror lay on the dressing table, and a rose-patterned jug and basin stood on the washstand. An easy chair was placed in front of the fire. A chest of drawers held nothing but two white nightdresses, a dressing gown, and a lavender bag. The only notable thing about the room was the absence of a wardrobe; an ottoman sat at the foot of the bed. I looked about for a door that might lead to a closet, but there was none. Again, the window would barely open. I looked outside at the world going about its business, passing by without even a glance at my window.

I nearly fell over my suitcase as I left the room; I had not heard Billy come up. I shunted it into the sitting room and closed the door behind me. There were no more rooms on this floor. The next flight of stairs led to a cold white bathroom which I shivered at the thought of using; the other doors were locked. Only the attics remained. Yet another locked door, and one which opened into a neat, plain little room which must be Billy's. A dog-eared penny dreadful lay on the bed: *The Boy Detective*.

I visited the floor below mine, where the doors were again locked and the rooms sheeted. The ground floor, on which I assumed there would be a parlour and dining room, was the same. On an impulse, I moved to the front door and attempted to open it. The bolts at top and bottom slid back, but the door was locked.

I jumped at a cough behind me. 'I'm sorry, ma'am,' said

Billy. His face was bright red. 'I have been instructed to keep the front door locked.'

'Why are so many rooms closed up, Billy?'

'This is a large house, ma'am, and closing off rooms makes it easier to keep clean.' Billy's ready answer suggested that he was prepared for the question.

I sighed. 'Is the kitchen downstairs?'

'That's right, ma'am. Would you like to see it?'

'I would.' I followed Billy down the basement steps to a warm, well-appointed room, with a bright fire and a homely table and chairs. I imagined this was where Billy spent most of his time. I walked through to the scullery and back again.

'I will serve dinner at half past seven, ma'am, if that is convenient?'

'It is, Billy.' I looked round the room again.

'I shall bring it to your room, ma'am.' I went upstairs with a distinct feeling of dismissal.

For the next hour I sat with an open book on my lap, but my mind was as blank as the white dust sheets which shrouded most of the house. Billy's return came as a welcome relief, and I took the tray gratefully. There was a pork chop, boiled potatoes and buttered carrots, with a slice of fruit cake to follow. Ten minutes later, it had all disappeared. I rang the bell for Billy to take the tray and took up my book again, but I could not concentrate. I discovered a pack of playing cards in the drawer of the writing desk and dealt myself a hand of patience. It would not come out; nor would the next, or the next. I rang the bell again. 'Billy, I am quite tired. I shall go to bed.'

'Of course, ma'am. I will bring up hot water.'

I tossed and turned in the strange bed, and sleep would not come. This was my whole life: a house of locked doors, filled with books which I had either read or would not care to, and with no wardrobe for my clothes. The omission puzzled me, but my mind could not find the reason for it, since there was a sheeted wardrobe in the locked room. A firm tread passed the window. That would be the policeman.

Eventually I did sleep, for I woke to the weak light of breaking dawn. I felt both restless and exhausted: too tired to rise, but weary of my bed. I swung my feet to the floor and went to the chest of drawers for my dressing gown. I slipped the gown on and tied the cord about my waist. Then I understood. Wardrobes have hooks and rails. Dressing gowns have cords. The inspector suspected I might hang myself.

I gasped in horror. But as I watched the light strengthening, and the day beginning in earnest outside my window, I wondered if death would be an escape. I imagined making the knot, slipping it over my head, fastening the other end to a rail, and the jolt. I would have to kneel on a chair and push it away, and hope that my neck would break. Or there were the banisters… I saw myself a staring corpse swinging in my nightdress, and put my hands over my eyes.

I barely ate that day, and did not sleep at all. Long shadows crept across the room and every creak chilled me to the bone. I cried out for Jack once, before I remembered that he would not come. He might never come again.

One night I must have fallen asleep through sheer exhaustion. I awoke to a rough shaking. Billy was standing over me with a candle. It was dark.

'What is it, Billy? Why have you woken me?' The words hurt my throat.

'You were screaming, ma'am.' Billy's face wore the blank expression again.

'Perhaps I was having a bad dream.' And as I said it, the dream flashed into my mind. I was locked in a room and the inspector was watching me through the window, which was curtained with dust sheets. The window smashed and Jack climbed into the room – but Jack was a drowned man, holding a dressing-gown cord. I screamed at the touch of his clammy fingers on my throat, and Billy shook me again.

'It isn't the first time, ma'am,' he said, gently. 'I'll get the doctor to come tomorrow.'

The doctor came early. I heard the muffled knock, but it was some minutes before Billy showed him into my sitting room. I had used the time to try and make myself presentable, but there was not much I could do; my eyes had sunk deeper, and the shadows beneath were dark as a fresh bruise.

The doctor frowned. 'It is as you say,' he remarked to Billy, as if I were not there. He took my pulse, examined my tongue, and shone a light into my eyes. 'You should rest, Mrs Hudson,' he declared. 'You must go back to bed.' I tried to protest as he led me back to the bedroom, but I was too weak to resist. I started to cry as Billy pulled the covers back. The doctor took a small bottle from his coat pocket and put some drops into the glass of water by my bed. 'Drink this.'

I knew it from the first taste. 'Laudanum,' I said. I paused for a moment, then drank it down. Nothing could be worse than my present state. Warmth spread through me, and suddenly all I wanted was to go to sleep. I got back into bed and Billy helped me with the covers. The room was shifting a little, but it stopped when I closed my eyes. I began to drift with it, like a boat on the river.

Billy's voice sounded muffled. 'How often should I give it to her?'

The doctor's voice sounded even further away. 'Whenever she needs it.'

CHAPTER 15

Clerkenwell, 12th January 1881

'Where are we going?' I muttered under my breath, as Napper walked me along the street. His grip on my arm was less painful, but still firm.

'Police station,' he said, out of the side of his mouth. 'It isn't far.'

'Are you mad?' I hissed. 'Someone might recognise me!' Jack and Napper had started out at the local police station, and I had attended several of their social events.

Napper laughed, and his grip on my arm tightened again. 'I didn't believe it was you until I got you under a light. We can get a private room there; I'll pretend to caution you.' We walked on. 'Anyway, where else can I take you?'

We passed beneath the blue lamp. 'Act frightened, speak when you're spoken to, and keep your head down.'

'Who's this, then?' I knew that cheery voice, with its slight lisp, but I could not look at its owner. 'Napper Jenkins! What brings you here?'

'Found this old lady making a nuisance of herself, so I've brought her in for a talking-to. Have you got a room?'

'We can put her in a cell for the night, if you'd rather.'

I started to sob. Napper let go of me and walked over to the man at the desk. 'She's not worth locking up. A good fright should do the trick,' he said, in a whisper which carried to my ear.

'Right you are.' The policeman took a bunch of keys down and passed them to Napper, who grabbed me again and shook the keys in my face. 'Room two's available, sir.'

Room two was bare except for a table and two chairs. The barred window looked onto a brick wall. Napper closed the door and slid the observation window closed. 'Where the hell have you been?' His voice was low but furious. 'What do you think you're doing?'

I sank onto a chair before my legs gave way. 'Napper, I've been practically a prisoner for over two years. You have no idea what I've had to do to reach you tonight. I'm not dressed like this for amusement. If he finds out—'

'If who finds out?' Napper's voice was incredulous. He took his helmet off and sat down opposite me.

I took a deep breath. I had to tell him, or this whole pretence had been for nothing. 'Inspector Lestrade.'

Napper stared at me. 'The inspector's keeping you prisoner?'

'After he told me Jack was missing, I woke up in a nursing home. I – I had been pregnant, and I lost my baby, and they gave me laudanum to make me sleep.' The words came out in a rush. 'The inspector made me promise to live as a widow, away from my friends and family, or I would stay locked up. I have never had any news of Jack. This is the first time I have been more than a mile from the house since I entered it. I cannot live like this any more, with no husband, no friends, no occupation, no family. I have to know the truth, even if it is that Jack is dead. Please help me, Napper.'

Napper's gaze searched my face. Then he reached across the table and took my hand in his. 'Nell . . . is that your real hair?'

I almost laughed. 'It's a wig,' I said, pulling a strand of my brown fringe down.

'And are those your own clothes?'

'They were bought for me.' Why was Napper asking such trivial questions?

'I see.' He continued to hold my hand. 'Nell, you've just told me that you have been all but a prisoner, and yet you have managed to obtain a disguise, leave the house and get to Clerkenwell. It doesn't make sense.'

'Napper, I have had to lie, and steal, and disguise myself to find you! Why don't you believe me?' Anger, hurt, and shame fought inside me.

'I am sorry, Nell.' Napper sighed and looked away, though he still held my hand. When he looked back at me, his bright-blue eyes shone with tears. 'If I tell you what I know, will you promise not to tell anyone that we have met?'

'I promise,' I said. I knew already that it would not be good news.

Napper took a deep breath. 'I was badly hurt on the day that Jack – disappeared. I woke up in hospital, and the doctors told me afterwards that they expected I would die. After some weeks, I was moved to a convalescent home.' He looked down at his hand on the table, which shook a little. 'The inspector visited me there and told me that Jack's body was found in the river a week after he had vanished. His pockets were weighted with stones.' He looked at me, as if waiting for me to cry. But I felt numb.

'Do you remember anything from – that day?'

Napper shook his head. 'The last thing I recall is running up the stairs of the opium den. Everything else has gone.' He bowed his head, and suddenly looked up at me from beneath his eyebrows. 'You don't believe me, do you?'

'I do,' I said. I believed that Napper was speaking the truth, but why had Inspector Lestrade lied? Why had he kept me in the dark about Jack's death? Why hadn't he let me go back to my family to grieve?

'I can tell you don't.' Napper pulled his hand away.

'Are you calling me a liar?'

'No!' he cried, then slumped back in his chair. 'I hoped it wasn't true,' he muttered.

'That Jack had died?' I cried.

'Not that... I can't, I can't tell you.'

'Tell me what? What is it, Napper?'

'It will do no good.' Napper's eyes glistened. 'I hoped the inspector was lying—'

'What did he say?' I looked at him, bewildered.

Napper dashed a hand across his eyes. 'After he told me about Jack, the inspector said you had been taken ill at the news. When he came again I asked after you, and the inspector said that you had lapsed into a brain fever. Eventually I returned to light duties, and Inspector Lestrade called me in.' Napper's voice cracked. 'He called me in and told me that, for your safety, you had been committed to an asylum.'

'What? That's a lie!' I shouted.

'Calm down, Nell. Please...' Napper made a shushing motion with his hands. 'Lestrade told me you behaved in such an – uninhibited manner in the hospital that they had to restrain you. I cannot tell you all he said.' He looked at me curiously. 'You don't remember any of it, do you?'

'Of course not! It didn't happen! It's all lies!'

'You refused to believe that Jack was dead, and flew at anyone who tried to tell you otherwise. You assaulted your own father when he visited you. Just look at you, Nell.' Napper's voice was hard as iron. 'Your fists, the way you are breathing. You would hit me now, if you could.'

'That isn't true!' I uncurled my hands and stared at the nail marks in my palms.

'I wish I could believe it.' Napper shook his head. 'I hoped for better news, and many months later the inspector told me that you had undergone treatment which, while harsh, had cured your hysteria, and your – urges – and you had been moved to a nursing home.' He paused, and looked at me. 'Preparatory to being kept in a quiet house, with an attendant, where you could do no harm.'

I remembered the dragging pain in my stomach when I had awakened at the nursing home, and clapped a hand to my mouth. Could it be true? I shivered, and my teeth chattered.

'The inspector asked me not to look for you, but he warned me that you might escape and find me, and that you would tell me a tale of imprisonment which a child could see through.' Napper took my hand. 'But above all, he said that if I did meet you, I should treat you kindly; not as the woman I once knew, but as a stranger in need of protection and understanding.'

I burst into tears. Billy's kindness, the policeman outside the door, the little controls that had angered me, the inspector's insistence that I stayed away from family and friends, even the books chosen for me – Napper's explanation made far more sense than my own.

'Would you like to go home, Nell?' Napper's voice was soft. The sort of voice you would use to an overtired child.

'Yes!' I wailed. I was disgusted at myself. I saw what I truly was; a woman who had lost her mind and become a delusional, hysterical, violent creature, if not worse. I wished I could crawl into my room and never come out.

'Come.' Napper rose and held out a hand. 'I will put you into a cab. You will have to tidy yourself in there as best you can.' He helped me to my feet and put his arm through mine. 'It is a good sign, I believe, that you show remorse. Perhaps the inspector was right, and one day you will be able to live a normal life again.'

Seven years echoed in my head. Inspector Lestrade had decided, after I refused to believe that Jack was dead, to maintain the fiction that he was missing as the kindest way to confine me.

Napper leaned down to me. 'I will not tell the inspector that you have visited, but please, Nell, do not come to me again in this manner. The constable here will arrest you if you do.' His smile was weak as winter sunshine. 'If you would like to talk over old times, and that will make you more settled, I am sure we can find a way.' He raised my chin gently and his bright-blue eyes seemed to look through me. He muttered, low, 'And yet your eyes are just the same...'

'What has become of my family?' I whispered.

'They moved away after the – unpleasantness. I don't have the address.' I shuddered, and gulped down my sobs. Crying would do them no good now. They probably wished I was dead, like Jack.

We passed back through the police station and the police officer called out to Napper, 'Looks like that talking-to did the trick! She's walking to heel now, eh!'

'Goodnight,' called Napper, and led me outside. He whistled for a cab. 'What address?'

'221B Baker Street.'

'Hmm.' He reached into his pocket and gave me a handful of coins as the cab drew up. 'That should just be enough. Goodnight, Nell, and good luck.' He looked sad and weary, and as he walked to the cabman's box his limp was more severe than before.

In the cab I ripped off my battered bonnet and wig. My pocket-mirror showed that I had cried most of the talcum away. I scrubbed my face with my handkerchief and resolved that I would never do such a stupid thing again. I had thought myself so clever, and all the deception proved was that I had used low cunning to break everyone's trust. Jack was dead, I could never return to my former work, and all that I did have was through the inspector's kindness.

Before long the cab was slowing down. I got out, put all the money into the cabman's hand and walked up the steps with a heavy heart. I rang the bell and checked my watch. Seven o'clock.

'You're early, ma'am,' said Billy. 'Did you enjoy it?'

'I enjoyed the knitting demonstration, but I am not used to staying out so late.' I took off my bonnet and kept my face turned away in case Billy saw I had been crying.

'I kept some dinner warm, ma'am. Shall I fetch it?'

'That would be very kind,' I choked out, blinking furiously. I went upstairs, washed my face in cold water, and put the elements of my disguise beneath the spare underthings in my drawer. I wanted to remove every trace of that horrible creature – of the whole day, if I could.

Billy knocked and served me a helping of the stew and dumplings I had prepared earlier. 'I cannot eat it all,' I said. 'I am quite tired.' When he left the room I took a spoonful, but barely got it down. I feared that if I ate any more I would be sick, and pushed the rest round my plate. I put the tray on the landing and got ready for bed. Tomorrow I would throw myself into housekeeping and do my best to be – not the woman I had been, but a good, hardworking and obedient patient.

73

CHAPTER 16

221B Baker Street, October 1878

I knocked again, then lost my patience and hammered on the door. 'Billy! Wake up!' I heard a grunt, and a few moments later the door opened. Billy stood in his shirt, hair on end.

'What is it, ma'am?' He rubbed the sleep from his eyes. 'Is something wrong?'

'I cannot sleep,' I said, pulling my dressing gown about me. 'I need some more laudanum.'

Billy frowned. 'But you had your usual dose before bed. I brought it up to you, don't you remember?'

'Well, it hasn't worked.' I shivered, despite the dressing gown, and scratched my arm. 'I need some more.'

Billy sighed. 'You can't have more, ma'am. Perhaps if you go back to bed for a while—'

'What do you mean, I can't have more? A new bottle came two days ago!' I shook Billy's hand from my arm. 'The doctor said I could have it when I needed it, and I need it now!'

'I can't! You've had the full dose already, and any more will make you ill.' He sighed. 'Please ma'am, go back to bed, and I will bring you hot milk.'

'Can't I even have two drops? One drop?'

'Ma'am, I—'

I flung my hand up. 'Very well, Billy. Since you won't help me, I shall go back to bed. Don't bother about the milk.'

He gave me a strange look. 'Yes, ma'am. Goodnight.' By then I was halfway down the stairs.

I returned to my room and banged the door shut so hard that it opened again. Then I sat on the bed and counted to a thousand in my head. The house was silent. I rose and, moving as quietly as I could, I took a couple of hairpins from the dressing table and crept out to the landing. I knew every loose floorboard, every creak of the stairs; cooped up as I was, there was nothing for me to do but study the minutiae of my daily existence. I reached the ground floor and the tiles chilled my feet. One more flight of stairs and I was in the kitchen.

Billy kept the laudanum in the high corner cupboard; I had sneaked down once before and peeped in when he was preparing my draught. He wore the key on a chain around his neck; upstairs, the glint of metal had showed against his collarbone. I placed a chair next to the cupboard, making a tiny clack. I listened while I counted to a thousand again. Nothing. I climbed up on the chair and set to work with the hairpin. All else was forgotten as I jiggled the pin in the lock. If I bent it a little, then—

'Get down at once!' I had never heard Billy shout before. He was standing in the doorway and the light from his candle showed a face like thunder. I scrambled down and stood by the chair like a naughty child.

Billy marched over and held out his hand. 'Give me that.' He examined the bent hairpin. 'Now go upstairs.'

'But I won't sleep—'

'I said go up!' He caught me by the wrist and pulled me to the stairs. I could not resist; his grip was like an iron band. I stumbled after him, my teeth chattering, until Billy sat me down on my bed.

'Stay there.' I watched as he walked around my bedroom, opening drawers, lifting the mattress, checking pockets.

'I won't sleep.' I folded my arms.

'You'll have to try, ma'am.' He picked up the rest of the hairpins, my scissors, and a small nail file, pocketed them, then turned the bedcovers down.

'I must lock you in tonight, ma'am.' Billy towered over me. 'Please ring the bell for me first thing.' I realised as he left that he had my dressing gown over his arm. The key turned in the lock, and I lay back on my pillows prepared for a sleepless night. Billy was moving about in the kitchen downstairs, probably looking for somewhere to hide the laudanum. I made a list in my head of all the places he might choose. The lock scraped and Billy came in, holding a cup. 'Drink this, ma'am.' I took a sip, hoping he had relented, and tasted the blandness of warm milk. 'Sleep well, ma'am.' And he was gone.

It was the longest night of my life. I kept my eyes closed so that the shadows would not frighten me. I whispered poems and nursery rhymes to myself, I recited the kings and queens of England, I went through multiplication tables, I set myself sums in long division. When I finished, I started from the beginning again. Sometimes I lulled myself into a half-dream as I murmured my litany; more often I startled awake and looked about me in panic. But at last the blackness lifted into a dark, dark grey, and I knew that morning was on its way.

When Billy came into my room he looked exhausted. He stayed close to the door, as if he might have to run out and lock me up again. The thought made me smile; I was too weary to move. 'Would you like some tea, ma'am?'

I sighed. 'Yes, please.' I knew better than to ask for

laudanum; I did not want him to shout at me. Billy left without another word, and the lock snicked again.

He brought the tea tray and placed it on the dressing table, then stood by the bed. 'Ma'am, I've been thinking.'

I stared at him.

'I was told to attend to the household business, leaving you to regain your health as you saw fit.' He looked away for a moment. 'But you shouldn't be so much alone.'

'I have no choice. I am a widow, and must remain out of society.' I was caught between anger at Billy for stating the obvious, and pity at my own friendless state.

Billy poured me a cup of tea. I sipped it, but the warm liquid had no effect on the cold inside me. I glared at him and put the cup back on its saucer. 'I need something stronger than tea.'

'I will bring hot water, ma'am,' said Billy. 'When you are dressed, ring for me.' He disappeared again.

I did as he asked, wondering how I had come to be ordered around by a youth in livery. This time Billy did not close the door behind him. 'Breakfast is ready in the kitchen, ma'am.'

We sat facing each other, eating toast and boiled eggs. The meal was over quickly; I had nothing to say, and Billy concentrated on his food. I did not look at the corner cupboard, even though it probably did not matter now.

'Are you cold, ma'am?' I realised that I was shaking.

'No. Just tired.' I hugged my elbows, then let go to scratch my arm, which had started to itch again.

'Are you in pain?'

'No! Just leave me alone.' My eyes strayed to the cupboard. 'With something to take the edge off.'

Billy rose and took the plates. 'I will give you a small dose, ma'am…'

'You will?' I was happier than if he had handed me the key

to the front door.

'If you choose a book, and read to me while I work.'

I ran upstairs, pulled out the first book I saw – *David Copperfield* – and returned to the kitchen. 'Can I have it now? I shall read better if I am calm.'

Billy sighed. 'Yes, ma'am.' He fetched the bottle down and I watched the drops spread through a glass of water. They were the colour of blood. 'You know that this is poison?' He indicated the label.

'Of course I do,' I said. 'It's medicine, too.' I took a deep draught and the cold inside me ebbed away.

Billy indicated a chair placed near the fire. 'Would you like to start?'

I opened the book. 'Chapter One: I Am Born,' I read.

And so we began. I read while Billy washed the breakfast dishes and tidied the kitchen. I read in my sitting room while Billy cleaned the grate and relaid the fire. We returned to the kitchen, and I read while he polished the fire irons. Sometimes he would ask me to repeat a sentence or two, or would ask a question, but mostly I read without interruption. At first I had stumbled over the words, unused to hearing myself. As the morning went on, though, I became lost in the story, and read without self-consciousness.

We came to the end of a chapter, and Billy looked up. 'It's lunch time. After we have eaten, we'll go to the park.'

My mouth dropped open. 'Outside?'

'Yes, ma'am, outside.'

He made sandwiches of cold roast beef, and made me sit until I had finished mine. He helped me on with my cloak and bonnet, including the heavy black veil, and at last the door was open! I breathed in smoky London air. The noise was terrific; rattling carriages, clacking hooves, shouting voices, running feet. I clutched Billy's arm. 'This way, ma'am,' he said, and pointed. There was a park at the end of the street, and Billy steered me through the bustle towards it.

There was so much to see, even through my veil, and we walked until I was tired. Billy talked about the park, and his family, and the sights in London, and I was glad just to listen. Then he asked me what my favourite meals were, and before long we had agreed to make a shopping list when we went home. I read to Billy again while he prepared dinner, and he allowed me another small drink of laudanum before bedtime, although he said the fresh air would help me sleep.

Over the next few weeks we read *Vanity Fair*, *Romola*, and *North and South*; we walked in the park on fine days; I took control of the meal plans and shopping lists; I taught Billy how to make a Victoria sandwich and how to fry fish the way I liked it. I found that I only shook a little in the mornings now; my arm itched less, and the skin was not so raw. I slept better, too. I still had bad dreams sometimes, when I would wake to find Billy shaking me, but they came every few days, rather than every night. I never tried to pick the cupboard lock again, and in return I had a drink of laudanum each night, though Billy put in a drop less. In the mornings he asked me to wait until after breakfast for my drink, then till mid-morning. Some days we were so busy that I only realised during our walk that I had missed my drink.

One day after dinner Billy asked if I would read another chapter of *Barchester Towers* while he cleared up. I was not tired at all, so I agreed. Billy finished his work and sat at the table with me, and it was only when he yawned that I realised how late it had grown. 'I should go to bed,' I said, laying the book aside. 'Will you prepare my drink, please?'

Billy frowned. 'Do you really need it, ma'am?'

'I worry that I won't sleep without it.'

Billy got up, stood on his chair to unlock the cupboard, and put the bottle down on the table. 'You can make it yourself, ma'am.'

I looked up at him, and he nodded. 'Go on.'

I fetched a glass of water and set it down on the table. My hand shook as I reached for the little bottle. *Just one drop*, I told myself. The label was stained and partly worn off, but – I looked more closely. *Aromatic bitters*, I read. *Angostura*.

I looked up at Billy, who was watching me from the doorway. 'The bottle of laudanum ran out two weeks ago, ma'am.' His voice was soft.

Gratitude rushed up in me, and I opened my mouth to pour out thanks. Then I saw how Billy bit his lip, and blinked. I put the bottle down, and stood up. 'Thank you, Billy. Goodnight.'

'Goodnight, ma'am.'

CHAPTER 17

221B Baker Street, 13th January 1881

I had expected to spend the night after my misadventure tossing and turning in bitter reproach. Instead I fell fast asleep and did not stir until persistent knocking awakened me. 'Morning tea, ma'am,' called Billy.

'Oh. Oh yes.' Then yesterday's events flooded in on me, and I had to look away when Billy carried in the tray. 'What time is it?'

'Just after seven, ma'am. I've taken hot water to Mr Holmes, and as you weren't down I've started breakfast.'

'I'll do it, Billy. I'll come down as soon as I'm dressed.' I would start the day as I meant to go on. I hoped that learning Mr Holmes's plans for the day would allow me to replace his stolen belongings, and put yesterday behind me for good.

Mr Holmes had said that he liked bacon and eggs for breakfast above all things, so that was what I cooked. He was reading the newspaper when I entered the room, and his face lit up at the sight of the plateful I set before him. 'Mrs Hudson, you have done me proud today.' He picked up his knife and fork and set to.

'Will you be in to luncheon?'

Mr Holmes swallowed hurriedly. 'Yes. I am making a call on an old associate at ten o'clock this morning, and then I shall return here. I have some reading to do.' He dabbed at his mouth with the napkin. 'Dr Watson will be out this morning too, but in any case he will lunch at the club.'

My heart leapt. I could replace the wig this morning, and no one but myself would be any the wiser. 'Thank you, sir,' I said, and withdrew.

Dr Watson rang for his breakfast at nine. When I brought his tray up I found him smart and nervous in a dark suit, while Mr Holmes lay on the settee reading a novel. He looked at his plate of bacon and eggs doubtfully, took his jacket off, and spread a napkin over as much of his shirt-front as he could. I wondered what the occasion for the suit was, but of course a good landlady would not pry. As I went downstairs I heard Mr Holmes say 'I'll walk over there with you, if you like.'

I pottered around in the kitchen listening for movements upstairs. At around half past nine I was rewarded by descending feet and the bang of the front door. I finished wiping the table, and said to Billy as casually as I could, 'I'll go and clean out the gentlemen's fireplaces.'

Billy looked up from the pair of boots he was cleaning. 'I'll do it later, ma'am. That isn't a job for you.'

'I'll go and do it now.' I gathered up the necessary equipment and left before Billy could say any more. Apart from anything else, a morning of hard, dirty work would be an appropriate start to the penance I should serve for my many transgressions.

I knocked at the gentlemen's sitting-room door, and there was no answer. Then I looked into the adjoining bedrooms, which of course were empty. I ran upstairs to my room and retrieved the wig, almost laughing with relief. Mr Holmes's room was just as it had been the day before; the trunk had not moved, and the catches clicked open. I pulled the wig from my apron pocket – and something creaked behind me. The wardrobe doors swung open and out stepped Mr Holmes, looking furious.

He snatched the wig out of my hand. 'Mrs Hudson, explain yourself.' His voice was low, but the tone of it was sharp as a knife.

'I – I...' I stammered. I was frozen to the spot. There was no explanation I could offer, nothing I could say to excuse my behaviour. I was caught red-handed. I trembled as I thought of what the inspector would say, and imagined the blacked-out carriage rattling through the streets towards me.

'Mrs Hudson!' Mr Holmes looked calmer, and even a little pleased that he had caught me. 'Sit down, please.' He motioned to the easy chair. I sat down, but he remained standing. 'I would like an explanation.'

I twisted my hands in my lap while I racked my brains, but nothing came. 'How did you know?' I whispered.

'I am a detective, Mrs Hudson. It is my business to know. You have observed that my trunk is not locked. However, I make a point of placing a hair across the lid. On my return home yesterday I observed that the hair had been disturbed, and quickly discovered what had been taken. Unless we have been visited by a burglar specialising in grey wigs, the culprit was a member of the household: Dr Watson, Billy, or you.'

His eyes bored into me. 'You were not at home when I returned last night, which is most unusual, and I recalled that you had enquired about my plans at breakfast. I also remembered that you had encountered me in disguise – wearing this wig, indeed! – and knew where it was kept. Billy told me you were at a knitting class you had mentioned earlier that day, and my suspicions were confirmed. When you asked about my movements again this morning and cooked my favourite breakfast, I presume out of guilt, I could only conclude that you planned either to put back the wig or to take something else, and so I set a trap. I am glad that I did not have to spend more than a few minutes in the wardrobe.'

I shuddered at how easily Mr Holmes had deduced my silly little scheme. 'I am very sorry, Mr Holmes. I will never do such a thing again.'

Mr Holmes looked down his long nose at me. 'I dare say you will not, Mrs Hudson. But I should like to know what you were doing with my property.' He shook the wig at me.

I looked at the floor. 'I cannot say, Mr Holmes. But I give you my word that it will not happen again.'

'So I shall have to solve the case of the thieving landlady myself?' His eyes gleamed. 'Let me think…' He began to pace. 'Yesterday evening you went to a place where you did not want to be recognised.' He stopped, held up the wig, and raised an eyebrow. 'You pinned this back under a bonnet?' I nodded, and he resumed his pacing.

'Billy's lack of dissembling means that he is not in on your secret, so you disguised yourself en route.' He looked at me expectantly.

'A ladies' public convenience,' I muttered.

'Ah, of course. I sometimes resort to a lavatory myself. You were back by seven, too early for dinner or the theatre – and why would you disguise yourself for that? This house proves that you are a woman of means; therefore your motive is not petty crime.' He smiled. 'Besides, Inspector Lestrade would not have recommended you as a landlady if he had the least suspicion about your moral rectitude.' My mouth twisted at the irony of this, and last night's nausea rose in me again. 'And yet… The obvious explanation is that you were meeting someone in secret. An assignation, perhaps?'

'No!' My face grew hotter and hotter.

His eyes flicked towards my half-mourning. 'I understand that such a thing would be a delicate matter.'

'I swear it was not that!' I cried. 'I was meeting someone, but it was an – an old friend.'

'And of course you would lie to your servant, steal from me, and disguise yourself to meet an old friend.' The amusement of Mr Holmes's tone was undercut by sharpness.

'I had my reasons,' I said. 'It shall not happen again. If you wish to give notice, or to take proceedings, Mr Holmes, I will understand.'

Mr Holmes stared at me. 'So you would risk your good name rather than tell me the truth?'

'It does not matter now. I will lose my good name, either way.' *A name that isn't even mine.* Tears welled up, and I was too broken in spirit to do anything but let them fall.

I felt Mr Holmes's hand on my shoulder, and a handkerchief being pressed into my hand. 'I do not believe it can be as bad as all that,' he murmured.

'It is! It is worse than I could have imagined!' I buried my face in the handkerchief and sobbed.

Mr Holmes was silent, and when I eventually looked up at him, his face was grave. 'Mrs Hudson, from what I have seen, you appear to be a sensible person. If you say that a matter is serious I am inclined to believe you, and the strangeness of your actions bears it out. Now, you left some cleaning materials outside. I shall take them down and inform Billy that you have gone to bed with a headache and do not wish to be disturbed. When I come back, you will tell me the truth.'

'What if I won't?' My voice rasped in my throat.

'Then I will put the matter into the hands of the police.' He stood looking down at me for a moment, then turned and left. The pail clattered outside. My head throbbed as I sat waiting. There was no escape, and every second I waited added to the agony.

He returned, beckoned me through to the sitting room, and pointed to the basket-chair. 'Sit there, please.' Mr Holmes took his seat opposite, and gradually, falteringly, I told him the whole sorry tale, from the day of Jack's death to my return yesterday evening. I had meant to keep the worst of it back, but his questions laid me utterly bare. He watched me the whole time, his face devoid of any expression, any reaction. I tried to remain calm, but I cringed and wept as I spoke of the terrible things I had learned the night before. I wished that I could have died before I heard the truth about myself.

My voice died away and I waited for Mr Holmes to ask me another question, or to deliver his verdict. But he did not speak; he sat motionless, his eyes still fixed on me. Finally he rose and went to the bureau, where he scribbled a note and placed it in an envelope. 'Stay there.' He rang the bell and moved to the door. 'Deliver this at once, please,' he said to Billy. Mr Holmes closed the door and resumed his seat, and I waited for the hammer-blow to fall.

CHAPTER 18

Clerkenwell Library, 1871

'Hoi, you! Leave her alone!' Those were the first words I heard my future husband say, and I was profoundly grateful to him.

I was eighteen, and coming to the end of my apprenticeship as a pupil-teacher. I would have to sit the Queen's Scholarship for teacher-training college; and I would need a second-class scholarship to have a hope of going. The examination was a month away and I had already reached the point of desperate cramming, though my supervisor told me I should not worry.

I had stayed longer than I meant at the library. Lottie had packed her books up at five minutes to four, and I told her to go without me, as I had one more thing to look up. The one more thing led to several more things, and the discovery of a large gap in my knowledge. By the time I was shooed out, it was growing dark outside. I hugged my books to my chest and set out at a good pace for home. Mother would be cross at my lateness, as would Susan, who would have twice the work as a result. I wished that somehow I could be both a good student and a good daughter, without the constant pull of guilt between the one and the other.

The library was on a well-lit, busy road, so when I heard footsteps behind me I was not afraid. But the footsteps were joined by others, and when I turned the corner into a quieter road, they followed me. *It is a well-used road, and it is early evening*, I told myself. Yet when I quickened my pace, the footsteps did not fall back. I passed a group of men drinking outside a tavern. They laughed and catcalled, but I did not turn my head. *It is only a fifteen-minute walk home. Ten, if I hurry.*

The street lamps were further apart now, and there were dark places between them. I walked as fast as I could and cursed my foolishness, while my heart beat loud as a drum in my ears. Then there was a low laugh, a dirty laugh, and a whisper, and I broke into a run. Feet thudded behind me and there was no more laughter. But my books hampered me; my foot caught in the hem of my dress, and I fell headlong. The books were scattered and my hands throbbed under my gloves; but that was nothing compared to what I feared would happen next.

They stood in a circle around me. One reached out a hand to me. 'Here, missy,' he said. 'Don't be scared, now.' When I took his hand he jerked me to my feet so roughly that I fell against him. 'Oh, you're forward,' he laughed. 'I like a forward girl.'

'Let go of me!' I tried to pull free, but he stood firm.

'Let's have some fun, hey!' I looked around for help, but the street was empty. I screamed, and he twisted my arm up behind my back. 'Don't do that again, dear,' he whispered in my ear, 'or I might have to hurt you.' Another man started to pull at the fastenings of my dress. 'Wait yer turn,' said the man holding me, and pushed me towards an alleyway.

'Please don't,' I begged. 'Let me go, and I will tell no one.'

He laughed, and kept moving. A rattle sounded, then a shout, and as quickly as they had seized me the men were gone, pelting down the street like a pack of wolves.

'Are you all right?' the voice shouted, and as he came towards me his buttons twinkled.

'I . . . think so,' I said, and when I realised what I had just escaped my legs buckled under me.

'Whoa!' The policeman reached my side just in time to hold me up. 'It was lucky I came along. You shouldn't be out alone here at this hour,' he scolded.

'I won't do it again,' I said.

'Wait, I know you.' He peered into my face. 'You're the girl from the library!'

'Am I?' I tidied myself while he retrieved my books from the pavement.

'Yes, you are.' He held my books in a little pile. 'I've started going there with my mate to study, and you're always in there with a heap of books. I thought you were a librarian at first.'

I looked at the smiling face beneath the helmet. While the light was dim, I distinctly recalled two lads I had seen there more than once; one with his head down reading, the other looking round the room. This policeman was the second of the two.

'I have an exam to study for,' I said.

'I'm just trying to keep my job,' he said. 'I scraped through the written tests, and they said I could come in on probation.' He laughed. 'I always wanted to be a policeman since I was a boy, but if I'd seen all the paperwork I might have changed my mind. Anyway,' he held out a hand, 'Constable Villiers, at your service.' He looked at me inquiringly.

'Nell Marsden,' I said, and shook it, though my palm still tingled. His hand was large and reassuring.

'Well, Miss Marsden, I'd better walk you home in case you get into any more scrapes.' He proffered his arm, and a few minutes later I was back at my own front door. By that time I had learnt that Constable Villiers's first name was Jack and his friend was called Napper, and he had asked me when I usually went to the library. 'I expect I'll see you there soon,' he said. 'Goodnight, Miss Marsden.'

'Goodnight, Constable Villiers.' When I turned to close the door he waved, and I watched him down the street. I saw him at the library more often; he said it was on his beat, and that libraries were surprisingly criminal places. He always offered to walk me home, in case anyone stole my books. Within six months we had moved from Constable Villiers and Miss Marsden to Jack and Nell, and he had kissed me in the reference section, and I had allowed him to.

CHAPTER 19

221B Baker Street, 13th January 1881

'I do not believe it.' Mr Holmes looked at me over the steeple of his fingers.

'I beg your pardon?' I stared at him in amazement. 'Why would I invent such a story against myself?'

'I did not say that I do not believe you, Mrs H – *Villiers*.' He unlaced his fingers. 'I do not believe *it*. I do not believe that the woman who devised and executed yesterday's intelligent, rational plan was ever locked up in a lunatic asylum.'

'But all the evidence points to it,' I said, mechanically. 'Napper said I had received treatment—'

'Which you remember nothing of.' Mr Holmes leaned forward. 'Describe the police work you performed for Inspector Lestrade.' He reached for a notebook, and I spoke of the statements I had analysed, the reports I had written, the cases I had worked on. Occasionally he would interject that he remembered a particular case; on a couple of points he debated my conclusions with me. I had never had such a conversation with Inspector Lestrade. I felt as if my mind was being stretched, gently but firmly. It was a welcome escape from the ocean of sadness and guilt I had been immersed in for the past few hours.

The front door banged, and the stairs creaked. Mr Holmes closed his notebook. 'Unless I am much mistaken, my second opinion is here.' There was a rap at the door, and Dr Watson hurried in.

'I came as soon as I got your note—' He looked in my direction, then at Mr Holmes, puzzlement on his face.

'It is quite all right, Watson,' said Mr Holmes. 'I apologise for calling you in at such short notice, but I knew that your interview would be a formality.'

'You were right, Holmes.' Dr Watson grinned. 'I start on Monday.'

'Excellent!' Mr Holmes's face showed genuine pleasure for his friend, and I wished fervently that I could have – or be – as good a friend. 'Mrs Hudson, Dr Watson is a competent doctor with general and surgical experience. I believe he is exactly the person to reassure you on the matter we have discussed. Would you permit me to give Watson a brief précis, then allow him to examine you?'

My head was in a whirl. In the abstract, I supposed that a medical examination was the right thing to do – but Dr Watson was my lodger. His eyes shifted between me and Mr Holmes, and he appeared both bemused and uncomfortable.

Mr Holmes leaned forward to me. 'Mrs Hudson, on my part – and I am sure I speak for Watson too – whatever the result of the examination, it shall never go outside this room without your permission.' He cast a look at Dr Watson. 'Isn't that right, Watson?'

'Of course,' said Dr Watson, though his face was wary.

'Do you promise, doctor?' I asked.

Dr Watson studied the carpet for some time, then raised

his head and looked me full in the face. 'I do. I trust Mr Holmes's judgement.'

'In that case, I agree.' My voice came out very small indeed, but the deed was done.

'Well done, Mrs Hudson,' Mr Holmes said quietly. 'Sit, Watson, for I have a case history to relate. Mrs Hudson, if I am inaccurate on any particulars I urge you to correct me.'

Mr Holmes's account, while factually identical to mine, was a simple presentation of the two sides of the story. He did not judge; he did not attempt to persuade. He referred to me by my assumed name throughout. It was like listening to the history of someone I had never met. At first Dr Watson sat back in his chair like a doctor hearing a patient out. As the narrative continued he moved to the edge of his seat and his impassivity vanished. Bewilderment, astonishment, and doubt flashed across his face.

'So, Watson, you understand why I summoned you so urgently, and why your medical judgement is required. I shall step outside, in order that you may conduct your examination.' Mr Holmes rose and left the room, with an encouraging smile in my direction.

Dr Watson proceeded to question me. He asked after my health, and my family history. He administered a memory test. He asked about the details of my treatment, and whether I remembered the name of any of the doctors who had attended me. When I mentioned Dr Hayward, who had written my first laudanum prescription, he merely commented that he had known him at Bart's. Then he paused. 'Mrs Hudson, I shall show you some pictures. Please name the objects if you can.' He selected a textbook, leafed through it, and presented a page of what appeared to be surgical instruments. I could feel him watching me. 'Have you ever seen any of these things, Mrs Hudson?'

I shook my head.

Dr Watson turned to another page. 'Or this?' He showed a picture of a strange jacket with long arms ending in straps. 'No,' I said. 'What is it for?' He said nothing, but closed the book and replaced it in the bookcase.

'Excuse me a moment, Mrs Hudson.' A murmur of conversation outside, and then Dr Watson returned and sat down opposite me, looking most uncomfortable. 'Mrs Hudson, would you permit me to conduct a brief physical examination? I apologise, but it is necessary.'

'Why?' The blood rushed to my head, and when I glanced at Dr Watson, he was blushing too.

'It is to look for signs of any medical treatment you may have received which you do not remember.' He paused. 'I shall only examine you as far as is necessary to obtain a proof either way.'

I was none the wiser. 'Will you tell me what you are going to do, before you do it?'

'Would that help?'

'I would prefer it.'

'Then yes, I shall. If you are uncomfortable at any point, Mrs Hudson, ask me to stop.'

I bit my lip, and nodded. Dr Watson locked the door, drew the curtains, and turned up the lamp. First he examined my wrists and ankles. Then he asked me to undress to my underclothes, so that he might examine my stomach. He pressed around it gently, which felt extremely strange. Finally he produced a tiny torch, and asked me to unfasten myself below, lie on the settee, and raise my knees. 'I'm afraid it is necessary,' he said, his face pink. Mystified, I complied. After kneeling and peering for a few seconds, Dr Watson stood up. 'My examination is complete, Mrs Hudson. I shall leave you to tidy yourself.' He hastened from the room, and I wondered whether he was as shy with all his female patients.

I dressed again and sat down to await Dr Watson's verdict. While Mr Holmes's account of the case had calmed me, Dr Watson's examination had roused me to curiosity and concern.

There was a light tap at the door. 'Enter,' I called, and the two men came back into the room. Dr Watson had resumed his expression of professional calm.

Mr Holmes looked at Dr Watson. 'Have you reached a conclusion, Watson? I am sure you will respect Mrs Hudson's feelings in your answer.'

'I have.' Dr Watson glanced across at me. 'There is no evidence at all that Mrs Hudson has suffered from a mental illness, or that she has received treatment in an asylum. Her memory and faculties are excellent, as is her general health. When shown pictures of common treatment devices for hysteria she shows no sign of recognition. There are no physical marks of the procedures used to treat severe mental disorders in women.' He paused. 'Mrs Hudson mentioned Dr Hayward, whom I know well. He is not a specialist in mental illness; he is an obstetrician.' I remembered the dragging pain in my stomach, and bit my lip.

Mr Holmes broke the silence. 'It appears, Mrs Hudson, that the story you were told by your old friend yesterday was just that. A story, and a particularly malicious one. There are further checks to be made, but unless they uncover sound evidence to the contrary I consider them a formality.'

'But how can you be sure?' I was relieved that Mr Holmes thought as he did; but a black cloud of doubt still hung over me.

'Your friend's story is based entirely on hearsay.' Mr Holmes leaned forward. 'Your regard for a trusted friend, the stress of your journey, and the emotions you felt on hearing his tale would naturally weaken your judgement.'

A horrible realisation dawned on me. Napper had lied to me, or…

'You are right, Mrs Hudson,' said Mr Holmes. 'You have been lied to, and we have two suspects. Your friend Napper, or our mutual acquaintance, Inspector Lestrade.'

CHAPTER 20

5 St James's Terrace, Clerkenwell, May 1878

'Come to bed, Nell,' Jack massaged my shoulders. 'Some of us have an early start in the morning.'

'It's only half past nine.' I blew on the sentence I had just written. 'If I finish this tonight, you can give it to the inspector in the morning.'

His breath was on my ear, and his arms slid around me. 'Or you could come to bed with me.'

'Jack…' He kissed my neck, and his warmth stole through me. I pushed my papers aside and kissed him back, and he lifted me to my feet.

We walked upstairs hand in hand, and undressed each other. My hand went to the lamp. 'Don't,' he said. 'I want to look at you.' In bed he moved above me, his broad dark shape blocking out the light, and handled me like a piece of china, just as he had from the moment we met. Then suddenly he grunted, and tensed. 'I'm sorry.' He withdrew, and flopped down beside me on the bed. 'I was excited.'

'It's fine, Jack,' I said. I got up and washed myself quickly before extinguishing the light and getting under the covers.

After a while he sighed, and got into the bed too. 'Did you enjoy it, Nell?'

'Yes,' I said, although the truth was that I had been getting ready to enjoy it when the end came.

'It's been a while.'

When we had first moved into our little house we had made love at every opportunity; first thing in the morning, often when Jack came home, and sometimes he would surprise me in the kitchen and carry me off to bed without warning. It was such a novelty to be in our own home, without the fear that our creaking bedsprings would make Mr Peabody bang his stick on the ceiling, as he had in the flats. I had dreaded encountering his beady stare when we passed each other on the stairs.

I tried to remember the last time; perhaps on Saturday, or on one of the mornings before.

'I reckon you're overworking.'

'I don't think so, Jack. Remember when I was teaching all day, then studying with you, and running the house?'

'I s'pose.' There was silence for a moment. 'But when we have a family…'

'Mm,' I said. We had been married for five years, and as yet there was no sign of a baby. I had grown used to the reassurances from friends and family that it would happen when it was meant to happen. Jack was disappointed, though he never said a word, but what could we do about it?

'Things will change. I mean, you'll stop working.'

'I suppose,' I said, warily. 'I hadn't thought about it.' Jack earned well over a pound a week as a sergeant; but we would not have been able to live as comfortably as we did without the fifteen shillings a week I brought home. How would we cope if I did have a baby?

'Goodnight, Nell.' Jack leaned over and kissed me on the

cheek, then turned over.

'Goodnight, Jack,' I said into the darkness.

Next morning I was woken by whistling. Jack was sitting with his back to me, shaving in the glass. When he saw me watching in the mirror he paused, then finished the stroke he was on before setting the razor down. 'Good morning, sleepyhead.' His face was still half-lathered.

'Good morning.' I yawned.

He resumed shaving, turning his face this way and that. Then he wiped the lather away and reached for his shirt. 'There's tea in the pot,' he said. 'I'll bring you a cup in bed, if you like.'

I always made the morning tea. 'What time is it?' I sat up.

'Nearly eight. I couldn't wake you, you looked so peaceful.' He kissed me on the mouth, and ruffled my hair. 'Bye, Nell.' He thudded down the stairs, and the whistling started again as the front door closed.

I reached for my dressing gown and padded into the kitchen. The teapot stood on the table next to my unfinished work. Half an hour more, and the inspector could have had it today. Perhaps Jack was right, and I was overworking. The inspector had increased my wages to match the thicker bundles of papers that Jack brought home. London was suffering from a criminal heatwave; the newspapers screamed of crime sprees, super-villains and gangs, though they shunned the streets of Clerkenwell. Jack said the rags were just trying to sell more copies. 'There's no point analysing it, Nell,' he laughed. 'Some days there's more crime, some days there's less. It's just how it is, and it's my job to stop it.'

I poured myself a cup of tea and pulled the papers towards me. There had been a spate of housebreakings, and the inspector had asked me to look for a pattern in the last two months' reports. He had also warned me that I might find nothing at all. I had worked on the papers for hours and the findings were no different from what I would have expected, save in one respect.

I had separated robberies involving violence from the other crimes. Among these I had found a small but distinct sub-group – robberies where no one had been at home, but the premises had been smashed up. They occurred at all times of the day, and were sprinkled throughout the city. There were perhaps ten cases in this group, and the value of the stolen goods was much less than the cost of the damage: windows and furniture smashed, clothes and curtains ripped, and in one case a wall brought down. I could not see the point, and that in itself made the group worth investigating further.

I wrote my conclusion, blotted the last sheet, and sat back. It was not my job to dwell on the paperwork, simply to do as I was asked and move on to the next case. Yet I found myself wondering why burglars would break up someone's house when it would increase the risk of their being caught. Did they get satisfaction out of it, or were they following orders? Could it be an act of revenge? A warning? I considered adding a sheet of possibilities, then laughed at myself; the inspector understood criminal motivation much better than I did. And besides, the house needed cleaning. For a while I scrubbed, swept and straightened happily enough, but I hoped that Jack would bring home more work for me.

His key turned in the door a little after half past five. 'Evening, Nell!' he called, and his eyes flicked to the novel in my hand. 'Taking it easy?'

'It isn't time to start dinner.' I said, perhaps a little defensively.

He laughed as he hung up his coat. 'I asked Lestrade to let me go early. All work and no play makes Jack a dull boy, you know. It's Friday night, Nell! We'll go to the theatre and have supper.' Jack unbuttoned his uniform jacket as he climbed the stairs, and his voice floated down to me.

I went up after him. 'Didn't the inspector mind?'

'Put your blue dress on,' Jack's voice was muffled as he pulled his shirt off. 'You deserve a night off, Nell. I told him he was working you too hard.'

'Oh Jack, you didn't!' I bit my lip to keep myself from saying more.

'He just laughed and said he needed your brains, and I said he'd wear you out if he wasn't careful.'

I took the blue dress from the wardrobe and unfastened my print frock, which was faded and out of fashion. 'That won't happen, Jack,' I said, as neutrally as I could.

'I'm not running the risk.' I heard Jack's tread behind me and hastened to button my bodice. His face fell a little, but he said no more.

I cannot remember the play we watched that night. Jack ordered champagne, and after a glass or two on an empty stomach I was far too giggly to pay attention. The play must have been a comedy, as I recall laughter around us. We ate at Simpson's and I marvelled at the joints of meat parading round the room on silver trolleys, but I made a poor supper. Jack talked and laughed enough for both of us, his face red with wine and good humour, and exclaimed often at the fine night out we were having. I must have fallen asleep in the cab, as the next thing I remember is lying on the bed while Jack undressed me, swearing under his breath at my corset.

I woke the next morning with a bad headache, and winced as the sun caught my eyes. Jack was still asleep, snoring a little. I propped myself on my elbows and looked at the bedroom. The blue dress lay on the floor beneath my underthings, and Jack's clothes were scattered everywhere. So much for tidying the house. Perhaps a cup of tea would help the pain in my forehead and settle my gnawing stomach.

Downstairs I lit the fire and set the kettle to boil. At least it was Saturday. A day off for Jack this week, and no church. *A rest day...* Jack's words, 'All work and no play,' came back to me, and his conversation with the inspector. Inspector Lestrade usually sent work to me on Monday, Wednesday, and Friday. Jack would come home, extract the packet from his inside pocket, and announce 'A missive from the inspector'.

Jack's coat was in the hallway, and it was the work of a moment to slip my hand inside. The pocket was empty. I sat down at the kitchen table and speculated whether the inspector had had no work for me, Jack had forgotten it, or he had left it behind on purpose. Then I shook myself mentally. No good could come of it, and I could not ask. But I looked at the undelivered report in front of me and wished that I could deal directly with the inspector. My stomach growled. I made some toast and boiled an egg, but when I came to eat it the sight and smell of the yolk revolted me, and I pushed it away untouched.

CHAPTER 21

221B Baker Street, 13th January 1881

'Mrs Hudson, I congratulate you,' said Mr Holmes. 'I often bemoan the simplicity of the puzzles which Scotland Yard bring to my door. This one, though, is most interesting. A double mystery.'

'Mr Holmes, I doubt I can afford your fees.'

'Mm.' Mr Holmes's eyes glittered. 'I believe there may be a way round that. I have a little proposition for you.'

I sat bolt upright. 'A proposition?' I repeated. I had no idea where this conversation was going.

'Yes.' Mr Holmes smiled. 'I need an assistant.'

'What?' Dr Watson and I exclaimed in unison.

Mr Holmes's grin became as wide as the Cheshire Cat's. 'Most of the work Lestrade brings me is bread-and-butter stuff. It requires some intelligence, but it is hardly stretching. Now, if I had an assistant versed in police work who could undertake the simpler aspects of these cases, I could focus on the complex cases which will build my reputation. What do you say?'

'I – I…' I was completely taken aback. 'What would you

expect me to do?'

'Oh, this and that,' Mr Holmes said airily. 'Much the same as your old job, I expect. Perhaps some occasional fieldwork…'

'Holmes, is this wise?' Dr Watson looked as nervous as he had that morning at breakfast. 'I am not denigrating Mrs Hudson's intelligence or capabilities in any way, but – a woman, doing this sort of work!' His eyebrows were halfway up his forehead. 'I feel it is inappropriate.'

Mr Holmes sighed. 'Mrs Hudson has undertaken police work before…' He paced for a few seconds. 'Aha! I have it. I shall set a test. If Mrs Hudson agrees to this and I judge that she has passed, will you give the arrangement your blessing?'

Dr Watson's brow furrowed. 'I suppose I shall have to. In any case, Holmes, you know your own mind.'

'Mrs Hudson, do you agree to undertake my test?'

'I do.' My initial astonishment had been displaced by annoyance at Dr Watson's objections, and I was eager to prove myself.

'Excellent!' Mr Holmes did not appear to have noticed his friend's reticence; or if he had, he ignored it. 'Mrs Hudson, if you will go to your sitting room I shall fetch you when the test is ready. Dr Watson, it is a surprisingly fine day, so I suggest that you repair to the park. I will set the test for Mrs Hudson, then join you while she completes it.'

My mind raced as I walked upstairs. What sort of test would Mr Holmes set? I hoped I could remember sufficient of my former skills to pass muster. If I did not, it was a judgement on my sex, and a vindication of Dr Watson. I strained my ears to hear the conversation downstairs, but it was merely a faint buzz. I heard two sets of footsteps go downstairs, and one come back up, continuing to my door. 'Come in!' I called, my heart racing. Mr Holmes closed the door behind him and leaned against it, his hands behind his back.

'Mrs Villiers, I have your test ready.' I rose. 'It requires a little preparation.' There was what I can only describe as a twinkle in his eye. 'I have sent Billy on a long errand, and we have the house to ourselves for at least the next hour.' He laughed at my surprised face. 'Have you guessed what I would like you to do?'

'Mr Holmes, I have no idea.' His face was full of mischief, and I racked my brains for what might amuse him. Then it dawned on me. 'No!'

'You have worked it out.' He drummed a little tune on the door. 'Mrs Villiers, here is your test. You will dress as you did last night and take a stroll in the park. I have arranged to meet Watson at the first bench on the left after the entrance. You will walk past, drop your handkerchief, and he will return it to you.'

'Mr Holmes, I don't understand—'

'Dr Watson does not know what the test is, Mrs Villiers. The test is that he continues not to know.'

I stared at my taskmaster in horror.

'Your task complete, you will return to Baker Street and resume your normal appearance. I shall return after a reasonable interval with Dr Watson, and we shall take matters from there.' Mr Holmes smiled. 'Is that all quite clear?'

'It is, Mr Holmes.' Sweat prickled on the back of my neck and my palms, and I wished that Mr Holmes could have administered a written examination.

'Excellent! I shall expect you downstairs shortly, dressed appropriately.' He bowed slightly, and was gone.

It was a matter of minutes to whiten my eyebrows, change into an old black dress and catch up the shawl, basket, and battered bonnet. I drew a handkerchief from my pocket, and on impulse changed it for one with a deeper black border. I moved quickly to distract myself from the embarrassment creeping over me. *This is your chance*, I told myself. *This is the only way to find out what happened to Jack.* And suddenly excitement coursed through my veins. It was a chance to catch Dr Watson out, a game, a play. I regarded myself in the mirror, and laughed that I would play that dismal old woman again.

'Enter!' called Mr Holmes. He had the wig ready for me. 'Is that all you need?' He sounded a little disappointed.

'Do you have a snuffbox?' I called, as I tucked my hair into the wig.

'Yes.' He came through with it, and watched me settle my bonnet, putting my face in as much shadow as possible. I was not used to such scrutiny, and at first I looked down, away – anything to avoid meeting his eyes. But then I realised Mr Holmes was not watching me in the way that a man sometimes watches a woman. His face showed interest, but a curious interest. A professional interest.

'I am almost ready,' I said. He held out the snuffbox to me. I opened it, took a heaping pinch, and Mr Holmes retreated as I sneezed six times in succession. 'Ugh. Please excuse me, Mr Holmes.'

'Your dedication is commendable, Mrs Villiers.' His face was expressionless. 'I shall join Dr Watson in the park.'

My heart was pounding. Mr Holmes's steps faded away, and the front door thudded shut. I watched the minute hand of the clock inch forward more than once. Could I do it? Could I fool Dr Watson and pass the test? I looked at the stooping figure before me. There was no way to know but to try.

I descended to the kitchen and as I opened the back door my wedding ring flashed in the light. I put it in a pocket, and dirtied my hands on the kitchen floor.

It was a relief not to have to brave the main street at once. I shuffled along the alley, perturbed by a new worry. My previous expedition had taken place in dusk and darkness; this time I would be in daylight. I hoped my disguise would hold up.

The park was a short walk away. I meandered through the flowing river of people, caught by an elbow or two as people brushed past in their haste. No one apologised, and I took this to mean that I was suitably invisible.

I sniffled and crept, and with every step I advanced closer to the bench on which Mr Holmes and Dr Watson were sitting. Dr Watson sat neat and straight; Mr Holmes was sprawled with an arm over the back of the bench, and his long legs crossed at an angle. They were facing away from me, but soon I would be within their range of vision. I pulled out my handkerchief as I ambled along and blew my nose heartily, then indulged in some more snuffling before stuffing my handkerchief into my sleeve, fumbling it half-out again. A moment later it fell. I was level with the park bench, and I willed myself not to quicken my pace, not to dawdle.

'Excuse me!' It was the moment of truth. I came to a stop and turned my head as I had once seen a gigantic old tortoise do in the Zoological Gardens.

'Excuse me!' Dr Watson was pointing behind me. 'You dropped something, ma'am.' His voice was raised, and his words more clearly enunciated than usual.

I turned myself round to the handkerchief, 'Oh! Thankee, sir,' I growled. I began to shuffle back towards it, throwing in an occasional sniff. After a few seconds the doctor sprang up, pinched the handkerchief between finger and thumb, and held it out to me. 'Thankee, thankee.' I took the handkerchief, bobbed something halfway between a curtsey and a bow, and made as if to blow my nose.

'No!' he shouted, and snatched the handkerchief away. 'It's been on the ground in the dirt, for heaven's sake! Here.' He pulled a large white handkerchief from his trouser pocket and flapped it at me. 'Use this.' I took it and buried my nose in it, honked twice, then held it out towards him. 'You may keep it,' he said, stepping back with a look of distaste. 'How long have you had this cold?'

Before I could answer, Mr Holmes called out from the bench, 'Do leave that old hag alone, Watson, you'll catch the plague.'

Dr Watson ignored him and waited for my answer. 'Week or two, sir,' I mumbled, keeping my head down and wishing he were less conscientious.

'Well, if you want to be well again you must help it on its way,' he proclaimed. 'Fresh air, clean linen, beef tea, and camphor. Do you have any camphor?'

I considered, and shook my head.

He tutted in exasperation. 'Wait.' He took out a small notepad and scribbled a few words, then tore the sheet out and thrust it under my nose. 'Take this to the druggist.' He dug into his pocket and brought out half a crown. 'And while you're at it, buy yourself some oranges.'

I bobbed again. 'Thankee *kindly*, sir!'

'She'll only spend it on drink!' Mr Holmes heckled. I shook a grimy fist in his direction.

He snorted and stood up. 'Come, Watson, let us take a turn in the park.'

'Now, do you remember what you must buy?' Dr Watson asked me sternly.

'Yessir. Camphor'n oranges, sir.'

'That's right. Good day to you, ma'am.' He inclined his head to me and strode after his departing friend. I looked down at the coin in my hand, bright as a new-minted moon, and shuffled on my way, willing myself to stay stooped and slow.

I thought I would never reach the safety of the tradesman's entrance, but at last I turned into the short alley and eased open the familiar door. I peered in; all was quiet. My walk in the park seemed to have lasted an eternity. I pelted up the stairs to my room and changed back as speedily as I could. Had I done enough? Had I passed muster? Mr Holmes's eyes had gleamed more than once, but I had not been able to interpret it. Amusement? Contempt? Approval? Dr Watson might have guessed and humoured me, and the pair of them might be laughing about it now. My stomach twisted itself into a tight knot.

The front door opened and I heard laughter. Then the door below opened, the conversation ceased, and one pair of feet came upstairs. 'Come in,' I called, and steeled myself.

Mr Holmes walked in, his face serious. 'Mrs Villiers, I have some bad news.' Then he paused.

Why didn't he just tell me? I was a grown woman; I had heard far worse things than the results of a stupid test. I had done all I could, and if it was not enough, I had tried my best. 'Well, tell me then!' I burst out.

His mouth twitched. 'Mrs Villiers, I am afraid that you have lost a handkerchief. Watson put it in the first rubbish bin that we passed.' A broad grin spread across his face. 'He would like you to bring up some hot water, so that he can scrub his hands clean.'

'He didn't guess?'

Mr Holmes's face was incredulous. 'Of course not! You were magnificent! When we left you he even rebuked me for my ungentlemanly behaviour.' He chuckled. 'When I am next in a low mood, Mrs Villiers, I might ask you to repeat the performance. It was one of the most cheering spectacles I have attended for a while.'

I found myself smiling in response to his laughter. 'I am not sure that I would care to do it too often.'

'Mrs Villiers, I would not ask you to.' He was all seriousness. 'Deceiving our friends is a bad habit to form. I wouldn't have asked you to do it today, but I had to judge how you would cope under pressure. If the good doctor had recognised you it would have been embarrassing, but far better than a failure when someone's life depends on it.'

'My husband's life may depend on it,' I answered, looking up at him. He looked away, and shifted from foot to foot.

'Quite. Could you attend to the hot water, Mrs Villiers, and I shall tell Watson that you have passed your *written test* with flying colours.' He opened the door for me. 'Oh, and one more thing—'

'Yes, Mr Holmes?'

'Dr Watson knows from your history that you have another name. I have not revealed it to him, as I did not have your permission. Do you wish to tell him?'

I reflected. Dr Watson was a good and trustworthy man; yet he might slip, and address me by it in front of Billy, or someone else. 'Perhaps in the future; not at present,' I said.

'Very well.'

I went downstairs to boil the kettle for Dr Watson's hot water, a little flustered. Only three people knew that Mrs Hudson was Nell Villiers: Inspector Lestrade, Napper, and Mr Holmes. Now I was beginning to appreciate that 'Mrs Hudson', whom I had viewed as blotting out my real self, could be a useful cover for Nell Villiers, and I liked the thought that at Baker Street my real identity was a secret shared only with Mr Holmes. I could not say why, exactly – but I liked it.

CHAPTER 22

5 St James's Terrace, Clerkenwell, July 1878

The parlour cushions were plumped, the rug straight, the fire irons polished and the fire bright. A tray laid with our wedding china stood on the sideboard. I had put on the blue dress and the gold necklace that Jack had given me on our anniversary. There was nothing to do now but wait.

Jack had come home late on Monday evening, the shoulders of his coat damp with rain. With a quick 'Evening, Nell,' he went to get changed. I finished the sock I was darning, closed my workbox, and took it upstairs to put away.

Jack pulled his braces into place as I walked into the bedroom waving the sock. 'I have something for you, Jack.'

'The inspector's coming round on Thursday.'

'Did he say what it was about?'

'No.' Jack took the sock from me and shoved it into the drawer.

'It isn't about finishing early on Friday?'

Jack snorted and slammed the drawer. 'Of course not! If Lestrade was going to tell me off about that he'd call me in, not drag himself out here!' He turned to go downstairs, muttering something under his breath.

'I didn't quite hear you, Jack.' The tone of my voice reminded me of my former life as a teacher, when I had a disruptive pupil.

Jack faced me, standing in the doorway. 'I said, Nell, that for a clever woman you can be bloody stupid sometimes.' He sighed. 'If he's coming to the house, it isn't me he wants to speak to.' His feet clattered downstairs, and after a moment or two I followed. Jack was sitting at the kitchen table. I fetched his dinner from the oven. 'I shouldn't have snapped at you,' he said. 'I'm sorry.' He pulled my hand towards him and kissed it.

I ruffled his hair. 'It's all right.' I sat down with him. 'It's probably nothing.'

Jack swallowed a large forkful of cottage pie. 'Like I said, he wouldn't come out here for nothing. He's a busy man. Very busy, at the moment.' He took another mouthful, got up, and walked into the hall. When he returned he had a thick brown envelope in his hand. 'He gave me this for you. Open it; perhaps he's written you a note.'

We walked back into the kitchen and Jack resumed his dinner while I slit the envelope and pulled out the contents. The usual sheaf of papers, and the inspector's instructions. 'More robberies,' I sighed. 'Is anything left unstolen in London?' I read the instructions, dashed off in the inspector's spiky hand, and put them by Jack's plate. As before, he asked me to look for any pattern to the crimes, which this time were all from District 1.

'North of the river,' said Jack, pointing at the inspector's note with his fork. 'Stepney, Whitechapel, Thames, Islington. Does he say anything else?'

'Only that the report's due by Wednesday.'

'He's a wise old owl, the inspector.' Jack scooped up the

last forkful of pie from the plate. 'He'll want to know what you make of this little lot beforehand. But there must be something afoot, or he wouldn't have booked himself in to visit us.'

'Did you give him my report today?'

'This morning.' Jack mopped up the gravy on his plate with a piece of bread. 'Could that be something to do with it?' His voice was casual, but his eyes searched my face for clues.

'It might be.' It must be! The pattern must mean something.

'What did you write? Did you find anything?'

'Nothing conclusive. Just—' I hesitated. 'You won't tell anyone, will you?'

'Course not, Nell,' Jack reached for my hand. 'Come on, what did you find?'

'I wasn't even sure that it meant anything. Just some robberies where the houses had been smashed up. Not to get in or get at belongings, but as if it was a message. I didn't try to work out why; I just noted the pattern and wrote a list of the cases that fitted.'

Jack squeezed my hand. 'Maybe a protection racket? Were the cases in the same area?'

'No, they were scattered around London. That's why I didn't make much of it.'

'That makes no sense.' Jack's voice was indignant.

I put a hand over my mouth to stifle a yawn. 'Sorry, I'm more tired than I realised.' It was a quarter past ten.

'I've kept you up,' said Jack. 'Go to bed if you're tired, Nell. I won't be long.'

I put the papers back into the envelope, stood up, and stretched. 'I'll leave the lamp on for you.' Upstairs I undressed slowly, folding each item as I took it off. I was unpinning my bun when I heard what I had been listening for: the *slip* of paper being removed from an envelope. Jack was reading my papers. I got into bed a little more noisily than usual and coughed as I settled down.

Jack came upstairs perhaps five minutes later, and burrowed into the bed to kiss my forehead. 'You look comfortable in your nest.' He was ready quickly, and put the light out. I lay in the dark, wide awake and annoyed. Jack didn't discuss his work with me; yet now he pressed me to share my findings with him. I had feigned tiredness to avoid further conversation, and Jack had read the inspector's papers when I was upstairs. I swallowed the anger as best I could, but it was a long time before I slept that night.

The next morning I tried not to show my impatience to have Jack out of the house so that I could get to work. The front door had barely closed before the papers were spread all over the table. I read greedily, as I would have devoured a new work from a favourite author, and scribbled as I read, covering sheet after sheet. I ate a biscuit and read through my scrawl. These cases were more serious than the previous set. In several the house had been occupied when the break-in occurred, and the inhabitants had been beaten, knocked out, tied up... While the cases came from a smaller area, they were widely scattered within it; no area was more concentrated than another.

I needed to find a way in. I laid the statements in a patchwork on the table and let my gaze wander over them. A name caught my eye. Arthur MacAleer, a shopkeeper known to the police for receiving stolen goods; I had probably read about him before. His shop had been ransacked in the early hours. His cries alerted a passer-by at seven in the morning, and he was found tied to a chair. He did not recognise his attackers. He had not been knocked out; instead they had beaten him around the legs, shattering his kneecap and breaking an ankle. It read like a revenge attack, yet MacAleer said he did not recognise them. Was he telling the truth? *Known to the police…*

I scanned the documents again. In five cases the victim had a police record. Assault, pickpocketing, causing a nuisance, receiving stolen goods, damaging property. I laid the other documents aside and took a fresh sheet of paper. In each case the victim had been alone when the break-in occurred, and they had all been injured in some way. Two were found unconscious; all had been beaten with a thick club of some kind. I read through the list of injuries: fractured skull, broken right wrist, two broken ribs on the left side, cracked left kneecap… *Wait.* I picked up MacAleer's case. Broken left ankle, shattered left kneecap. I scrabbled at the papers.

All five victims had a broken left kneecap. My hand shook as I wrote the words down.

All of the crimes had been reported by someone other than the victim.

None of the attackers had worn a mask or a hood.

None of the victims could think of a reason why they would be attacked. No one bore a grudge against them; they had no enemies.

Those were the common themes. Sometimes there was one burglar, sometimes a gang. The value of the stolen items ranged from ten shillings to three hundred pounds. Two victims lived in slum dwellings; one lived in the best house in the neighbourhood. I could not tell if the motive was revenge or a warning, but there was coordination and planning behind the seemingly random attacks.

I spent the rest of the day searching through the other cases for connections and patterns, trying to find something I could understand. There was nothing. My final report was two pages long. Instead of my usual objective presentation of the facts I wrote to convince the inspector that there was a significant pattern potentially linked to my previous report. I signed my name, found an envelope, and sealed the report inside.

When Jack got home that night he asked whether I had found anything. I replied that a few cases were linked but I was uncertain of the significance, and couldn't say more until the inspector had read my report. He accepted it, and for the next three days I wondered whether I had made too much of my findings. Had I been led astray by a coincidence? Had I strung together a pattern from a few odds and ends?

And now it was Thursday and Inspector Lestrade was coming home with Jack. Jack's key scraped in the door, and butterflies flew upwards in my stomach. Soon I would know. Soon we would both know.

CHAPTER 23

221B Baker Street, 17th January 1881

'So, Mr Holmes…' I looked around the sitting room, half of which was as disarranged as ever, 'what would you like me to do?'

It was Monday morning. Dr Watson had departed for the first day at his new job: *locum tenens* at Bart's Hospital. I had brought a good breakfast for the gentlemen, and he had fallen to with relish. 'I am looking forward to being back in harness,' he said, wiping egg from his moustache. 'A man needs occupation.'

So does a woman, I thought to myself. And soon I would have an occupation again, a way back to myself, and, hopefully, to Jack. I performed my morning duties with a light heart, then tripped upstairs to discover what Mr Holmes had in store for me. He was lying on the settee, scraping at his violin, but sat up and put it aside when I entered.

'First things first.' Mr Holmes looked about him in a way which suggested that I would be tidying the room, then sprang up. 'We must purchase your equipment.' He picked up his overcoat from the arm of the settee.

'I beg your pardon?' I imagined a typewriter, or a dictating machine.

'I apologise, Mrs Villiers, I am getting ahead of myself. Let me explain.' He flopped down on the settee again, and waved me to Dr Watson's chair opposite. I sat down, straight-backed, and folded my hands in my lap.

'Ah, you are worried at what I shall say next!' Mr Holmes chuckled. 'And perhaps you are right. Mrs Villiers, do you recall the day when you surprised me in costume?' He spoke without embarrassment.

I laughed. 'Indeed I do.'

'The profession of consulting detective is a strange one.' He gazed at the ceiling. 'It divides roughly into four quarters. A quarter research, to write monographs which will build my reputation. A quarter drumming up business: obtaining my cases. A quarter racking my brains and forming my theories...'

'And the other quarter?'

'Being someone else.' Mr Holmes sat bolt upright. 'Following people, hanging around on street corners, picking up gossip, drinking in taverns, waiting for something to happen . . . the thing that proves or disproves my theory, the key to the mystery.' He snapped his fingers. 'For that I require equipment. And so do you.'

I glanced towards Mr Holmes's bedroom door, behind which squatted the trunk.

'Yours will not be as extensive,' he said. 'I wouldn't ask you to venture into half the places I frequent. Besides, I have noted that you have several plain dresses which will serve my purpose admirably.'

'Thank you.' I bowed. He did not appear to notice.

'Just a few accessories.' He bounded up. 'Let us go.'

Sudden panic glued me to the seat. 'But I—'

'What, Mrs Villiers?'

'I cannot just leave the house with you! I must have a reason, for Billy.'

'In that case, I have asked you to help me choose a present for my aunt and uncle's silver wedding anniversary. Come along, now.'

Billy wished me good luck with the shopping, and two minutes later Mr Holmes and I were in a cab. His mood improved as soon as we had left Baker Street behind. 'I apologise, Mrs Villiers,' he said. 'I am impatient, and sometimes I forget the proprieties.'

'It is quite all right.' I looked out at London whizzing past us. 'I have spent so long shut away that I fear the open door.' I glanced at him, afraid that I had said too much, but he was looking out of the other window. 'Where are we going?'

'Here.' He rapped on the roof with his cane and the cab rolled to a stop. He helped me down, and took my arm. 'It is a minute's walk this way. Your name at the establishment is Miss Amelia Jones. I trust them, but it is as well to be careful.'

'Is this Covent Garden?'

'Seven Dials.' He steered me under a large awning. The sign beneath read *Angel and Son: Theatrical Costumiers*.

The shop was enormous, with rack upon rack of garments in all styles and colours. It was like a riotous flower garden. A small woman hurried up to Mr Holmes, beaming. 'Mr Harwood!'

'Mrs Keen!' He took her hand with a flourish and raised it to his lips. 'How are you?'

'All the better for seeing you, my dear. Mr Angel will be so sorry he missed you! And who might this charming young lady be?' She regarded me with bright birdlike eyes.

'Allow me to introduce my cousin, Miss Jones. She's in the

business too.' Mr Holmes's voice had a note of swagger and a slight London twang, and I realised that he had moved a little differently since we entered the shop. 'Rep mainly, and understudying.'

Mrs Keen clasped her hands. 'Wonderful! And are you shopping today, Miss Jones?'

'She is,' said Mr Holmes. 'What can you show us in wigs?'

'Come through to the dressing room!' Mrs Keen opened a plain wooden door, behind which was a small but well-lit room with a dressing table and two chairs. 'I'll bring a selection,' she breathed, and bustled out.

Mr Holmes leaned across. 'She will dress you up like a doll,' he muttered. 'Just let her do it; but we shall pick and choose.'

'I had no idea you were so famous, Mr Harwood.' I laughed. 'Understudying, indeed.' I felt far more relaxed in this shop, as Miss Jones, than I did in my own home.

He grinned. 'I did warn you that I spent a lot of time pretending to be other people.'

'Here we are!' Mrs Keen's arms were full of boxes. 'Now you sit before the mirror, dear, and we'll try them on.'

I did as I was told, and submitted first to a tight stocking-cap over my hair, then to fitting, styling, pinning, and teasing. My hair changed from its usual light brown to fair, then chestnut, dark brown, and black, and I saw myself with a chignon, a plaited coronet, and other styles which I would never be able to reproduce.

We left the shop with several parcels: the chestnut and dark-brown wigs, and some accessories. Mr Holmes had chosen two light patterned shawls, a short grey jacket, a large handbag, and a plain winter bonnet. They were in the current fashion of cut and colour, of medium quality, and utterly commonplace. Mr Holmes had also picked out a few things for himself while Mrs Keen gossiped to me about the famous actresses who had visited in the last week. I was doubly glad that we were under an alias. He paid in cash and waved away the change, and whistled for a cab as we stepped outside.

'Does being a detective pay well?'

The cab rattled along for a few seconds while he considered my question. 'It varies,' he said. 'But I have to pretend to the outside world that money doesn't matter to me. And of course it is always preferable to deal in cash when using a false name.' He glanced out of the window. 'When we return to Baker Street I shall summarise the case you will assist with tomorrow. In the morning you will read through the case notes; in the afternoon you will shadow someone.'

'Is it the criminal's wife?'

'It is. I have been courting her lady's maid, and while she knows nothing of importance she loves to gossip about her mistress's plans.'

'Is that necessary?' I shifted in my seat.

'Not for you,' he snapped. Then he sighed. 'Mrs Villiers, I am a gentleman, and I only do what is necessary to obtain the information. There will be no damage to the girl's feelings.'

We were silent until the cab drew up in Baker Street. I informed Billy that the shopping trip had gone well and went to take off my outdoor things, glad of a few moments away from Mr Holmes.

When I went downstairs Mr Holmes had recovered his good humour. 'Take a seat, Mrs Villiers, and I will tell you about the case. No, not here.' He waved a hand at the bedroom. 'In there.'

I remained where I was. 'Why in the bedroom, Mr Holmes?'

'So that we can settle your costume for tomorrow at the same time. I have a call to make later this afternoon, so it is

121

best to do it now.' I followed him into the bedroom, where he placed a chair for me so that I sat in full light. 'The chestnut, or the dark brown?'

'The chestnut.' I replaced my own hair with a rich mane which I tamed into a bun on the top of my head.

'Good. Mrs Villiers, I apologise for asking you this, but . . . have you ever worn make-up?'

'Of course not!' I snorted, then blushed.

Mr Holmes opened one of the parcels we had brought home. There were little pots and pencils, and I had no idea what to do with any of it. 'Do you remember what I said in the cab, that I would only do what is necessary?'

'Yes,' I wondered what courting maids had to do with painting my face.

'This is necessary to keep you safe. You must not be recognisable either as Mrs Villiers or Mrs Hudson. If the inspector, or Billy, or a former friend saw you—' He sighed. 'When we have solved the mystery of your husband's disappearance I hope you will be able to live a normal life, with no connection to the strange things you have undertaken in pursuit of the truth.' I could appreciate Mr Holmes's reasoning; but the reference to keeping me safe touched a nerve. Then again, I reflected, sending me out in disguise to track a criminal's wife was hardly wrapping me in cotton wool.

'Don't worry, Mrs Villiers. I promise not to paint you so that your features can be made out from the back row of the theatre. You have a rare quality which it would be a pity to waste.'

I raised my eyebrows and Mr Holmes laughed. 'You are capable, when you wish, of being superlatively inconspicuous. Your height is normal, your features regular, your appearance pleasant but not striking. Some of us are not so fortunate.' He stood tall and waved his long arms around, and I could not keep from laughing. 'I am paying you a compliment! Yet it is more than that. When you played the old woman a few days ago, you were just like a hundred old women who shuffle about the streets. I behaved shamefully in heckling you, but I wanted to see what you would do, and you reacted beautifully. Watson could never have carried it off; he is too much himself. You must look different from your usual self, but not stand out.' He passed me a hand mirror. 'I shall begin, then you will finish the process.' He picked up a pencil and I flinched as it approached me. 'I will be as gentle as I can, Mrs Villiers.'

I watched in the mirror as my right eyebrow changed its shape a fraction, and matched the chestnut wig. 'Now it is your turn. Little strokes, as though you were drawing the hairs on.' My hand shook as I made the first mark. 'It will come easier with practice,' said Mr Holmes, watching. I took a deep breath and did my best to match the two brows. 'Not bad for a first try, Mrs Villiers.' Next my colour grew a little higher and I acquired two small moles, and finally I had to keep very still indeed as my eyelashes darkened. 'That will do.' Mr Holmes delved into one of the parcels and presented me with a pince-nez. 'They are plain glass. Use them or not, as you wish.'

I fixed them on my nose and regarded myself in the mirror. I did not look painted at all; just different, and perhaps a few years younger. I tried a few expressions, and they looked different too. 'I had no idea that my eyebrows were so much a part of me.'

He smiled. 'It is strange, is it not, the little things that make us. Now, choose your accessories for tomorrow, and I will tell you about your quarry. Her name is Mrs Euphemia Stanley; her husband is Emmett Stanley, a convicted embezzler. There have been financial irregularities at the

Bank of England lately, and Mr Stanley is nowhere to be found...' I settled on the grey jacket as the best match for the dress I planned to wear the next day, and put the bonnet on at a fashionable tilt. 'She is taking afternoon tea with a friend at Brown's Hotel, around four o'clock. If you can get a table nearby, do; otherwise, see if you can trail her when she leaves. I shall expect you back no later than half past six. Here is money for expenses.' He dug into his trouser pocket and put a few pound notes and some loose change into my hand.

'Is there anything in particular I should watch for?'

Mr Holmes considered. 'Any talk of different parts of England, or of abroad. Otherwise, just keep your ears and eyes open. It is most likely that you will hear nothing useful at all.'

'What if something significant is happening and it is time for me to return? Should I remain?'

He shook his head. 'No; come home. When I am in character I feel as if I am in a house of mirrors; I imagine myself at every angle, and it is a strain on the nerves. I am fit for nothing after a day of being somebody else, and I am used to it. I would not have you make a slip through tiredness. Now, can you get yourself ready tomorrow, more or less the same?' I nodded. 'Then it is time for you to go back to being Mrs Villiers for the afternoon. Cold cream will take it off.' He retired to the sitting room.

I removed the wig and set about cleaning my face, which was easier than I had anticipated. Five minutes later I had re-dressed my hair, and was ready. I gathered up the elements of my disguise and opened the bedroom door. Mr Holmes was stretched on the settee, reading. 'Mrs Villiers!' He beckoned me over, and got up. He examined me closely, then pulled out his handkerchief, turned my cheek to the light, and wiped a trace of something away. 'You missed a bit.'

I thanked Mr Holmes, went upstairs, and after I had hidden my new possessions I lay down on the bed. A few minutes' rest would do me good, I told myself, and it had been an exciting first day. Of course I was tired. I had been shopping; I had learned new skills; I had been given my first undercover assignment. That was why my heart was racing. That, and climbing the stairs too fast. I closed my eyes and tried not to think of the warm, light touch of Mr Holmes's fingers, or the care with which he had wiped away the paint. It was nothing but caution. Nothing at all.

CHAPTER 24

221B Baker Street, 13th September 1880

'Do you know what day it is today, Mrs Hudson?'

I had been startled by a single hard knock at the front door at half past eight in the evening. It could be only one person. I racked my brains for a reason for Inspector Lestrade's visit. I had not asked for anything lately. Since I had been permitted to join the library six months ago I had occupied my leisure time well, introducing Billy to several new authors.

I looked at the calendar on the mantelpiece. 'That is not what I meant,' said Inspector Lestrade. His tone was level. 'Today it is two years since Sergeant Villiers disappeared.' He looked at my black silk dress. 'You may assume half-mourning, if you wish to.'

I could not believe I had been at Baker Street for so long. 'I had not realised.'

'Neither had I. It was a chance remark from one of the sergeants which alerted me.'

'I take it there have been no developments in the case.'

'No, I am afraid not. No developments, and no news.' The inspector looked up at me, his eyes like jet beads. 'All the

126

trails have gone cold.' It was the first time he had been so open with me. 'I am sorry.'

'I'm sure you are doing all you can, Inspector.' I said the words mechanically; it was the platitude I usually trotted out on these occasions.

'As much as we can, yes.' The inspector rose. 'You can remain in full mourning if you prefer, of course.'

'I shall make the change, Inspector.' The words were out of my mouth before I had thought about them.

'Very well, Mrs Hudson.' The inspector inclined his head. 'I shall leave it to you to arrange matters with the outfitters.' I rang for Billy to show the inspector out, and he wished me a good evening.

Two weeks later I was the owner of three new dresses: one grey, one purple and one lilac. I cannot describe how marvellous it was to take off my black dress and step into the soft grey folds. The fabric was probably of equal weight, but a heavy mass had been lifted from my shoulders. The dressmaker fussed around me, checking the fit of the dress; I would not have cared if it had hung off me like a sack. 'That's better, isn't it, ma'am,' she said, arranging my skirts. The dresses were all trimmed with black, but I felt transformed, and thanked her profusely.

When she had left I turned this way and that in the glass. It was not that the dresses were particularly flattering, although deep black had drained the colour out of me. It was that I was a person again, and not an object of pity. There might, after all, be a life ahead of me; some way out of the pretence I was living under. The inspector had never allowed me to arrange my own appointment before, and I hoped fervently that this might be the beginning of the end of it all. Then I felt a stab of guilt that I was so ready to move on, to cease mourning Jack, and slough him off as a snake does its skin. Yet I had never been able to mourn him with a quiet heart. If Jack had known what was happening, I told myself, he would not have expected me to mope around in black for ever. I pushed it to the back of my mind, and went down to speak to Billy about the butcher's order.

Billy was in the scullery when I entered, and when he turned at the sound of my voice he jumped as if I were the ghost of myself. A slow smile spread over his face as I talked about chops and cutlets, and a small joint of meat for Sunday. 'Yes, ma'am,' he said, when I had finished speaking. 'I'll go now.' He picked up his livery coat from its peg. 'Will you come too, ma'am? It is a fine day.'

I was about to reply that the errand did not require two of us when I remembered that I had read all the books I had borrowed from the library. 'What a good idea, Billy. I shall be ready in a few minutes.' I hurried upstairs to fetch my books and my bonnet, and left the house in fine spirits. We passed the policeman on his beat and he raised his helmet to me, which he had never done before. The butcher's eyebrows shot up when we walked into the shop. I suspect that if I had gone alone he would not have recognised me. At the library Mr Rogers fumbled over my books, nearly dropping one of them as he stamped it. On the way home through the park I spied two women whom I had seen in the next pew during my infrequent visits to church, and we exchanged a few words.

When we had parted I looked across at Billy, who had a silly expression on his face. 'What is it, Billy? Have I said something amusing?'

'Not at all, ma'am.' His grin broadened. 'Shall we take another turn round the park?'

'Why not?' We strolled along, watching the ducks in the pond and the children with their sailboats, and I realised I could behave like a normal person again. I did not have to hide behind a veil or black drapery. In a few months I would not have to wear any black at all; I never wanted to wear black again.

'Billy, what are the inspector's latest instructions to you?'

Billy scratched his ear. 'Well, ma'am, he said that now you were in half-mourning you should go out more. Broaden your interests. Make some friends. Those are his words, not mine, ma'am,' he added hastily.

'I see.' We walked on. The sky was almost cloudless and birds sang in the trees. My black clothes had smothered me in a fog of grief, and now that they were gone everything was brighter and clearer. I could not return to the life I had lived – not yet, at least – but I could make a new life, and hopefully make it worth living. 'I shall need visiting cards, Billy.' I wondered what the extent of the inspector's new boundaries might be. I remembered myself cowering in the house, a frightened black fledgling wanting to fly but too scared and sad to do it.

When we arrived back in Baker Street I went upstairs to take off my bonnet and put my new books in the sitting room. My bedroom door was open, and the black dress was a puddle of darkness draped across the easy chair. My first impulse was to tear the vile thing apart, but I told myself that such a destructive action belonged to the frustrated, trapped, half-crazed woman I had been. I picked up the dress and folded it until it was as small a bundle as it could be. I took the clothes from my bottom drawer and thrust the dress to the back. The other black dress joined it, and I flung the black cloak and petticoats into the drawer above. I would never have to look at them again.

CHAPTER 25

221B Baker Street, 18th January 1881

'A table by the window, madam?'

'Yes, please.' The waiter led the way and pulled out my chair. 'It is most unlike my friend to be late,' I commented, looking around the room for that fictitious person.

'I am sure she will not keep you waiting long,' said the waiter smoothly. 'May I take your name, so that I can direct her when she arrives?'

'I am Miss Fry.' He bowed and withdrew and I turned my attention to the menu, taking care not to stare at the two women sitting at the next table.

Thus far all had gone to plan. I had read Mr Holmes's case notes that morning, and purchased more wool at the haberdasher's. On that errand I had also visited three Ladies' Rooms to assess their facilities and lighting. On my return I invented another class at the Institute, and upstairs I knitted an inch of a scarf as a proof for later. I wondered how Mr Holmes had got on that morning and whether I would see him – indeed, whether I would recognise him.

After lunch the time dragged and I willed the hands of the

clock to turn faster. When the time came I fairly jumped out of my chair. I called goodbye to Billy and set out: first in the direction of the Institute, then diverting into a ladies' room to assume my new identity. It was quieter than on my previous excursion, so I called to the attendant for more lavatory paper and slipped out when her back was turned.

Brown's Hotel was a mile away. It was a fine, crisp day and I enjoyed my walk in the sunshine, window-shopping and watching passers-by through my pince-nez. I turned into Albemarle Street and the cream-coloured facade of the hotel rose before me. 'Afternoon, miss.' A tall man in livery hurrying past touched his cap to me, and I realised that Mr Holmes had just gone off duty. My watch said that it was five minutes past four. I took a deep breath, and walked into the tearoom.

Mrs Euphemia Stanley was just as Mr Holmes had described: a short, stoutish, dark-haired woman of about forty, elaborately dressed. But she had an open, pleasant face and an amiable manner. Her friend was around the same age, fair-haired and slim, with the air of a thoroughbred horse. I listened to their conversation while I studied the menu, deciding with regret that since my friend had deserted me, perhaps I should not treat myself to a full afternoon tea. The waiter returned, and I ordered a pot of tea. 'Which cake would you recommend?' I asked.

'The lemon sponge is popular,' he replied.

'Oh!' interjected Mrs Stanley's friend. 'If you're only having one cake it should be the Dundee, my dear. Exquisite!'

'A slice of the Dundee then, please.' I disliked almonds; yet if it meant establishing friendly relations with the next table, I would eat a slab of cake with pleasure.

'On your own, dear?' Mrs Stanley looked sympathetic.

'My friend was supposed to meet me here. I wonder where

she can be…'

My innocent remark opened the door for a flood of speculation and anecdote from Mrs Stanley and her friend: the iniquities of London cabmen, the beastly Underground Railway, going to the wrong hotel, and the time when Mrs Stanley had been kept waiting at a shop twenty minutes for bottle-green ribbon. 'Apple-green they tried me with, Kelly green, olive green… Oh, I was fuming, but I kept my countenance, of course.' She assumed a distant, serene expression, and I could not help but laugh. My tea and cake arrived, and I made appreciative noises as the almonds cracked between my teeth.

The Dundee cake apart, I could not remember when I had last spent such an agreeable afternoon. When I entered half-mourning I had made and received calls from a few ladies in the church congregation, but I was out of practice in the social graces. 'Mrs Hudson' constrained me so much that I only managed a handful of pleasantries and platitudes before making my excuses. Here the conversation flowed freely and I let it wash over me, doubting that any of it would be useful, but enjoying it for what it was.

The two ladies called for the bill. I could not follow them; that would be too obvious. 'I hope your friend turns up safe and well,' said Mrs Stanley.

'Oh, I am sure she will, thank you.' I sipped my tea and toyed with my cake, trying to avoid another mouthful.

Mrs Stanley reached into her bag. 'Oh!' She frowned and pulled out a crumpled letter. 'I have forgotten to post this, and the carriage will be here directly!'

'I can post it for you.' I took another sip of tea. 'I pass a pillar-box on my way home, and I have a letter to post too.'

'Oh, would you, dear? That would be so kind.' Mrs Stanley held out the letter and I put it into my handbag without looking at it. 'I am terribly forgetful. I put a stamp on it ready, and I told myself that I should tie a knot in my handkerchief, and— Ah, here is John now.' She waved to the footman at the door, then shook my hand. 'Lovely to meet you, Miss—'

'Fry,' I said. 'Amelia Fry.'

'Effie Stanley. I'm sure we'll meet again; I'm always bumping into people!' She and her friend rose, laughing.

I took ten minutes to drink the rest of my stone-cold tea, then pushed the rest of the cake away and paid my bill. The walk home was far less pleasant; every passer-by must know I had the letter in my bag, and that I did not intend to post it. I hurried on, head down, and the pink in my cheeks was no longer rouge alone. I hoped the letter was innocent, as Mrs Stanley had seemed so nice; I wanted and did not want to read it.

I chose a different public lavatory to change myself back, examining myself carefully for traces of paint, and left on the tail of a little group of women who chattered like starlings. Amelia Fry was no more, and she would not reappear; much as I liked Effie Stanley, I did not plan to bump into her again. I breathed a little more easily, but the letter still lay in my bag.

I found Billy peeling potatoes at the kitchen table. 'How was the knitting class, ma'am?'

I waved my inch of knitting at him. 'I have begun a scarf, and I sat with two nice women whom I would like to call on.' It was close to the truth; I would have liked to know Mrs Stanley and her friend better, if I had not been spying on them. 'I shall take off my things, then help with dinner. How many are we?'

'Three upstairs, probably. Dr Watson isn't back yet, but I'm expecting him. Mr Holmes, definitely.' Billy picked up another potato.

133

The gentlemen's sitting-room door opened as I reached the landing. 'Mrs Hudson, can you spare me a moment?' said Mr Holmes, in a carrying voice.

'Of course, Mr Holmes.'

He closed the door behind me. 'How was it? Did you get close to them?'

I pulled the letter from my handbag and held it up. His eyes widened. 'How did you get it? Wait, I will find some gloves.' He hunted in the drawer of the occasional table.

'I offered to post it for Mrs Stanley.'

Mr Holmes stared at me. 'You didn't!' He sounded both horrified and amused.

'We got talking, as we were on adjacent tables. It may be nothing important,' I said, as he pulled on a pair of kid gloves.

Mr Holmes examined the letter. 'Addressed to a Mrs Davies in Surrey... Handwriting appears feminine, a good-quality gummed envelope from Dickinson's...' He selected a glass flask from the selection on the sideboard, filled it with water, and lit his bunsen lamp. 'We shall have to steam this open.' Waiting was an agony, but eventually the flask bubbled merrily, and Mr Holmes worked at the flap of the envelope with a letter opener. Eventually the flap lifted, and Mr Holmes pulled out two sheets of paper.

The letter was in a flowing hand and appeared to be written to an old friend, as Mrs Stanley had come across a mutual acquaintance in town. It was friendly, gossipy and entirely characteristic of the woman I had met that afternoon. How silly I had been to think it such a prize! 'I thought I had secured something worth having,' I said ruefully.

'We are not finished yet.' Mr Holmes read the letter through again. 'The language is informal, which suggests that there is no code or cypher. There are no dots or marks on the page to indicate particular words or letters. Hmm...' He brought the letter close to his face, sniffed, and shook his head. 'Or could it be…?' He went back to the bunsen lamp, turned the flame down, and held the first page of the letter above it. I feared that the paper would catch, but Mr Holmes's hand was steady. 'There.' I peered at the paper and could just distinguish faint blue writing between the lines in a different, spidery hand.

'Cobalt chloride.' Mr Holmes picked up the second page of the letter. 'It will fade again after a while. Well, Mrs Villiers, you have certainly found something worth having.' He read in a low voice. 'All ready for 14th. Catton in place with Old Lady. Bags via night mail to Rattray. No notes.' He wrote down the message and laid down the letter. 'My suspicions about Mr Stanley and the Bank of England appear to be justified. I shall post this in the Albemarle Road pillar-box as soon as the ink has faded.'

'You will send it on?'

'Of course. I will inform Inspector Lestrade of our find and continue my investigations. The inspector will be pleased with today's work.' He turned the bunsen lamp off. 'It is a shame that you will get no credit, but then again, neither shall I.'

'Really?' I remembered my former, private work for the inspector.

Mr Holmes blew gently on the paper. 'The glory will be Lestrade's. He buys my silence at a good price, though.'

'I must go and help Billy.' I picked up my bag, then remembered the rest of its contents. I retrieved the wig and the rest of the paraphernalia and handed them to Mr Holmes. 'That is everything.'

'I believe so.' He smiled. 'Did you enjoy it?'

I considered for a moment. 'Yes, I did.'

'I thought you would.' He opened the door, which I took as dismissal. 'Oh, Mrs Hudson.' His tone was sharp.

'Yes, Mr Holmes?'

His next words were a whisper. 'I keep a record of who I have been, and where. It will be as well for you to do the same.'

CHAPTER 26

5 St James's Terrace, Clerkenwell, July 1878

The parlour was quiet when I entered with the tea tray. I had expected Inspector Lestrade and Jack to be talking, but the parlour's formality had affected them. I poured the tea and handed the cups, glad to have something to do, and the men watched in silence.

'Your latest report, Mrs Villiers.' The inspector looked at me over the rim of his cup.

'Yes, Inspector?'

'It confirmed my suspicions almost exactly. The pattern of the left kneecap—' He grimaced. 'It could be the title of a penny dreadful.'

'Excuse me, Inspector?' Jack was looking from one to the other of us. 'The left kneecap?'

The inspector nodded. 'One of the cases had stuck in my mind. When I encountered another robbery with violence and a broken kneecap, I went back through the files. It is an unusual injury; I do not remember more than a handful since I became a policeman. I wondered if I was being fanciful, so I pulled out the cases, with a selection of others, to see if Mrs

Villiers would reach the same conclusion as I did. And she was as fanciful as me.'

'Can I ask what you made of my previous report, Inspector, where the houses were smashed up?'

'The connection is perhaps more tenuous but yes, I believe it is related. The cases were more scattered, but the crimes have the same air of deliberation about them. This second batch of cases is more focused, and of course more serious, and I am concerned as to what the next wave of crimes will be.'

'What's behind it, Inspector?' Jack looked a little dazed.

'In her last report Mrs Villiers suggested that it might be a warning or a punishment. I am inclined towards both. A punishment for those who have transgressed in some way, and a warning for anyone tempted to do so.' The inspector pinched the bridge of his nose. 'For a few months now I have felt that something strange was in the air. Just a hunch, no more – but I have learnt that there is often something behind my hunches. When Mrs Villiers's previous report came in, I reread the cases and requested any files from the preceding three months which might fit the pattern. In three-quarters of the cases a kitchen window had been smashed. Sometimes it was one of many, sometimes the only one, but it was consistent enough to be noticeable. There is organisation behind this, I am certain. And now that I am certain, we must move more quickly.'

The inspector's eyes darted from Jack to me, and back again. 'You'll both work full-time on this. We must progress from piecing together past crimes to understanding the mind behind them, until we can predict his next move. Previously I have assigned you to different cases; I did not think it wise for a husband and wife to share their work and their domestic life. However, in this case I am willing to run the risk, in the hope that two heads are better than one.'

Jack looked at the floor, then at me. 'I'll do it, Inspector, of course I will, but are you sure I'm the right man for the job? I mean, Napper – Sergeant Jenkins – is more used to this sort of desk work than I am.'

'Did I say it was desk work, Sergeant?' The inspector put his cup down. 'You need to be sticking your nose in where it isn't expected, reporting to me daily, and bringing back new intelligence for Mrs Villiers. That doesn't sound like desk work to me.'

'Nor me, Inspector.' Jack smiled. 'Thank you for explaining.'

The inspector's beady eyes shifted to me. 'Mrs Villiers, you will be kept very busy – possibly too busy to run the household as you normally would. Your pay will increase in line with your hours, so you can engage a charlady if you wish. I hope that is acceptable.'

I glanced at Jack. Anyone who did not know him as I did would have seen nothing, but the muscles of his jaw pulsed. 'I shall think it over, Inspector.'

'As you wish, Mrs Villiers. I shall not take up any more of your time, as I am sure you are both ready for your dinner.' The inspector stood up and shook hands with us. 'You'll be in first thing tomorrow, Sergeant. Mrs Villiers…' The inspector reached into his jacket and handed me a thick brown envelope. 'These will keep you occupied tomorrow, and then you and Sergeant Villiers can put your heads together. Good evening.'

Jack and I watched from the doorway as the inspector's straight black back receded down the street. 'Well!' I said.

'What's for dinner? I'm starving.' Jack walked through to the kitchen and I followed.

'The end of the mutton, potatoes, and cabbage. You'll have to wait for it, though.' I reached for my apron.

'Go and get changed, Nell, for heaven's sake. You'll spoil that dress if you cook in it.' Jack sat down at the table and opened the envelope which the inspector had given me.

'You don't have to look at that now.' I kept my tone light. 'Inspector Lestrade's given us the night off.'

'Mm.' Jack was already reading. 'I may as well start getting the facts.'

I went upstairs and changed into the shabbiest dress I had. I flung the gold necklace into its box and slammed the drawer on it. Jack wasn't happy, and neither was I. I couldn't tell whether Jack didn't want to work on the case, or whether he didn't want to work with me. If he proposed to order me about, then I didn't want to work with him either. Downstairs I banged a pan on the stove, then fetched some potatoes and put them on the kitchen table. 'I'll get you a knife.'

Jack raised his eyebrows. 'I didn't realise I'd have to get my own dinner.'

'If we're both working full-time, you should help. Unless you'd rather I hired a char.'

Jack's brow furrowed. He stuffed the papers back into their envelope and rolled up his shirt-sleeves, taking his time. 'The sooner this case is over, the better.'

I turned my back on him and chopped the cabbage far too small. I had got what I wanted, a mandate for my work, yet I was still unhappy. I told myself that this would blow over and Jack would get used to it, and I wished I could believe it.

CHAPTER 27

221B Baker Street, 14th February 1881

The next few weeks were a blur as I fitted my domestic duties between the various assignments which Mr Holmes set for me. The shadowing itself took up comparatively little time, but there were excuses to invent, case notes to read, disguises to practise, and after the event, a discussion with Mr Holmes. It was a long way from the desk work I had undertaken for Inspector Lestrade. Even lying in bed, I was knitting away at my scarf, ready for the next class I would supposedly attend at the Institute. Yet I was not tired – I was full of energy, in a way that I had not been since the busy days of my life with Jack.

My whole life had new purpose. When I put my hair up in the morning, I tried a new arrangement before I put it into its usual high bun. When I walked into a room I attempted to remember the order of the books on the shelf, or the objects on the sideboard, to improve my observational skills. I carried out my house-work swiftly and efficiently; I could not afford to waste a moment.

Sometimes I sat for hours in a teashop or a restaurant and

learned nothing at all – but that was not the case. I might not have secured any evidence, and yet I was still learning. I was learning about people and society: seeing their emotions, the little tells, the half-truths they told. It was like returning to a world I had forgotten about, and it made even the dullest-seeming assignment fascinating.

I had spent most of one afternoon in a Holborn teashop, to little profit, and returned to Baker Street. As I took off my bonnet there was a creak above and Mr Holmes appeared. 'Can you come up?' I glanced towards the basement steps. 'Billy is out. He said he had an errand to run.'

I followed Mr Holmes up the stairs and into the sitting room. 'Mrs Villiers, I have some news.' He remained standing, but nervous energy pulsed through him. 'I have heard from a contact of mine who has access to the records of the General Register Office. I asked him to look for anything which could relate to your husband's disappearance. After a thorough search, he has found nothing. There is no death certificate to support your friend's story.'

I tried to speak but no words would come. Jack might still be alive. Or— There were too many possibilities. My legs trembled, and Mr Holmes guided me to a chair. 'I am sorry, Mrs Villiers, I should have let you sit down before I told you.' He sat down opposite and watched me as though I might faint at any moment.

'It is quite all right,' My voice seemed to come from somewhere outside myself. 'I was not expecting it.' I breathed in and out, and my head cleared. 'Your contact – he is sure?'

'Absolutely sure. Your friend was certain that Jack Villiers had been found drowned in the Thames a week after his disappearance. Such a death would have been recorded in full, and there is no conceivable match for over a month. It throws the whole of your friend's story into doubt. I knew it.' Those last words were muttered to himself, and his face was grim.

'What happens next, Mr Holmes?' I needed to concentrate, to stop the thoughts and notions crowding in on me.

'We work out the possibilities and test our theories, making as little noise as we can, so that we disturb neither your friend nor Inspector Lestrade. We try to find your husband. And we carry on working as normal, for I must still earn my bread and butter.' He paused. 'Mrs Villiers, you look all in. If there is nothing urgent to report, I suggest you rest for a while. I am sure dinner can wait until Billy gets back.'

'Thank you, Mr Holmes.' I got up from my chair. 'I shall just check what is left to do downstairs.' I shut the door gently on his look of disapproval. I had expected to find some signs of dinner, but there were none. Perhaps Billy had been delayed. Then there was a tap at the back door.

I opened the door to a grimy little boy. 'Are you Mrs Hudson, mum?'

'I am, yes.'

He held out an envelope. 'This is for you, then.'

'Thank you.' I took the letter, and looked for a penny for him, but he was gone the next moment.

'Mrs Hudson, 221B Baker Street,' I read. I never received letters. The handwriting was rushed but well-formed, in black ink. The envelope was white, except where the little boy's fingers had been. There was no stamp or franking mark. I sat down, and opened it.

Nell, we must meet. Meeting you again has stirred such memories, I cannot sleep for nightmares. I will be at the Rising Sun Inn on Tottenham Court Road from eight tonight, and each night for the rest of this week. I hope that you can slip out and come to me there.

James Jenkins (Napper)

I stared at the paper. Did Napper really expect me to sneak past Billy and the policeman outside, and go to a public house at night, alone? I reread the letter and noted how the writing had been dashed off, as if it were an impulse he was fighting against. What could the nightmares be? Did Napper mean that he had remembered something more about Jack's disappearance? I slipped the letter into my pocket. I would ask Mr Holmes's opinion, but I would go.

As I left the kitchen, the back door clicked. I turned, thinking I had not closed it, and came face to face with Billy. He started, but said nothing.

'I didn't know you were going out this afternoon, Billy.'

'I had something to do, ma'am.' He took off his coat and went to hang it in the scullery. When he came back his face had the expressionless look I remembered from my first days at Baker Street.

'Billy, is something wrong?' I sat back down and indicated a chair.

'No, ma'am.' He remained standing. 'I went to visit my cousin, who is a footman in Kensington. The family are seeking a second footman, and as I am a close match to my cousin in height and looks they have offered me the job. I will give a month's warning, unless you can let me go earlier.'

'You can't leave! Billy, how would I cope without you?'

Billy looked past my right shoulder. 'I will write to the inspector tonight.'

'Would you stay if I raised your wages? I'm sure the inspector would agree.'

'It isn't that, ma'am.' His face remained blank.

'Then what is it, Billy? Is it the work? The inspector is looking out for a maid to help...'

Billy sighed, and sat down opposite me. 'Ma'am, I may be speaking out of turn, but – I am not stupid. I have worked for you over two years, and since Mr Holmes and Dr Watson came, you have changed. You hardly left the house before, except to visit the library or the park. Now you go out at a moment's notice, often for hours at a time. You visit Mr Holmes often when Dr Watson is at work. Sometimes you are cheerful, sometimes you are exhausted, especially when you return from one of your trips.' Billy rubbed his face with his hands and sat back, looking thoroughly miserable. 'Something is going on. I should tell the inspector, but what would happen? I don't know what I should do, and now that this opportunity has come up, I shall take it.'

While Billy had been speaking tears had risen up, and I blinked as hard as I could to keep them in. He had looked after me so kindly – had probably saved my life – and I had repaid him with lies. 'You are right, Billy, in a way. Yet if you knew the truth, perhaps you would not think so badly of me.' I looked up at him, and his expression made the tears prickle even more. 'I do not want to lose you. If you promise not to tell the inspector then I will tell you the whole story, and you can decide whether you will stay or go.'

Billy swallowed. 'I promise.'

I took a deep breath. I was risking everything, but Billy had supported me through some of my darkest times. I hoped with all my heart that he would not desert me now, when some of the fog surrounding Jack's disappearance was beginning to lift. 'When was the last time you read a penny dreadful, Billy?'

He darted a surprised look at me. 'I'm reading one at the moment, ma'am. *The Black Band.*'

'Perhaps you will enjoy this story, then.' I paused. 'My name is Nell Villiers, and I do not know whether my husband is alive or dead.' Billy gasped, and as I continued my tale his expression moved between horror and bewilderment. The daylight faded and the room grew dark, but Billy did not stir, nor did his eyes move away from me, until I finished speaking.

CHAPTER 28

5 St James's Terrace, Clerkenwell, August 1878

'Jack, get up.' I shook him by the shoulder but he rolled over and buried his head in the pillow, mumbling. 'What did you say?'

Jack rolled onto his back and stared at the ceiling. 'Not well. Bad head.'

'I'm not surprised.' Even though he had just woken up Jack had dark shadows under his eyes, and they stood out more against his unusually pale face.

It had been past midnight when I heard a noise at the door. I opened it and Jack fell across the threshold. 'Sorry, Nell,' muttered Napper. 'I hope you weren't worried.'

I shook my head as Jack started giggling at my feet. 'Get inside, Jack.' I hadn't been worried; when eight o'clock had come and gone I knew only too well where Jack would be, and with whom. 'Napper, do you have to go drinking with him? Look at the state he's in.'

Napper ran a hand through his hair as he looked down at Jack. He himself looked a little dishevelled, but nothing more.

'He always says just the one to unwind, and then, well...
Come on, Jack.' He bent down, put his hands under Jack's
armpits and heaved him upright. 'Go and sleep it off.'

We watched Jack lurch towards the stairs and swing
himself up them, hanging on to the banister as if fighting a
gale. 'I don't understand it,' I said. 'He never used to go out
and get drunk like this.'

Napper leaned towards me. 'He's unhappy, Nell. That's
what it is.' I stared at him. 'When he's had a few, he opens up.
He's out of his depth on this case Lestrade's got you both
working on, and he's worried you'll show him up.'

'Me? Why would I do that?'

Napper's face was very serious as he looked at me. 'You
wouldn't do it on purpose, he knows that. But he always talks
about how clever you are, and how if anyone can crack this
case, it's you. He said once that the inspector wouldn't keep
him on as a sergeant if it weren't for you.'

'That's ridiculous!' I exclaimed.

'Sssh,' hissed Napper. 'If Jack knew I was telling you this,
he'd be furious. Just think about it, Nell. Maybe ease off a bit
on the work; Jack says you do twice as much as you're paid
for. Let him have a bit of the credit too.' He patted my arm. 'I
must go. I've probably said more than I should have.
Goodnight, Nell.'

'Goodnight,' I said softly, but Napper was already walking
away.

I closed the door, sat down at the kitchen table, and put my
head in my hands. Was I so taken up with my work that I
hadn't noticed how unhappy Jack was? I worked hard because
I wanted to bring criminals to justice; did I also do it to steal
the glory from my own husband? I thought it over for a long
time, sitting alone in the cold kitchen, and I did not like the
picture of myself that formed as I did so. Yet perhaps there

was still time to paint a better one.

Despite his hangover the next day, Jack was in better form once he had drunk a strong cup of tea. I waited until he was buttoning his tunic. 'Jack, come straight home tonight.'

He fastened the last button and looked up, his face neutral. 'I said I was sorry, Nell.'

'It isn't that; you have to help me with the case. I need you to tell me what you've found out during the day. I can't get any further on without you.'

'All right.' He took his hat from the hatstand, then came over and kissed me on the cheek. 'See you later.'

Jack did come home on time, with another packet of documents for me. I had dinner ready – his favourite, veal and ham pie – and afterwards we talked over the case with a pot of tea. I let Jack do most of the talking, and while he was hesitant at first he grew in confidence. I bit back my impulse to interrupt him with questions, and we discussed the documents he had brought home. I made notes of all his ideas, and thanked him for his help. Jack looked delighted, and I could have kicked my silly, vain self for not realising before how much he valued my attention and my praise.

There were still occasional lapses on a Friday or a Saturday night but things were much improved, and in my head I thanked Napper fervently. He had been a good friend to Jack for many years, and he was a good friend to me too, though I didn't deserve it. The intelligence that Jack shared helped greatly, and we grew closer the more we worked together. I was glad of it, for I had begun to feel nauseous almost every morning. In a few months, God willing, we would be a family of three.

CHAPTER 29

221B Baker Street, 14th February 1881

'Do you believe me, Billy?' It was dark outside now, and I could see no more than Billy's outline against the kitchen window.

He did not reply for some time. 'It's – too much like a story.' His voice was dull.

'I believe Mrs Villiers's story, Billy.' The voice came from the doorway and Mr Holmes appeared, silhouetted in the light from the stairwell. 'I apologise for listening at the door, but I came to find out why Mrs Villiers was down here and not resting as she should be.'

'Billy has formed his own ideas about my visits to your rooms, Mr Holmes,' I said, as lightly as I could.

'Really.' Mr Holmes entered the kitchen, turned up the lamps, and sat down on a third side of the table. 'Billy, I am surprised at you.'

'Well, sir,' Billy retorted, 'it makes much more sense that Mrs Hudson – *Villiers* – has been visiting you to disguise herself and spy on criminals all over London!'

I snorted. I couldn't help it. Billy and Mr Holmes both

150

looked at me reproachfully. 'I'm sorry,' I said. 'It is a serious matter, but put like that – I do not blame Billy for having his doubts.'

'Neither do I,' said Mr Holmes. 'Mrs Villiers, before we go any further, why have you told Billy the truth about your situation?'

'He has given notice due to my strange behaviour lately.' My voice wobbled a little as I finished the sentence. 'Billy has been a great support and help to me, and I decided to trust him with the truth to persuade him to stay.'

'Is that right, Billy?' asked Mr Holmes. Billy glanced up at Mr Holmes, and nodded. 'And if the story were true – the disappearance, and the mystery, and Mrs Villiers's work for me – would you stay?' Before Billy had a chance to answer, Mr Holmes held up a hand. 'I am getting ahead of myself. Come upstairs, Billy, and I can show you some things which will help you make up your mind.'

Billy did as he was asked, and presently was exclaiming over the contents of Mr Holmes's trunk. 'I knew you were a detective, sir, but I didn't think you went out in disguise! It's like I've stepped into the pages of a novel.'

Mr Holmes laughed. 'I suppose it is, Billy.'

'That reminds me,' I said. 'I didn't unpack my bag earlier. Not that it matters so much, now that Billy knows.' I fetched my bag from the kitchen and pulled out my knitting, which was quite bulky now, and the dark-brown wig. Billy's eyes were like saucers as I gave the wig to Mr Holmes, then drew out a shawl, and finally rummaged in the bottom of the bag for rouge and pencils.

'Where did you go, ma'am? Did you catch anyone?' breathed Billy.

'I was at a teashop, Billy. Nothing to report today, Mr Holmes. The shop was crowded; I could not get a table close enough to hear much.' Billy was shaking his head and staring at me, grinning like someone who has just understood the joke. Then I remembered the letter. 'But there is something else.' I drew the letter from my pocket. 'This was delivered while I was downstairs. My friend wants to meet me again.'

Mr Holmes held out his hand for the letter and scanned it, frowning. 'This sounds as if he has more information.'

'Yes.' I rubbed my forehead, which had begun to ache. 'But what if it is some sort of trap?'

'Is this from the policeman you went to meet, ma'am? The one who said your husband was dead?'

'That's right, Billy.'

'Then you should go, but not alone. One of us should come too, and make sure you come to no harm.'

'Just what I was about to say,' observed Mr Holmes. 'Mrs Villiers, are you of a mind to go?'

'I am. I cannot miss the opportunity.' Mr Holmes handed me back the letter, and I put it back in my pocket. 'Although I wish Napper had not chosen a public house. I shall not go tonight; I am too tired.'

Mr Holmes closed the trunk. 'I will pay a visit to the Rising Sun tonight and take a look at your friend. Not as myself, of course,' he added, as we stared at him. 'It will help us make arrangements for your visit.'

'Thank you, Mr Holmes.'

'Oh, my offer is mainly out of curiosity to observe your friend,' he replied. 'But there is one more thing to settle first.' He turned to Billy. 'Is all this enough to persuade you to stay?'

Billy looked from one to the other of us, and spread his hands wide. 'How can I leave with all this going on?' Relief washed over me, and I almost cried again. Then a shadow passed over Billy's face. 'I've worked for the inspector these last four years, and if I thought…' He looked stern, and years older; a man, not a youth.

'It is settled, then.' Mr Holmes clapped Billy on the back. 'And on that subject, Dr Watson will be home soon, and he is a man who appreciates punctual mealtimes.'

'Right away, sir.' Billy hurried to the door.

I started up. 'I'll help—'

Billy waved me away. 'I can cook dinner, ma'am. Anyway, you and Mr Holmes must have plans to make. Cases to discuss.' He shook his head, smiling, and clattered off down the stairs.

'You did the right thing, Mrs Villiers.' Mr Holmes said. 'Billy is a good-hearted lad, and he will help us both.'

I sighed. 'Telling the story grows no easier. I have to drag it out of myself.'

'Go and rest now. If my visit to the Rising Sun goes well tonight, you will need your strength for tomorrow.' I stood up, and Mr Holmes opened the door for me. 'Who knows, Mrs Villiers? After today's news, perhaps your story will end happily ever after.' He bowed me out of the room, and the door clicked behind me.

I went upstairs and obeyed Mr Holmes's orders by lying on my bed, but though my body was still, my mind tossed and turned more than ever. Could Jack still be alive? What did Napper have to tell me? Was the meeting a trap? I sprang up and went to help Billy in the kitchen. The only way I would get any rest that night was for my body to be as worn out as my brain.

CHAPTER 30

5 St James's Terrace, Clerkenwell, 22nd August 1878

'You're joking.' I gawped at Jack's delighted face.

'I'm not, Nell!' He pulled me up by the hand and flung his arms round me, squeezing hard enough to take my breath away. 'They've caught them!'

'But how?' I disengaged myself so that I could look up at Jack. 'I mean, I thought that we were on to something, but…' Slowly, carefully, we had narrowed our search to Stepney, the geographical centre of the activity we had identified, from which the cases spread out along main thoroughfares like the strands of a spider's web. Inspector Lestrade had sent extra men to patrol the area. Meanwhile, I pored through past cases to identify what might happen and when. I was still uncertain as to exactly what, but I had been confident that early in the coming month would be the time for action. Yet here was Jack, at two o'clock on a Thursday afternoon, telling me it was all over.

'It was the inspector,' Jack grinned. 'He said it came to him when he was talking the case over with someone. It's the

Mile End Gang.'

'Really?' I sat down. 'Aren't they just petty thieves?'

'They were, but they got a new leader, Sampson, a few months back, and from the sound of it he was trying to make a name for himself.' Jack sat down opposite me. 'Anyway, the inspector went out with a few men and they tracked him down drinking in his local. Apparently he sang like a bird.' Jack chuckled. 'I guessed you'd want to know, so I asked the inspector if I could pop home and tell you. Might have to work late tonight, though.'

'And that's it? That's the end?'

'Well, all bar the shouting. Sampson's already bargained his membership list for a lighter sentence, so the boys are out rounding them up – and that's where I should be.'

'Yes, of course.' I reached across the table for his hand. 'Thank you for coming to tell me the news, Jack.'

He squeezed my hand, and got up. 'The inspector said to pass on his thanks for all your help.' Jack picked up my papers from the table, stuffed them into their envelope, and put it in his pocket. 'For the trial. I bet you're glad to see the back of them.' He put his helmet back on. 'Bye, Nell!' he called over his shoulder, and the door slammed shut.

I stayed sitting at the table. It was over. They'd arrested someone, he had confessed, and all the heavy machinery of the law would creak into life. I should be glad, relieved, thankful to have done my bit, and yet I felt blank. No, not blank: cheated, as I would if I had arrived at a party and found them clearing away. *Don't be ridiculous*, I told myself. *As if you were going to go and catch the criminal!* A visit to my friend Lottie would put me back into spirits. I had neglected Lottie sadly lately, as I had been so taken up with the inspector's work. Indeed, I had kept away from my friends and family, so worried had I been that I might let something slip. Now was the time to put it right.

Lottie was in when I called, and proposed a walk to the park with the children. I helped her with the perambulator, then took two sticky little hands in mine, ready for the trip. 'You haven't visited us in ever so long, Aunty Nell,' said the oldest girl, Maria. 'Where have you been?'

'I haven't been anywhere,' I said. 'I've just been busy. I had lots of things to do at home. Now, if you're good, I'll buy you a lollipop.' Maria squealed in delight, my absence forgotten, and I wished that I could distract myself so easily.

Jack was home by nine, and there was a faint whiff of whisky on his breath when he kissed me. 'I had a quick drink with the inspector.'

'I didn't think Inspector Lestrade was a drinking man,' I said.

'He isn't, usually.' Jack hung up his helmet. 'He bought a round for all of us who were out this afternoon, though. He said we'd earned it.' I imagined a table full of policemen sitting in the pub, buttons gleaming in the gaslight.

'Did you round them all up, then?'

Jack yawned. 'We got all the big fish. Some of the others will escape but they'll come back in the end, and we'll track 'em down. They never stay away long.' He stretched his feet out under the table and nudged mine. 'I can't wait to get back to normal. On the beat again, with familiar faces. It's been an odd time, and I'm glad it's over.' He looked into my face. 'Aren't you, Nell?'

'I'm glad the gang got caught; I'm just a bit surprised. I didn't expect it to happen so soon.'

'That's why Lestrade's an inspector.' Jack matched his foot to mine. 'He's sharp as a needle, and you could fit what he doesn't know about policing on the point of one. Now, is there any food in the house?'

'Of course there is. I kept yours warm.' I stood up and went to the oven, and set the plate of beef stew and dumplings in front of him.

'Lovely.' Jack rubbed his hands. 'Arresting people makes me hungry.' He took a huge mouthful, then another, looking round the room as he chewed. 'I bet you'll be glad to get the house in order too.'

I followed his gaze. The kitchen was untidy and the floor needed a good scrub. The rest of the house wasn't much better. I had concentrated on preparing meals and let the house-work go until I had more time. Tomorrow would be a day of cleaning, I thought, without much relish.

'Not now!' Jack laughed and bolted the last spoonful of food. He walked round the table to me and pulled one hairpin out, then another, until my hair began to come down. 'Time for bed.'

CHAPTER 31

221B Baker Street, 15th February 1881

'Well, I certainly hope that no one recognises me.' I shuddered at my reflection.

'Trust me, Mrs Villiers, you will not stand out. Wait in the sitting room while I change, please.'

Mr Holmes had visited the Rising Sun the previous night. A man, well-muffled but matching my description of Napper, had been sitting alone in a dark corner of the snug. The inn was busy, but as far as he could tell there were no other policemen near. 'And now I have the measure of the place, I shall do some shopping tomorrow.'

'To the costumier's?' I asked.

Mr Holmes laughed. 'Nothing so grand, I am afraid.'

Mr Holmes had gone out the next day dressed as a workman. I awaited his return, curious to see what special thing he had bought. He was back within the hour and I cried out in dismay as he unwrapped a shiny, flouncy, peacock-blue dress. 'Where on earth did you get that?'

'Petticoat Lane,' he replied composedly. 'It should fit, and I believe it is more or less in the fashion. You must look like a woman who is quite accustomed to walking into an inn on her own. Watson is out tonight with a friend at my suggestion, so if you come down in the dress at half past six we can make ready.'

A quarter past six struck, and the dress still lay on the chair in my bedroom. I looked at it and sighed. I made sure the blind was down and the doors were closed, and put a chair under the doorknob. I cursed the previous owner of the dress, who was both smaller in the waist and larger in the bust, but after tight-lacing my corset and padding with handkerchiefs, the dress was on. The kindest thing I could say about it was that it was relatively modest in cut.

Mr Holmes answered the door to me and snorted at my expression. 'I am sorry, Mrs Villiers, but it has to be done. I doubt Inspector Lestrade will be there, but if he is, I hope you recognise him long before he recognises you.'

I looked down at myself. 'It's so unsuitable.'

'Yes.' He grinned. 'We shall have to suit you to it.'

I pinned up the dark-brown wig, leaving some loose curls to fall down the back, and Mr Holmes handed me some cheap jewellery. Then he set to work. When I opened my eyes I saw a bold-looking young woman, powdered and rouged, with suspiciously dark eyelashes. She was like an overblown peony. I had seen women like her when I had gone out for the evening with Jack. What would he say if he saw me now?

Mr Holmes was ready in a few minutes, and matched me well in his loud necktie and cheap coat. 'It is past seven o'clock. We must hurry.'

'Are we going to the inn before eight?'

'We will go for a drink nearby first.' He laughed at my shocked face. 'That expression does not suit you at all now. It will give you a chance to get used to the atmosphere.'

We went downstairs together. Mr Holmes went into the

kitchen first and Billy looked up in surprise, but he stared outright at me, then whistled. 'I wouldn't have known you, ma'am.'

'That's as well, Billy,' I said darkly. 'If I never come back, please do not remember me like this.'

'I won't,' he said, sobering up. 'Good luck, ma'am.'

Mr Holmes and I went out through the back door and he took me through a maze of alleys until we came out onto the road. 'That will do. There is a suitable inn a few minutes' walk away.' He offered his arm, and I took it.

In one way the garish dress had been a good thing, for it had distracted me from worrying about the evening itself. Now I walked along with Mr Holmes, trying not to stare at the sights of the city. Office workers and shop-girls hurried by, and young men lounged in groups at street corners. No one gave us a second glance.

'Before we go in, it may be as well to establish names. It will be useful if we are separated,' said Mr Holmes. 'A couple such as we appear would be on first-name terms; you can call me Tom. Shall I call you Nell? Something else might be safer.'

'Call me Annie,' I said firmly. I hated the idea of my name being attached to this peacock-blue creature.

The pub was already busy. Mr Holmes shouldered his way to the bar, returning with two glasses of something colourless. 'Is this gin?' I asked suspiciously.

'Keep your voice down,' said Mr Holmes. 'You don't have to drink it all.'

I took a sip. The harsh chemical smell filled my mouth and heated my throat as I swallowed. I tried not to make a face.

'Good. Now, study those two women near the bar.' Mr Holmes leaned against a pillar, surveying the pub.

The women were about my age and wearing the same kind of bright, cheap clothing. They were a lively pair, calling out to men who passed them on their way to the bar. Sometimes the men came over. They were flushed and laughing already, though it was early, and completely at home in their surroundings. They stood, heads high, displaying themselves to the crowd. I squared my shoulders, raised my head, and looked about me, placing a hand on one hip.

Mr Holmes leered at me, detached himself from the pillar and leaned down to whisper in my ear. 'Much better. Before we move on, some advice: let your friend do the talking. He may be trustworthy, or he may not. As far as he is concerned, nothing has changed and you know no more than the last time you met. I will take you through the inn and find a place where I can keep watch. If you need to call me over, come and set your glass down loud on the bar.'

I flashed a broad grin at him. He grinned in response and steered me to the door with his hand on the small of my back. Someone whistled and my cheeks grew warm, but I threw my head up and carried on walking.

'I shall have to keep a close eye on you, Annie,' muttered Mr Holmes as we strolled through the streets. 'You are more forward than I realised.'

'Sorry, Tom,' I said, and winked, which made him look away for a moment.

Mr Holmes dropped my arm just before we entered the Rising Sun. 'Follow me. I shall stop at the bar; you keep going. Head up, remember.'

I walked through the pub looking about me as if seeking a friend, when really I was watching for an enemy. Everyone seemed to be exactly what they were: workers relaxing after a hard day. But that was exactly what Mr Holmes seemed to be as he leaned over the bar and called to the barman for a pint. I walked past him towards the entrance to the snug. A couple were in there, sitting close over their drinks, and a man in an overcoat and scarf with his cap pulled low, reading a newspaper. His eyes flicked up and down again: bright-blue eyes.

I stuck a smile on my face, walked across and sat down beside him, on the side furthest from the other people. 'It's a chilly night out there; won't you buy a girl a warming drink?'

Napper stared at me over his newspaper for some time. Then he folded the paper, got up, and came back with two brandies. 'For God's sake, Nell!' he muttered. 'You look like a tart.' He gulped half of his drink. 'It makes me wonder what you are like underneath.'

I gasped. 'Not like this, I assure you. You shall have to take me as you find me, Napper.'

He passed a hand over his face. 'I am sorry, Nell. I was expecting the old woman to reappear, and here you are bold as brass.'

'It is paint and fabric, Napper, nothing more.' I sipped my brandy and leaned closer. 'Why did you ask to meet with me?'

'That night you came to me... When I clapped eyes on you I was certain that the inspector spoke true, and you were a deluded woman indeed – and yet I still felt a strong pull towards you. Once I had put you into the cab I walked home, and all the way I was thinking of your story and what I remembered of the time. I lay awake long into the night trying to understand it all. And when I slept there were nightmares: Jack falling, the stick coming for me, the hood slipping over my head...' He drank again, and his hand was shaking.

'But these are nightmares, Napper.' I said gently, 'They are not the truth.'

Napper removed his hat and wiped his forehead. 'It was when I woke... I remembered what led up to our visit to the opium den. I had planned to bring extra officers and storm the place: get the job done. Jack talked me out of it. He said the two of us could do it with a few men on standby. 'It will be like old times, Napper,' he said. 'You and me, on the beat together.' I thought Jack wanted to be a hero, and I indulged him. It was my case, and I should have trusted my own judgement. Perhaps if I had not let him talk me round…'

The room swam before my eyes. Napper put an arm around me and held the glass to my lips. The liquid burned, but it cleared my head. 'Jack was not a risk taker, Napper. He was reckless sometimes, but he would not have put you in danger.'

'No.' Napper's mouth twisted. 'I was beaten senseless, but not enough to kill me.'

'What are you saying?' I forgot myself, and my voice was loud enough to make the couple next to us look over.

Napper looked distraught. 'Jack arranged for the two of us to be there, and I remember nothing, and the inspector told me he was dead.'

'You think there is a conspiracy. You think that Jack is alive.'

Napper bowed his head, then took a deep breath. 'When the inspector visited me at the convalescent home, he offered me protection of a kind. I had forgotten it, but your tale brought it back. He offered to transfer me out of London; he said he feared the people at the den might come back for me. I refused. I would not run away.' He sighed. 'But I am not the policeman I was, nor shall I be again. The inspector keeps me chained to the desk. He believes me unfit for active work. Perhaps I would have been freer if I had moved away.' His tone was bitter, and he slumped like a defeated man.

At the other side of the pub there was a loud smash of glass, followed by cries and screams. I could not see what was happening for the gathering crowd. Then I heard rattles outside. The police! 'Oh my God!' I clutched at Napper.

163

'Quick, Nell, we must get away! If you were found here, like this—' Napper pulled me to my feet and we joined the tide of people now rushing to the door. I looked for Mr Holmes in the crowd but he had vanished.

Someone trod on my skirt and I stumbled. I would have fallen if the crowd had been less dense, but I was borne along into the open air. Napper was somewhere behind me, and I could not move against the surging crowd. The rattles sounded again, and a stern voice cried 'Stay where you are!' People were running, screaming and shouting, and in sheer panic I ran too.

'Annie!' Mr Holmes caught my wrist and jerked me to a halt.

I wriggled, but his grip was too strong. 'Let me go!'

'No. Walk with me.' His voice was low, grim. He drew me into an alley. 'Never run when you hear a police rattle; they will chase you like a dog. I learnt that the hard way.' The rattle came again and there was shouting in the street, but the shouting came and went. They were looking for something. For someone.

I whimpered as the shouting grew closer. Mr Holmes leaned down and muttered, 'Forgive me.' He pushed me up against the brick wall and kissed me so hard that our teeth clashed together. The rattles sounded again, and feet pounded like my throbbing heart. They stopped. Then laughter, and whistling, and they ran on.

CHAPTER 32

221B Baker Street, 15th February 1881

He kissed me until the footsteps had died away. He tasted of beer, and tobacco, and the gin we had drunk earlier. I could feel his heart beating against me, and I could scarcely breathe.

His mouth was still on mine as he whispered. 'Sorry – I didn't mean to be so rough.' He leaned back to look down the alley and I panted for breath. 'Stay close; they may come back.' I had no choice; he still pinned me to the wall. His breathing was quick as his heartbeat had been, and underneath the disguise his face was serious. 'I think we are safe,' he said, releasing me. 'This way.' He took my arm again and we went down the alley into a tangle of back streets. 'Wait.' He stopped under a street lamp and turned my face up to it. 'You're a little smudged,' he said, and drew his thumb along my lower lip. 'There. Am I all right?'

I examined him under the light. 'A bit—' I rubbed at the corner of his mouth with my finger. 'That's it.'

Arm-in-arm we walked on, and at the main road jumped into a cab. Ten minutes later we got out, crossed the street and took another cab to what I recognised as the Edgware Road.

My heart thumped the whole way, and I shivered at every shout. We hurried down dark roads, and a few minutes later Mr Holmes opened the back door at Baker Street.

Billy's eager face turned to dismay at our expressions. 'It has been a hard night, Billy,' said Mr Holmes, loosening his necktie. 'I suspect a trap, but we have escaped. For now.' His voice was clean and hard as steel. 'We must get changed; the quicker the better. Is Watson back?'

'He is, and eating supper.' Billy looked stricken.

'Bring hot water up for us as soon as you can, Billy. Supper too, if there is any left.' Mr Holmes ran upstairs. I walked up, my legs shaking, and carried on to my room.

I pulled the peacock dress off, my fingers fumbling at the buttons, and put on my dressing gown. I trembled all the while, and it was as if my mind shook too as I recalled the evening's events. Napper's words formed and reformed, then the smash of glass broke my train of thought. And on top of it all was the kiss.

Mr Holmes's voice, low, outside my door. 'May I come in?' I wrapped my dressing gown tightly about me and opened the door. Mr Holmes wore a loose white shirt and grey trousers, and held a can of hot water. 'Billy is worried about you,' he said. 'As am I.' He walked to the washstand and put the can down.

'Napper thinks Jack's disappearance was a set-up—'

Mr Holmes held a finger to his lips, then stirred up the fire. 'We can talk later. First, we must get rid of Annie.' He picked up the peacock-blue dress and the fabric shrieked as he ripped it apart – once, twice – and threw the pieces on the fire, where they flared and sent sparks up the chimney. He pulled the bright necktie from his pocket and threw it on top. 'Poor Tom and Annie, too conspicuous to live.' He patted the easy chair. 'Sit, and I will get rid of her.'

'Mr Holmes, I can manage—'

He took my hand and held it for a moment. 'You are shaking too much; you will poke yourself in the eye.' He lifted the brown wig gently off my head and put it aside. 'Close your eyes; I shall try not to scrub at you.' He was far gentler than I would have been, and when the paint was all gone he poured hot water into the basin. 'There, you are yourself again.'

'Whoever that is.' I reached for the towel, and when I emerged Mr Holmes was looking at me with a curious expression on his face.

'At the moment, Mrs Villiers, you are a porcupine of hairpins. Now, tell me what your friend said…' He reached up and eased out a pin, and I shut my eyes. I couldn't look at him, so close. I took a deep breath and told the story of my meeting with Napper, as one by one Mr Holmes took out the pins, and my hair came down.

'I am not certain that I trust your friend.' Mr Holmes picked up my brush from the dressing table, moved behind me, and ran it through my hair.

'But what does he have to gain?' I tried to look round at Mr Holmes, but he moved my head gently back, and continued to brush.

'Who knows.' The strokes were long and steady. 'He likes you, though. I saw the way he looked at you.'

'That was probably the outfit.'

'Perhaps. Perhaps not.' The hairbrush kept moving. Napper's words came back to me. *A tart . . . bold as brass*. I remembered my reflection earlier that day, and shuddered.

The brush paused. 'I prefer you as you are.' The strokes started again, gentle and slow, until I put my hand behind and drew my hair over my shoulder.

'My husband—'

167

The brush clacked down on the dressing table.

'You kissed me…' I couldn't look round.

'If there was a trap, they were looking for a woman alone, not a couple. It was the best way to hide you. So really it is more accurate to say that Tom kissed Annie, or that the detective kissed his client.'

It had meant nothing to him. It should have meant nothing to me. My face was on fire at what I had said, and what he would make of it. I closed my eyes and waited for him to leave. I hoped he would go before I started to cry.

'The kiss was a matter of expediency, and it was rough. I am sorry for that.' I jumped as his hand touched my shoulder. Then he knelt beside me. 'Tom was rather rude; not the kind of fellow to stand on ceremony. But he enjoyed the kiss very much, and I think Annie did too, since she kissed him back.'

'She did,' I whispered.

He leaned on the arm of the chair and brushed a strand of hair away from my cheek. 'Now if Mr Holmes kissed Mrs Villiers . . . or Sherlock kissed Nell . . . it would be different entirely.'

It was. Yet though the kiss was warm and gentle, I was just as breathless as before.

'The supper tray is outside. You must eat; we have things to do.' He began to get up, but I laid a hand on his arm.

'I have a confession. On the way home, when I rubbed off the smudge on your mouth . . . there was no smudge. I just wanted to touch you.'

Mr Holmes – Sherlock – looked down and smiled. When he looked up, a light danced in his grey eyes. 'That is too bad of you, Nell. But you are forgiven.' He kissed me again. 'Especially as there was no smudge on your mouth, either.'

CHAPTER 33

221B Baker Street, 15th February 1881

'Make a good meal, Nell.' Sherlock pushed the plate towards me. 'You will need it.'

'Why?'

'Because it is time for you to disappear.' I almost choked on my mouthful of cold chicken, and he poured a glass of water for me. 'It is not as sinister as all that, but you cannot stay here. I am convinced that tonight's fracas at the inn was a trap, though I do not know who set it, and now it is only a matter of time.'

I saw myself in the peacock-blue dress, dragged down the street by policemen, and drank some more water to try and fight the rising nausea. 'But where shall I go? Who can I trust?'

Sherlock pushed his hair back from his forehead. 'Do you trust me?' I nodded. 'That's as well, because I begin to suspect everyone. Watson I am sure of.'

'And Billy,' I said.

Sherlock leaned over to whisper in my ear. 'My heart agrees, but my brain says he is one of the very few who knew where you were meeting Napper.'

Revulsion hit me like a punch in the stomach. Had Billy played the faithful servant all along, waiting to catch me out? I remembered how he had looked after me when I was enslaved to laudanum. Had it all been an act? I shook my head, willing it to be false.

'I hope I am wrong. I cannot be sure, but this is one of the strangest things I have been mixed up in. Do you think friend Napper guessed you were accompanied?'

'He showed no sign of it... I cannot tell, any more.'

Sherlock sighed. 'Come, we had better get ready.' He pushed his chair back from the table. 'On this occasion travel as yourself, with a change of clothes. I will arrange the rest. Do not answer the door to anyone but me or Watson; put a chair under the handle. Billy knows to let no one in.' He strode over and kissed me, then was gone.

I was ready and packed within minutes, my hair twisted up anyhow, and all I could do was wait. My eye fell on the pack of cards lying on the bookshelf. I had not touched them since Sherlock Holmes had arrived at 221B Baker Street.

The front door closed and a tall thin figure strode away. I prayed that he would be safe. The usual policeman walked his beat, and the street looked the same as ever, but I found danger in every shadow, and sat by the window in the hope that he would be back soon. A minute passed, and another. Five, and something creaked downstairs. Was it...? Feet ran up, and the gentlemen's sitting-room door banged against the wall. A moment, and footsteps came to my door.

Sherlock's voice, an urgent whisper: 'Nell, let me in.' I opened the door to him, hat and coat on and valise in hand. 'It is time to go.'

Dr Watson was standing in the doorway of his sitting room as we passed, his face bewildered and concerned. Sherlock passed him without a word, and I judged that even his friend knew nothing of where we were going.

We entered the kitchen and I cried out, for Billy was blindfolded, gagged, and bound to a chair. 'I judged it as well to take precautions.' Sherlock's voice was calm. 'Dr Watson will untie Billy in half an hour.' Billy made a noise. 'Billy, it is for your own good.'

Sherlock pulled his hat down low and led the way through the alleys until we reached a horse and carriage with a boy waiting. Sherlock helped me in and closed the door. 'Put the shades half-down.' Someone climbed onto the box – was it Sherlock? It must be, surely. The crack of a whip, and the carriage moved off.

We drove steadily on main roads and I remembered how he had told me not to run, but my heart beat painfully fast to make up for it. What if we had been spotted? What if someone recognised Sherlock on the box? I pulled the blinds of the carriage a little further down. But there were no whistles, no shouts, and after a few minutes I fell to wondering where we were going. A train station, perhaps? But they might have our description. A friend? Yet even Dr Watson did not know what was going on. I wished I could be sure that Sherlock was driving the carriage. The journey had too many similarities with the blacked-out trip to Baker Street for my liking. But I had to trust him. I had no one else.

The carriage slowed down and the white stone of a row of townhouses appeared at the bottom of the window. We stopped, and Sherlock's face appeared. 'Wait here; I will be back in an instant.' I was so glad to see him that I would have done anything he asked. I wanted to peep out, but did not dare. After a minute or two the carriage door opened. 'Keep your head down.' The door of the nearest house swung open.

The footman shut the door with a barely perceptible click,

and we followed him into a book-lined study where a man was sitting behind a mahogany desk. The man was tall, broad, and somehow impassive-looking, as if he had heard everything and would never be surprised again. Sherlock shook hands with him, then turned to me.

'Mycroft, this is Mrs Villiers. Nell, this is my brother, Mycroft.'

Mycroft Holmes extended a large hand towards me, and I had to fight an urge to curtsey too.

Sherlock shrugged off his hat and coat. 'Could you ask your footman to change into these and return the carriage outside? It is from the livery stable in Gloucester Place Mews.' The footman took the clothes without a word and left the room.

'Well.' Mycroft indicated two leather chairs by the fire and moved his own chair to face them. 'Tell me why you are here, Sherlock. I assume it relates to the little matter I assisted with, concerning a man named Villiers.' His glance flicked towards me quick as a snake's tongue.

'That's it.' Sherlock sat down. 'We have made Baker Street a little too hot to hold us.'

'Ah.' Mycroft selected a pipe and began to fill it. 'I would offer rooms here, but I daresay the police will visit with a search warrant.' He tamped the tobacco down and looked up. 'Is it a police matter?'

'I'm afraid so.' Sherlock leaned forward. 'Mrs Villiers is meant to be living quietly under police protection.'

'Mm.' Mycroft reached for a match. 'Are they protecting you, Mrs Villiers, or themselves?' He struck the match on the leg of his chair and I watched the flame grow. He sucked on the pipe and shook the match out.

'Perhaps both. I am not meant to contact anyone from my former life.'

'And of course, you have.'

'Yes.' I felt exceptionally foolish, like a naughty schoolgirl.

'It is human nature.' Mycroft blew a smoke ring. 'Well, I had better pack you off before you are tracked down. I take it the incident happened this evening?'

'Yes, at around half past eight. Luckily we got away. We came home using cabs and back streets, and changed clothes at once. Our servant has been blindfolded, so he cannot describe our current appearance.'

Mycroft chuckled. 'Disguises again, Sherlock.'

Sherlock glared at him. 'Mrs Villiers could hardly go out in her own person—'

'Whatever you say, Sherlock.' Mycroft opened a drawer and drew out a large bunch of keys. 'Now…' He selected one and worked it off the ring. 'As you are in the thick of it, I assume you want to stay within London. This key opens most of the doors. You must lie low during the daytime – attic four in the North Wing is the best equipped – but at night you can have the run of the place.' He leaned forward and held the key out to Sherlock.

'Where are we going, please?' I asked.

Mycroft blew another smoke ring. 'Where I can keep an eye on you. The General Register Office at Somerset House. It is only a mile away. I suggest you leave through the scullery and use the Embankment; cabs will be too dangerous. I shall call tomorrow.' He pulled a document towards him, and leafed through the pages.

'Is he always like that?' I muttered as we walked through a dark square.

'Often more so. But there's a good heart under it all. We get on much better now that we're not under the same roof.'

'I can hardly believe that you're brothers. He's so – different.'

'In some ways. He's a government man through and through, but also quite ready to hide a pair of fugitives. It's a kind of legitimised lawlessness. Even if he got caught, he's senior enough for it to be brushed under the carpet.'

'A useful man to have as a brother, then.'

'Yes.' We came out onto the Embankment and Cleopatra's Needle loomed before us. 'I should have involved him in this earlier.'

I put my arm through his. 'He's involved now. And without you, I'd be shut up in Baker Street convinced I was mad.'

He squeezed my arm. We passed under a bridge and he steered me into the shadow of a stone archway, towards a small wooden door. He produced the key. 'Time to try this out.' I held my breath as Sherlock inched the door open. No noise inside, and only darkness. 'Come on.' He looked up and down the street, and we slipped inside.

The interior, dimly lit by the street lamps, was magnificent, but all I cared for was a hiding place. We crept up a grand staircase, along a passage, and up more stairs to the top of the building. A narrow corridor had box rooms leading off. We tiptoed to the door marked '4', and the key came into play again. The room had space to lie down, and a trunk held cushions and blankets.

Sherlock locked the door behind us. 'It is better than nothing.' He made two beds on opposite sides of the room. 'I would put them together for warmth, but...' He looked away, and I blushed for what people would think we were doing.

I lay down and spread my cloak over me. The floor was hard, but I could probably have slept on a clothes line. I listened to Sherlock's regular breathing across the room, and let myself slide into sleep.

CHAPTER 34

Somerset House, 16th February 1881

'Nell… Nell, wake up.' I could barely make Sherlock out in the darkness.

'What time is it?' I attempted to sit up, but all my bones ached from a night on the floor.

'After six. I am sorry to wake you, but I couldn't leave without telling you.'

'Leave?' I sat bolt upright.

'Only to find some food. I'll be back soon.' The key turned in the lock. I sank back onto the thin blanket and tried to sleep, but every little creak and groan of the building made me start and shiver.

I burrowed under the covers as I heard footsteps outside, and the key turned in the lock. 'I'm back, Nell.' Sherlock passed me a warm bread roll, and I smelt coffee as he unscrewed his hip-flask. 'Covent Garden never fails me. Would you like a saveloy? I have fruit, too.'

'No, thank you. Is that a newspaper?'

'Early edition.' He put it on top of my cloak. I peered at it, but it was still too dark to read more than the headline.

'Nell...' I looked up. 'You might want to use the lavatory before anyone arrives.'

I clapped my hand to my mouth. 'Oh! Indeed, yes.'

'There is one on the next floor down, near the offices. I shall find a, er, receptacle for later.' He gave me the key, and I crept out.

The building was silent, and after my initial trepidation I began to relax and to admire the grandeur of my surroundings as the light grew. *We must be the best-housed fugitives in London*, I thought. I hoped I would not have to spend another night on the floor, though, or need to use the lavatory again before the building was empty. I took the opportunity to wash my hands and face, tidied my hair, and scurried back to the attics. As I opened the door I heard quiet laughter. Sherlock was reading the paper.

'What is it?'

His eyes sparkled with merriment. 'Do you remember your first assignment?' He tapped the paper.

'The one where I watched Mrs Stanley? How could I forget?' I peered at the newspaper in the dim light. *BANK RAID FOILED. ROBBERS ARRESTED IN MIDNIGHT OPERATION. BANK OF ENGLAND SAVED.*

'You were right!' I remembered the pale-blue writing springing from the page as he had heated the letter. 'The Old Lady of Threadneedle Street . . . of course!'

'Lestrade has done well out of this. Listen: *The case was led by Inspector Lestrade of Scotland Yard. While he could not supply detailed information at this stage, it is our understanding that he tracked down and apprehended the ringleader, Mr Emmett Stanley, a known criminal in hiding, while a crack team from the Metropolitan Police lay in wait in the vaults of the Bank of England to arrest his accomplices.*' He snorted. 'Could not supply detailed information, indeed!'

176

I read to the end of the article. 'It is just as you said it would be. Lestrade is the only policeman named, and takes all the credit.'

'There are worse things to do,' said Sherlock. 'I cannot forgive him for his treatment of you, and if I find out he has been involved in your husband's disappearance...' He scowled and the edges of the newspaper crumpled in his hands, but the moment was gone as quickly as it came. 'Anger will not help us now. At least there is no mention of us, nor of the disturbance at the Rising Sun.'

'That may be in the later edition.' I pulled my cloak round my shoulders.

'Or not at all—' He broke off from what he was saying, listening with a finger to his lips. 'Noises downstairs,' he whispered. 'The early birds are coming in.' He inched the trunk away from the wall and made a nest of blankets and cushions behind it. 'Hopefully this will deceive anyone paying a casual visit. Rest some more if you can. We will be able to talk more freely later, when the building is empty.'

I curled up next to him. 'How long will we have to stay here?'

'Are you bored already?' He smiled down at me. 'I am sure that Mycroft will come to us as soon as he can. Come, Nell, read the paper with me.' We sat side by side, the paper in our laps. Once I caught him looking at me, and once he caught me looking at him. 'Here is another case of mine.' He ran his finger down the page. 'I am making the name of all the police inspectors in London today. It is Gregson this time, for unmasking a forger in Kings Cross.'

'No one below an inspector ever gets a mention in the paper,' I remarked, scanning the story. 'Jack never did, and neither did Napper. Not even when the Mile End Gang were caught. Jack and I worked really hard on that and I hoped that

Jack would gain some recognition, but no.'

Sherlock frowned. 'The Mile End Gang? When was that, roughly?'

'It was in August 1878, a few weeks before—'

'Before Jack disappeared?' His eyes were fixed on me now. 'Do you think there is a connection?'

I shook my head. 'How could there be? Jack told me that when Lestrade arrested the gang's leader he confessed immediately and bargained a list of his henchmen for a lighter sentence. It all tied up very neatly. And if the remainder of the gang had wanted revenge, wouldn't they go after Lestrade?'

'It all tied up very neatly, you say…' Sherlock pushed his hair back from his forehead. He seemed to be trying to make out something he could not quite hear. 'Nell, tell me everything you recall about the case.'

Speaking as low as I could, I talked of the patterns I had identified in the cases – the wrecked houses, the broken kneecaps – how the inspector had seen them too, and how Jack and I had both worked full-time on the case. I could not tell what Sherlock thought of my narrative, for his face was as inscrutable as it had been when I had told him my story.

I had just got to the part where Jack told me that the gang had been caught when his eyes widened and he put a hand to my lips. 'Shh.'

A knock at the door. We made ourselves as small as we could behind the trunk and drew my cloak over us. I was lying next to Sherlock, my face against his chest, and his heart thumped against my cheek.

The knock came again, then we heard a key in the lock. I put a hand over my mouth to keep from crying out.

The door opened and someone walked in. The door closed again.

We waited.

'Mr Mycroft Holmes presents his compliments, and would like you to join him in his office. Please follow me.'

CHAPTER 35

Somerset House, 16th February 1881

Sherlock threw off the cloak and we gaped at the speaker, a slight, clerkly man of about forty-five. 'Please follow me,' he repeated, and opened the door.

We followed his pinstriped back along the corridor to two doors facing each other. He opened the left-hand one, and we descended a flight of steep, dimly lit stairs. Halfway down the next flight of stairs he halted so abruptly that I almost walked into him. He grasped the banister rail, slid his other hand up the wall, and a door clicked open in the panelling.

We stepped into a dark little corridor, with another door at its end. The man opened it, but directly behind was yet another door with something hanging before it. He knocked, and Mycroft's voice called 'Enter!'

The man opened the second door, and the light which streamed in revealed the hanging object as an overcoat, which he held aside for us. We emerged blinking into a large square room lit by a massive window, against which I made out the shape of Mycroft Holmes seated behind another large desk. 'Thank you, Poskitt.' The man bowed, walked to a much

180

grander door across the room, and disappeared.

'Do sit.' We occupied the two wooden chairs in front of the desk. 'I hope you passed a reasonable night. Tea and biscuits are on the sideboard, if you care to help yourselves.' A china cup and saucer was already before him on the desk, so I poured tea for Sherlock and myself and brought the plate of biscuits over.

'So.' Mycroft leaned back and made a steeple of his fingers. 'Your outing last night was connected with your husband, I take it.'

'Yes. I met with a friend of Jack's, a colleague, as he had remembered something about the day Jack vanished. We were talking when there was a crash and the police arrived.'

'And do you trust this friend, Mrs Villiers?'

I remembered Napper's stricken face. 'He told me that it was Jack's idea for them to go together, with minimal back-up. He was beaten unconscious, left for dead—'

'Pardon me, Mrs Villiers, but you are letting emotion obscure the facts. Your friend says this, but who can back him up?' Mycroft paused, and his next words were spoken more softly. 'Your husband cannot defend himself. Perhaps there might be something in the paperwork.'

'That is not all,' Sherlock said. 'Nell was just telling me about the case she and her husband worked on before he vanished: the Mile End Gang, in seventy-eight. I recall now why it stuck in my mind. When the case went to trial, it collapsed.'

I gasped. 'So they arrested the wrong man?'

'Not necessarily, but they couldn't make the charge stick. Sampson changed his plea to not guilty and said he'd been forced into a false confession. It didn't do him much good, though. He was shot dead the year after.'

Mycroft consulted his watch. 'This is most interesting, but

I have work to be getting on with. My desk in Whitehall awaits.' He swivelled his chair towards me. 'Was your policeman friend involved in this case, too? Did he make the arrest?'

'No, he was working on other cases. Inspector Lestrade was in charge, and it was he who told me that Jack had disappeared, he who sent me to Baker Street—'

'Mm.' Mycroft took a biscuit from the plate. 'I have a proposition for you both. Sometimes I take it upon myself to conduct a departmental audit, which involves gathering in a great mass of documentation. Of course I only view the hundredth or thousandth of the whole that I am actually interested in, but it bypasses all those tiresome permissions while also demonstrating that I am an extremely busy man.' He smiled in a broad, satisfied way. 'I shall call in some papers including the Mile End case and, if you can give Poskitt the details, the case during which your husband vanished. I shall place the paperwork and this office at your disposal, and Poskitt can attend to your wants until I have time to visit again. I have ideas about how we should proceed, of course, but we shall check the official record first.'

'Thank you, you are very kind,' I said, and Mycroft's eyes twinkled with a mischief which, for the first time, showed a likeness to his brother.

'I imagine you will be glad to escape the attic, Mrs Villiers. I should not like to spend the night there myself.'

'Did you receive a police visit last night, Mycroft?' Sherlock spoke casually, but I could see the tension in his frame.

Mycroft shook his head. 'No calls at home or at work. You may have got away with it this time, Sherlock, but we shall take no chances. And on that topic' – he rose from his chair with surprising grace – 'a word with me in the outer office, if you would.'

Sherlock followed him through the grand carved door. I ate another biscuit, although if I had been asked I could not have said what kind. At last I would get at the papers surrounding the case! I prayed they would reveal the truth and put an end to the strange half-life I had lived for the last few years. But behind that hope was a great shadow. What terrible things would we find lurking behind the lies I had been told?

Sherlock strode back in, closing the door firmly behind him.

'You were right about your brother,' I said. 'There is a heart under that bureaucratic exterior.'

'Yes.' He flung himself into one of the chairs standing before the fireplace and stared into the flames. 'Although he does love to play the older brother with me.'

'Sherlock, is something wrong?'

'Apart from being on the run, you mean?' He glanced over and his expression softened. 'I'm sorry, Nell, that was uncalled for.'

'It's understandable.' I sat down in the other chair. 'What did Mycroft say? Was it about the case?'

'Not exactly.' He sighed. 'He was probably right, though. Nothing gets past him, unfortunately.'

'What do you mean?'

'I called you Nell earlier, and as soon as I had done it I saw that Mycroft had noticed. When we spoke outside he reminded me, in a kind but older-brotherly way, that you are a married woman and that I must think of you as such.'

'I don't feel like a married woman. It has been so long now, since Jack, that I don't know what I am.'

Sherlock smacked the arm of the chair. 'This situation is ridiculous!' Then he sprang up. 'Then let us work with it. I have been told to regard you as married, which means that

183

you have a husband somewhere.'

'But your brother knows less than we do about the case.' I watched Sherlock pace back and forth, thoroughly bewildered.

'Yes.' Sherlock stopped. 'But his caution has given us a hypothesis. If Jack Villiers has not been found dead, then he may be alive. If he is alive, where is he?'

'Perhaps he has somehow been imprisoned – as I have been, or in a different way.'

'It is possible; yet it is an effort, and expensive, to keep someone shut up where they cannot be found. What are the other options?'

'He could be hiding, but why? What would the reason be? Jack was not a man to be frightened. And if he were, surely he would seek the protection of the police?'

'Indeed.' Sherlock resumed his pacing. 'Unless the police were the problem. I keep coming back to the police. Your friend Napper is a policeman, as is Inspector Lestrade. At least one of them is lying, and until we find some evidence we have no way to prove it.'

Mr Poskitt entered with a bundle of newspapers. 'Excuse me, but Mr Holmes thought these might be a useful diversion while we procure your case papers.'

'Thank you, Poskitt.' Sherlock picked up the *Times* from the pile and scanned the pages. 'No news of us in any of these, I hope?'

'Not that I am aware of, Mr Holmes. Madam, could you come into my office so that I can take some details about these cases? I would like to make sure of the facts.'

'So would I,' I said, following him out. Mr Poskitt's office was smaller and plainer than Mycroft's, but still well lit and well appointed. How senior must Mycroft be, when his secretary's room was twice the size of my sitting room at Baker Street?

Mr Poskitt invited me to a chair and drew a notebook towards him. His questions were brief, relevant and impersonal. His pen flew over the paper making a jumble of shapes and squiggles. 'It is shorthand, madam. May I read it to you to check that I have it correct?' I nodded, and Mr Poskitt read back my words with the matter-of-factness of a grocery list.

'That is exactly right,' I said, and we both started up at a faint cry from the inner office. Sherlock opened the door, his face lit up. 'Nell, I have been a complete fool. Poskitt, can you get hold of some more documents for me?'

'I expect so, sir.'

'I shall make a list and bring it to you presently.'

'Very good, Mr Holmes.'

I returned to Mycroft's office to find Sherlock taking a seat behind the desk. 'What have you found?'

'Nothing yet. I was reading the *Times*, looking for any possible reference to either the incident at the inn or our disappearance – there was none – and my silly comment to Poskitt came back to me: *No news of us*. We leave a paper trail everywhere we go, Nell. Even Mrs Hudson has an address, a library card, and accounts with shopkeepers. I intend to explore all avenues, Nell, and if your husband is alive, I will find him.' His eyes glinted in a manner I did not like, and he began writing.

I sat down and took up a newspaper, but the words swam before my eyes. Perhaps the truth was hours away; perhaps we would never know what had happened in the opium den. I was happy that Jack might be alive somewhere, yet the happiness was smothered by apprehension at what we might find.

CHAPTER 36

Somerset House, 16th February 1881

'There.' Sherlock blotted the page. 'We have made a start.' He opened the door and waved the list at Mr Poskitt, who scanned it and frowned.

'Mr Holmes, some of these papers will take time to procure.'

'I understand, Poskitt. I know you will do your best.'

'Of course, sir. I can bring the newspaper immediately, as we have bound volumes for reference.'

'Wonderful. Oh, Poskitt—'

'Yes, Mr Holmes?'

'Is there another room I could sleep in tonight? Or a bed in the attic, perhaps?'

'I shall attend to it, sir.'

Sherlock watched him out of the room. 'I thought I should offer some proof to Mycroft that I do not intend to seduce you.'

I looked away. 'What papers did you ask him for?'

Sherlock sat down next to me. 'The sheet I gave to Poskitt covers the ways I could think of for a man to disappear.' He counted on his fingers. 'Admission records for all hospitals within ten miles. Shipping lists for the port of London. Prison admissions. Newspapers from September 1878 to the end of the year, in the first instance...'

I whistled. 'How long will it take us to read it all?'

'What else can we do, cooped up in here?' Sherlock pushed his hair back. 'I am sorry, Nell. I begin to understand your ordeal at Baker Street; the idea of venturing outside worries me.' He sighed. 'I hope Watson is safe. And Billy, if he is not mixed up in this – you see? I do not know who to trust. If nothing else, this will keep us from scaring ourselves with shadows lurking around every corner. We need to keep our wits about us.'

A few minutes later there was a thud at the door. Mr Poskitt staggered in under the weight of four large books and deposited them on the desk with a thump. '*The Times*,' he panted. 'Luncheon will arrive in half an hour.' He wiped his brow with a large white handkerchief and scurried out.

'Shall we take a volume each?' I asked. 'What should I look for?'

'Anything relevant,' said Sherlock, passing me September 1878. 'It is hard to say, but anything which catches your attention, or mentions an acquaintance, or even a story about the same area. We start by clutching at straws, but even a description of someone similar to your husband could bring back a memory. How old was Jack when he disappeared?'

'Twenty-six.'

'I had imagined him older.' He set a chair for me on the opposite side of the desk. 'I am twenty-six. It brings it home.'

I fetched myself paper and pen, sat down, and opened the volume. I turned straight to the day of Jack's disappearance, 13th September, but there was nothing that bore any relation to it. The following days were no better. Jack had vanished

187

without even a ripple.

Neither of us spoke until Mr Poskitt arrived bearing tea and sandwiches. 'There is fruit on the sideboard,' he said, waving his hand at a silver bowl stacked high with apples and oranges.

We ate lunch sitting before the fire, making small talk. I was glad to have a break from the endless pages of newsprint. But the time came when we would have to return to work. We retook our seats at the desk, and soon there was silence except for the turn of pages, the scribble of our pens, and an occasional sigh.

'I should have thought!' Sherlock's exclamation almost made me drop my pen. 'Did your husband have any friends or family outside London?'

I shook my head. 'Not at all. He was London through and through. His family and his friends are all here; he never even visited anywhere else.'

'Mm.' Sherlock bent again to his book, but he did not turn a page for some time.

Once I had got over the monotony of what I was doing and found a rhythm, time passed more smoothly. I had to break off to visit the bathroom; Mycroft had his own lavatory, behind another small door, which was far pleasanter than the ones downstairs.

As I washed my hands I looked in the mirror. I must have been running my hand through my hair as I read, for wisps had come loose from my bun, and several hairpins were half out. Then I realised – my hair looked as it used to when I was alone in the house at Clerkenwell, working. So much had happened since, and I still had the same untidy habits. I redid my bun and returned to my seat. Sherlock looked up at my entrance, and his smile broadened.

'What is it?' I asked, running my hand down the page to

find my place.

'You've pinned your hair up,' he said, grinning. 'I had made a guess at what time it would come down, and now you have spoilt it.'

I frowned at him and clasped my hands in my lap, so that I would not be tempted to disarrange myself again. But now it was my turn to read the same page over and over, and my scalp tingled at the memory of his fingers freeing the jammed-in hairpins one by one, then the long, gentle strokes of the brush, and then – my eyes flicked up, and met his. But when they did, instead of the desire which had coursed through me yesterday, I felt the shame I had when I saw myself in the peacock-blue dress.

He sprang up and went to the window. 'I am trying my hardest.' The bitterness was back in his voice – oh, the bitterness that I felt. 'It will be as well when this is over.'

I kept my head down then, ploughing through the thankless task. Eventually he returned to his seat, and the sounds of paper and pen indicated that he had resumed his work.

We worked on without speaking until Mr Poskitt arrived with a tray containing two plates of veal chops, mashed potatoes and peas. He placed it on the sideboard and glanced at the volumes on the desk. 'I would suggest that you have done enough for one day. Allow me.' He took note of the page numbers, then carried the books into his office. Then he set the plates out on the desk, facing each other. 'I shall ask you to retire after dinner, since I must secure the office before I set off home. Mr Holmes, a bed is made up for you in attic four; I shall escort you. Mrs Villiers, I have a camp-bed outside for you, which I shall require help to bring in.' He looked at Sherlock meaningfully, and left the room.

We ate, as we had worked, in silence. The food was good –

excellent – but swallowing it was strangely painful, and I put my knife and fork down with most of the food still on the plate. I got up and took the plate to the sideboard; I couldn't sit opposite Sherlock for another moment. More than anything, I wanted to be alone.

'I did not mean to—' His voice was tight, hard.

'What?' He looked utterly wretched, sitting at the desk on his own, a half-finished plate of food before him. He looked lost.

'It's always been fun before. Dull in parts, sometimes – often – dangerous, but fun. Meet the client, do the work, solve the case, move on. Even when I've been running through the back streets with a pack of thugs after me, there's the thrill of the fox escaping the hounds – and I've always escaped. I've been free to work as I like, and I've always known that in the end the police are at my back.' He spread his hands wide. 'But now the police are the enemy, Nell, and you're my client. If I solve the case, if I find your husband alive, that's it. We move on. We can't meet again.' His voice broke on the last word. He sprang up and strode to the bathroom.

After a minute or two came the inevitable tap at the door. 'One moment,' I called, wiping my eyes. 'Come in.'

'Have you finished, madam? Where is Mr Holmes?' Mr Poskitt looked around as if he might spring from anywhere.

'We've both finished,' I muttered. 'Mr Holmes is using the bathroom.'

'Ah.' He put the plates onto the tray. 'When he is quite ready, please tell him that I shall be waiting for him outside. To assist with the bed.'

Moments later I heard a tap running. Sherlock walked out, and while he was pale his face was composed. He walked through the room without a glance, and presently Mr Poskitt came in backwards with one end of the bed. 'Over there, please. That's it. And . . . there.' He dusted his hands off. 'Mrs Villiers, I trust you have all you require. Mr Holmes…' He gestured towards the leather valise lying in the corner, and Sherlock picked it up. 'This way.' He opened the cupboard door we had entered through that morning. 'Goodnight, Mrs Villiers.'

'Goodnight, Mrs Villiers,' echoed Sherlock, looking past me. He turned and followed Mr Poskitt through the cupboard.

'Goodnight, Mr Holmes,' I replied. The lock clicked, and their footsteps faded away. 'Goodnight, Sherlock,' I whispered.

CHAPTER 37

Somerset House, 17th February 1881

I woke the next morning with a pounding head and a damp pillow. At first I couldn't tell where I was, but the unfamiliar hardness of the bed told me that I was not at Baker Street. In the grey light I could make out two chairs and a desk… The previous day poring through the *Times*, and its wretched end, came back to me. I tried to shake it away, but it was lodged fast. I did the best I could with the cold water in the bathroom and emerged feeling more awake, if not more cheerful.

I had been dressed for perhaps half an hour when Mr Poskitt called, 'Mrs Villiers?'

'Come in, I am ready,' I said. The clock on the desk said a quarter past seven.

Mr Poskitt was as neat as he had been the day before. He cast an eye over me and I hoped that I passed muster. 'Good morning, Mrs Villiers. I have ordered breakfast for half past seven. Mr Holmes will join you shortly.'

'Thank you.' Mr Poskitt half-bowed. He was clearly a senior and trusted member of Mycroft's staff, but at times he had an odd little air of a butler or a valet about him.

He walked towards the cupboard, and paused. 'How is the work coming along, Mrs Villiers?'

I considered before I answered. 'It is a slow task, and not a happy one.'

'I have requested all the items Mr Holmes asked for, and I am hopeful that some will arrive soon. One in particular – I shall bring it to you both after breakfast. Let us hope for a better day.' He bobbed his head and left the room, and his quick, regular tread sounded on the stairs. I went to examine Mycroft's bookcase. It was an excuse not to look at Mr Holmes, as I should probably think of him again.

I was staring at the middle shelf when the cupboard door creaked open. 'Good morning, Mrs Villiers.' His voice was warm, friendly.

'Good morning, Mr Holmes,' I said, continuing to scan the books, though I could not have named a single title.

'I shall enquire after breakfast.' Mr Poskitt hurried away, and suddenly Sherlock was standing beside me.

'Nell, I am sorry for yesterday. I was thinking too much of myself, and not enough of you. Please don't be cold towards me.' Sherlock's voice and his words compelled me to look at him, and I saw the love and concern in his face.

'I cannot be cold towards you, Sherlock.' I laid my hand on his, and our fingers intertwined.

'My anger was born of frustration, and fear. I wanted to blame someone, and I took it out on you when I should have used it to spur me on. Poskitt is returning.' He walked to the window, and presently was proved right.

Mr Poskitt put down the tray, on which sat bacon, eggs, mushrooms, and a toast rack. 'A break from the newspapers would be advisable.' The corners of his mouth rose a fraction. 'I shall see what I can do.' And off he bustled.

Sherlock set the plates down on the desk, and I joined him.

'I wonder what he has for us. Something good, from the look of him.'

'Let's eat.' We fell to, and cleared our plates in short order. 'I shall grow lazy if we are here much longer,' I said, putting my knife and fork together. 'No cooking, no washing-up, no cleaning, no laundry.'

'No objectionable lodgers...'

Mr Poskitt came in. 'I gathered from the talk that you had finished.' He held a sheet of paper. 'I happened to pass the dock on my way in this morning and I had a word with the harbourmaster on duty, who has supplied a list of all the ships which left the port that week.' He put the sheet down between us. 'I expect some of the hospital records will come in today. They will make a fair copy and send it over.'

'Won't they find it strange that the General Register Office is requesting such things?' I asked.

'Oh, the papers will not come here at first. They have been requested by Whitehall's leading statistician, Dr Stamford Leach.'

'It is kind of him to make the time,' I said.

'Not really. I am afraid that he is an invention of Mr Holmes's. I imagine that his name strikes terror into the heart of any record-keeping organisation. Excuse me.' A sound which was half-cough, half-laugh escaped from Mr Poskitt as he left the room.

Sherlock picked up the sheet of paper and came round to my side of the desk. 'It is as I suspected.' He pointed with a long finger. 'Two long-haul ships left London that day: the *Achilles*, bound for Canada, and the *Valiant* for Tasmania. Now this list has many ships, travelling to many destinations, but I have a hunch that Jack Villiers may have been on one of these two, and I am inclined towards Tasmania.'

'Why?'

194

'Two men enter an opium den. When we catch up with them one is beaten half to death and one is missing, next to a window opening onto the river. What would anyone assume has happened to the missing one?'

I shivered. 'He has gone into the river.'

'Precisely. That is the sort of horrible, violent thing we expect to happen in an opium den, particularly when juxtaposed with the savage beating your friend Napper received. I have been puzzling away at this, picking at it every now and again, and I always come back to the same two points. The first is this: why would a criminal blindfold and beat one policeman and murder the other? And the second: if you had thrown someone into the river, you would close the window afterwards. Leaving the window open advertises what you have done, and positively invites the police to drag the river for the missing man. We were meant to jump to the conclusion that Jack Villiers was murdered and his body put into the river, but that was not the case.'

I swallowed. 'So you think Jack is alive?'

'I do. When there is a perfectly good way to kill someone on the spot, it would be stupid to take them somewhere else to do it. And that brings us to the next part of the mystery.' Sherlock paced up and down, buzzing with nervous energy. 'I put myself into the mind of the criminal. Napper was not intended to die; he was an unfortunate decoy left to signpost the open window. Perhaps they primed him with some useful talk when he was blindfolded, in order to send the police the wrong way. If so, they undid their work by beating him hard enough to induce memory loss. But what has happened to Jack in the meantime? It would be easier to kill him than imprison him in secret. We can only conclude that the plan was not to kill him, but for him to disappear.'

Sherlock came over to me. 'At one point I wondered if

195

your husband might have planned the disappearance himself' – he held up a hand as I began to protest – 'but I do not think so now. I remembered what you told me about the day he disappeared, and the thing that stood out was that for you, up to the point where Jack didn't come home, it was a normal day. If Jack had known what was coming he would have taken something personal with him: one or two of the everyday items which are almost extensions of ourselves. From what you said, he had a gun and nothing else. And he would have said that he might be late home, to prevent you becoming worried.' Sudden tears welled up in my eyes.

'So this is where I am at in my reasoning. Someone wants Jack to disappear. They do not want to kill him – murder is a serious crime – but they want him out of London. The obvious answer is to send him far away, to make his return as difficult as possible. And where is further than the other side of the world?'

I gasped, and Sherlock smiled with grim satisfaction. 'I perceive that you follow my argument. We shall examine the other records that I have asked for, of course, but this will be our main line of enquiry until proved wrong. I will ask Poskitt for the passenger lists of both ships, and a few other things that may be helpful.' He patted my hand, and went through to the outer office.

I saw rather than felt Sherlock's touch. Jack had not died that day. My instinctive revulsion at widow's weeds, my reluctance to accept my status, had been correct. The fog was lifting from one part of the mystery, but the greater part remained. Why had Jack disappeared, and why hadn't he come back?

CHAPTER 38

Somerset House, 17th February 1881

Sherlock entered the room with a wry smile on his face. 'If I achieve nothing else today, I have made Poskitt run. He sped off like a hare to fulfil my latest request; I hope his effort is not in vain.' He deposited a small stack of papers on the desk. 'The hospital admission records are coming in. These should have been checked at the time, but it is as well to look them over while we await Poskitt's return.' He divided the pile into two and slid half towards me.

After a few minutes Sherlock pushed the papers away and rubbed his eyes. 'Have you found anything, Nell?'

'Nothing definite. I am not sure what to look for. The obvious thing is some kind of severe head injury, but none of these entries fit.' I gathered up my papers, put them on top of his, and squared the edges.

'Neat as always.' Sherlock said, with a low laugh.

'I have been meaning to ask you . . . your bedroom is neat, while your half of the room you share with Dr Watson is quite untidy. Why is that?'

'Oh Nell, you have found me out!' Sherlock pushed his

hair back. 'It is a silly affectation of mine to demonstrate that my mind is on higher things. I associate neatness with that by-the-book approach of men like Lestrade. And now here we are working methodically through the evidence.' He leaned forward and whispered, 'If anyone hears of it, I shall blame you.'

'So you even pretend to Dr Watson?'

Sherlock raised an eyebrow. 'Are you the same to everyone, Nell? Of course not. During my first week at Baker Street you were brisk efficiency personified with me and Watson, but you and Billy were more like colleagues than mistress and servant. A little studied untidiness is harmless enough, and fits Watson's idea of what a great detective should be like.'

I sighed. 'It is harmless, but I don't understand why you need to put on a show to your friend.'

'Perhaps the show is all there is.' Sherlock made a minute adjustment to the stack of papers.

'You don't believe that.'

'I do sometimes when a case is going badly, or I am particularly low.' He frowned. 'If I tell you something, will you promise not to tell Watson?'

I sat back and folded my arms. 'That depends whether it is something he should know.'

'Absolutely not.' He grinned. 'It is harmless, but it will help to explain.'

'Then I promise. Tell me.'

'All right.' He was silent for a moment. 'I had known Watson half an hour when I invited him to the rooms in Baker Street. I am solitary by nature, and immersed in my work. But when I met Watson, a doctor and an army veteran, I thought he might be – not a partner, but an associate.'

I nodded, but my head was busy trying to reconcile steady

Dr Watson with some of the activities I had undertaken as Sherlock's assistant.

'We all make mistakes.' Sherlock laughed. 'Watson is intelligent, he is principled, and I am certain that he is brave. I am lucky to have him as a friend. But he is incapable of original thought and he does not have an unconventional bone in his body. If I asked him to disguise himself and follow a suspect round London . . . well, I would not ask him.' I smiled at the picture this presented. 'Early in our acquaintance I hinted at the sort of thing I had in mind, painting as attractive a picture as I could, but Watson reacted as a child might if you told them a story of dragons and princes. He was delighted, but he had no idea of being part of it.'

'Ah.' I considered. 'He is a spectator at the play, and you are the star of the show.'

'Precisely.' Sherlock scratched his ear. 'It sounds rather conceited, put like that.' Then he laughed. 'But you are in the show too now, for better or worse. The heart of the show, indeed.'

There was a rap at the door, and Mr Poskitt brought in an armful of papers. 'I have telegraphed the shipping offices and the British Museum, and requested the documents by return. I have here the full documentation for the Mile End Gang case, and all that is on file regarding the opium den incident.' We cleared space on the desk for him to put them down. 'I shall get some tea sent in.'

'Thank you,' I said. 'Before you go…'

'Yes, madam?'

'Everything seems to be happening very quickly. Is that usual?'

'When it is expedient, the wheels of bureaucracy can move with surprising speed. I will go and hurry up that tea.'

I glanced at Sherlock, who was watching Mr Poskitt's

retreating back with an amused expression. 'He's excellent at giving answers which aren't answers,' I said, resignedly.

'He's an excellent civil servant,' said Sherlock. 'It comes to the same thing.' He examined the pile of paper, separating the two cases out. 'Shall we each take one, then swap cases? Which would you prefer?'

'I am not sure that prefer is the right word.' I looked at the piles. 'I can take the Mile End papers. I shall probably remember some of them.' I slid the pile towards me. 'I was surprised that he had telegraphed directly, that was all.'

'Clearly it was expedient.' Sherlock stressed the last word. 'Mycroft likes to move in mysterious ways, but I would wager he shares our view that this case is about more than one disappearing policeman.'

'I just wish— If I could have seen this paperwork, or done anything before now to discover the truth…'

Sherlock reached out and touched my hand. 'At least we can do it now. Let us read, and see what we find.'

I burrowed into my heap of papers. There were reports, multiple witness statements, a report of the trial proceedings, and a newspaper clipping from the *Daily London Messenger*. *MILE END GANG CASE COLLAPSES*, the headline screamed. *JUDGE THROWS CASE OUT, RINGLEADER GOES FREE*. The cutting was dated 24th October 1878, around six weeks after Jack had vanished. By then I would have been shut up in Baker Street, with no access to news. Napper would have been in hospital or a convalescent home. I noted that Inspector Lestrade's name was not mentioned in the article.

I put it aside and turned to the reports. I leafed through, looking for my handwriting. It wasn't there. But then a sentence from one of the reports leapt out at me: *The criminal activity appears to radiate outwards from the borough of*

Stepney. I remembered writing it. I felt the pen in my hand, and saw the ink stain on my forefinger. And here the sentence was in a different hand, a careful clerk's copperplate. I turned to the next page, and at the bottom was a signature in a different hand. *Inspector G Lestrade, 6th August 1878.* I scrabbled through the rest of the reports, and his signature was on all of them. 'Ha!'

Sherlock looked up, eyebrows raised. 'What is it, Nell?'

'You were right about Inspector Lestrade taking the credit. My reports are here, recopied and signed as his. All the reports are signed by the inspector except the report of the trial itself. That is signed by a stenographer, J Willis.'

'That is interesting.' Sherlock moved round to my side of the desk. 'Which reports are yours, Nell?'

I flicked through the pile and separated mine into another stack, around two-thirds of the whole. 'These ones are mine.'

I made another pass, and found the reports Jack had written; I knew them, as he had always asked me to read and correct them before he handed them in. I made a stack of those. 'These are Jack's.' Then I removed the trial report from the original pile. Only a few pages remained. One report, dated 23rd August 1878. The day after Jack had come home to tell me that the case was solved. 'This is all that is left.'

Side by side, we read through the report. It was in the same copperplate hand. The style was plain, without flourish or ornament. The report stated that the author had, in the course of a conversation about an ongoing case, developed a fresh insight into the events in Stepney: *The author applied this insight to the existing documentation, and this narrowed the pool of suspects to a considerable degree. A further examination of this pool indicated that the group called the Mile End Gang was the most likely to have been responsible for the crimes, since it was large and well-organised, though there had been no known gang activity for some time. The author of the report arrested Richard Sampson, the ringleader of the gang, on suspicion of orchestrating and participating in the crimes. Mr Sampson readily confessed his involvement and provided a list of key individuals who had worked under his direction, in exchange for future leniency.*

'An open and shut case, it would appear . . . except that now we know better.' Sherlock leafed through the report again. 'Do you think Lestrade wrote this, Nell?'

'It is possible. He would write his instructions to me when I worked for him, and the style is similar.' I looked down at the page. 'A conversation about an ongoing case...' I tapped the paper. 'I wonder who he was talking to when he had this sudden insight.'

'So do I. Lestrade is not the sort of man to leap to conclusions. He is steady, careful, methodical.'

Something in Sherlock's tone made me look up from the report. 'What do you mean?'

'One of two things, and I am not sure which I believe. Here is my first theory. You have seen Lestrade's unpleasant habit of stealing the glory. It would be easy for someone to drop a hint or plant some information, safe in the knowledge that they would never be named in the official report.'

'And what is your second theory?'

Sherlock sighed. 'My second hypothesis is that there was no conversation with a colleague. Lestrade set the whole thing up. But it makes no sense. Why would a man who claims every success set himself up to fail?'

'He wouldn't,' I said.

'I agree. Unless...' Sherlock frowned. 'Unless the incentive was big enough to justify it. Lestrade would have received a severe reprimand. What would make the sacrifice worth it? Only a huge reward of money or power worth more to him than his professional reputation. Framing the wrong gang would allow whoever did commit the crimes to carry on.'

'So he might have taken a bribe, or—'

'Or been involved in criminal activities.' Sherlock pushed his hair out of his eyes. 'I can't imagine it either, but nothing is impossible. Either Lestrade was set up by someone – and that could only be a colleague – or Lestrade is not the man I thought he was at all.' His mouth twisted. 'And I cannot work out which is worse.'

CHAPTER 39

Somerset House, 17th February 1881

Mr Poskitt manoeuvred the tea tray expertly through the door. 'Any leads, sir?'

'They keep ending in blind alleys, Poskitt.'

'Ah.' He put the tray down on the sideboard. 'I have just taken delivery of the *Valiant's* passenger register for the second half of 1878.' He went out and returned with a large book bound in black leather, while we moved the piles of case notes onto the floor. 'I expect the register for the *Achilles* will arrive soon.'

'Thank you.' Mr Poskitt cast a lingering glance at the register before withdrawing.

We hurried to the desk. Sherlock opened the book and turned the pages. 'Now my hunch will be tested,' he murmured. 'Let us hope for a conscientious master... Here we are! 13th September 1878, from London to Hobart Town. Let us see if we can find Jack Villiers, or someone like him.' Our heads were so close that his hair tickled my ear. 'Could you describe him to me, Nell?'

I tore myself away from the book. 'He is tall – perhaps an

inch or two shorter than you – broad-shouldered and well-built. His hair is dark brown, and it was cut quite short. He is clean shaven, and his eyes are blue.' My use of the present tense surprised me.

'Does he have any distinguishing marks? Moles, scars, anything like that?'

'No – wait. He had cut himself on the thumb with his penknife a few days before. It was not a deep cut, but still healing.'

He had come into the kitchen with a handkerchief wrapped around his hand, biting his lip to keep from swearing. He swore when I cleaned the cut with iodine, though, spitting the words out through gritted teeth. When the bleeding stopped I bandaged it for him, and kissed the bandage. 'All better, Jack.'

'Oh, Nell.' I started at Sherlock's voice, and blinked. I had forgotten he was there for a moment. 'Is this too much for you?'

I shook my head. 'I'm sorry. Just…'

'I understand.' He reached out for me, then stopped and patted me on the arm. 'Come, let us read.'

The register held much more information than I had anticipated: name, age, marital status, education and trade, and the amount paid for passage. In addition, someone had written a brief description of each adult passenger: '35, tall, long face, fair hair.' I read. It was not Jack, but somehow it cheered me that someone had troubled to record the details of voyagers who would almost certainly never return. I pushed my fringe back and scanned the columns for men of around Jack's age. I reached the bottom of the page and looked at Sherlock.

'Anything, Nell?'

I shook my head. He turned the page and we read on, skimming the columns faster and faster as we grew used to the process. In the first few pages there were two men who could have been Jack. One was twenty two, one thirty-one; both were tall and dark-haired, but both had families. One was a Roman Catholic and could read but not write; the other had a dash under Education. I copied the entries down, but neither felt right.

The page turned again. *36 . . . 42 . . . 24—*

My finger paused.

John Smith, 24, single. Tall, heavy-set, dark hair, clean-shaven. Religion: Protestant. Education: R&W. Native place: London. Trade: labourer. Name of person on whose application sent out: Thos. Jones. Remarks: £10 paid.

The back of my neck prickled. I fumbled for my pen.

'Could it be...?'

'It could be,' I replied as I wrote. I put the pen down and looked at the words. *John Smith, 24.* 'It could be.'

'We must keep looking. There could be more people answering the description.' Sherlock bent his head to the book again and I did the same, though my heart was convinced that I had found Jack.

We read through page after page, but none of the records spoke to me as that one had, though there were a few more possible matches. We reached the last page of the entries for September 1878, and looked at each other. I felt light, giddy, a little dazed.

'You believe it, don't you?' Sherlock said softly. 'You believe it is him.'

'I do.'

He stood up, offered me a hand, and lifted me to my feet. 'Then we shall have a word with Poskitt.' He took my arm, and smiled down at me.

Mr Poskitt was dealing with correspondence when we entered his office. 'Have you...?' His mouth widened into an

O. 'You have found something!'

'It is a strong possibility.' Sherlock escorted me to a chair. 'Have you had word of the papers, Poskitt? Are they on the way?'

Mr Poskitt looked uneasy. 'There is a slight hitch, Mr Holmes. The British Museum replied to my wire. They have the papers, but due to the volume they are not prepared to send them here. We shall have to go to them. I must accompany you,' he replied to my look. 'Unless one of you has brought a reading-room ticket with you.'

'Is it safe?' I looked from Mr Poskitt to Sherlock, and back again.

'Oh yes, madam. We will use the private entrance, and the museum's people have agreed to let us have the use of a room.' Mr Poskitt consulted his watch. 'Luncheon is due in a few minutes. I shall order a conveyance for half past twelve.' He leapt up and ran out of the office.

'Twice in one day,' Sherlock remarked. 'That I have made him run, Nell.' His words were light, his tone less so. 'Perhaps we really are nearing the end now.' He got up and walked to the window.

His words pierced my heart. 'Oh, Sherlock…' He did not turn. I joined him, and took his hand. 'Whatever happens, whatever we find, I am so grateful to you. You helped me when no one else would, you listened, you gave me hope.' I could barely speak through the lump in my throat. 'Kiss me, even if it is the last—'

His arms were around me, his mouth on mine, and we both kissed as if we would never see the other again. We broke, panting, and stared at each other. Sherlock reached out and tucked a strand of hair behind my ear, never breaking his gaze. Mr Poskitt had to cough before we noticed him, so transfixed were we.

CHAPTER 40

The British Museum, 17th February 1881

Mr Poskitt opened a small grey-painted door, revealing a plain but respectable carriage waiting at the kerb. I blinked at the rush of air and light, and the icy blast pummelling my face. I shrank into my cloak and pulled the hood up.

'The journey should take no more than a few minutes,' remarked Mr Poskitt. 'Normally I would walk, but under the circumstances...'

I wondered how much longer we would have to be in hiding. It had been only two days, but it seemed like months. London flew past outside and corresponding images flitted through my head: walks in the park with Billy, nights out with Jack, walking the streets in disguise during my work for Sherlock. We were slowing down before I knew it. Through the window iron railings appeared; behind them stone glowed near-golden in the sun. As I got out the huge mass of the British Museum towered above me, and I felt small as an ant.

'The private door is this way.' Mr Poskitt took out a key and fitted it into a tiny hole in the railings. In a fold of the building, sheltered from passers-by, was a door painted to match the stone. Mr Poskitt rapped on it, with a peculiar jolting rhythm, and I heard bolts slide back in answer.

'I did not think you would be here so soon.' The speaker was a youngish, portly man with slicked-back hair and white gloves. 'This is all most irregular.'

'Thank you for accommodating us, Mr Ransome.' We followed Mr Poskitt inside. 'Mr Ransome is the Senior Under-Librarian of the Museum.' The man puffed up a little more as his title was spoken. 'Do you have a room ready for us?'

'I have closed off an anteroom adjacent to the Newspaper Room, Mr Poskitt.' He enunciated the words so sharply that the capital letters were audible.

'Excellent.' Mr Poskitt motioned to Mr Ransome to lead the way.

We passed from the small vestibule into a series of galleries. I had visited the British Museum before and I did not remember any of these rooms, but Mr Ransome walked too quickly for curiosity. We passed through a door behind a curtain, and through another set of smaller, plainer rooms until we came to a closed door. Mr Ransome produced a key attached to his watch chain, and stood aside to let us pass in. Then he followed us and locked the door behind him.

'Is this really necessary, Ransome?' asked Mr Poskitt.

'I do not allow unsupervised access to people without a reader's ticket.' Mr Ransome rocked back and forth on his heels.

The room was small, and made smaller by the glass-fronted bookshelves which lined it. In the centre was a large baize-topped table, with a chair on each side, and on the table were five large slim volumes, bound in maroon leather. *The Mercury* was stamped on each spine in gold, with the year of publication underneath. Sherlock reached towards the nearest. 'Gloves, please!' Mr Ransome strode to the table, pulled out a drawer, and withdrew three pairs of white cotton gloves, laying them on the table with a frown in Sherlock's direction. Then he returned to his post by the door. 'The museum closes at four o'clock today, and I shall escort you from the room at a quarter to four.'

'And if we have not concluded our business?' Sherlock pulled out a chair, but remained standing square on to Mr Ransome.

'Then you must arrange another appointment.' The corners of Mr Ransome's mouth twitched upwards. 'On a Monday, a Wednesday, or a Friday.'

I sat down and reached for the gloves. 'We had better get started. Here is the list of potential matches.' I took the paper from my pocket and placed it in the centre of the table. 'Please could we have some paper and pens, Mr Ransome?'

'We do not allow pens,' intoned Mr Ransome. 'Pencils only.' He opened another drawer in the table and gave us two sheets of paper and a pencil each.

I drew the nearest volume towards me. *The Mercury, January-June, 1880.* 'Wait – we should look for the *Valiant*'s arrival first.'

'I have the volume for the second half of 1878 here.' Sherlock opened it and turned the pages, watched like a hawk by Mr Ransome. 'If the ship left London on the 13th of September, it would have taken at least two months to get to Tasmania. Now, shipping . . . no...' He continued to leaf through the pages. 'Carry on, I will tell you when I find anything.'

I watched the top of Sherlock's head for a while, then bent to my own volume. I was not sure what to look for. *The Mercury, Hobart Town.* My eye leapt to the deaths on the first page, hoping that Jack was not there, that none of the names we had gathered were there. They were not. Then came the advertisements, a jumble of hotels, life assurance, hats, groceries and situations vacant. On the second page, shipping, mail and commercial news, followed by a long and impassioned editorial which had something to do with a schoolroom, then overseas news, which I skipped. On the next page I browsed through council news, letters and more advertisements which continued onto the back page, for sales of crown land, horses out to stud, and livestock auctions. Tasmania had sounded so impossibly exotic; *The Mercury* brought it right down to earth. I sighed and turned the page, scanning for a mention of John Smith, Simeon Rogers, Thomas Haycraft, Robert Pascoe, Joseph Davies, Joshua Naismith – but for John Smith most of all.

I was beginning February's papers when a low exclamation made me jump. 'I have it.' Sherlock pointed with a gloved finger. 'Arrived November 22nd,' he read. '*Valiant*, 491 tons, H. Wyatt, from London. Passengers...' His finger moved down the page. 'They are here; they are all here. Davies, Haycraft, Naismith, Pascoe, Rogers and Smith.'

'They arrived safely,' I breathed. 'Mr Ransome, could we have a window open? It is stuffy in here.' Mr Ransome nodded stiffly, unpeeled himself from the door, and set to with a window pole.

The names ran through my head like a litany as I scanned the pages. The men all had labourer or farm labourer for their trade; even if we found nothing in the papers, there might be more information at the shipping office. There must be something . . . but I had to keep reading or we would never finish before the museum closed. Davies, Haycraft, Naismith, Pascoe, Rogers, Smith. Sometimes the names popped up, but attached to accountants or marine surveyors or gentlemen's outfitters, and I read on. There was no sound but the gentle rustle of turning pages.

'It is like looking for a needle in a haystack,' muttered Sherlock.

I read through March, April and May; I was coming to the end of the book. 'Mr Ransome, do you have the papers for July 1880 onwards?'

Mr Ransome looked down his nose at me. 'They have not been bound yet.'

'But can I see them, please?'

He sighed. 'I shall enquire, madam.' He unlocked the door and closed it behind him, and I turned the page.

It leapt out at me from the top-left corner of the front page: '*John Smith*'. The words blurred before my eyes. I put my finger on the page to hold the words and myself steady. I closed my eyes for a moment. *There must be hundreds of John Smiths in Tasmania. It means nothing. It means nothing.*

I took a deep breath, opened my eyes, and read where my finger pointed:

BIRTHS
SMITH: On June 5th, at Home Farm, near Hobart Town, to the wife of John Smith, farmer: a son, James Jenkins.

I felt an arm around my shoulder and someone lifted my hand from the newspaper. Mr Poskitt's voice floated behind me. 'Is it he? Can we be sure?'

'Beyond a doubt,' said Sherlock. 'Damn him.'

CHAPTER 41

The British Museum, 17th February 1881

I was in the eye of a hurricane. I shivered and sobbed, but inside I was empty and silent. Mr Ransome had come back, and after a few angry words Mr Poskitt had sent him out again. Tea came, and after a few teeth-chattering attempts I took a few sips of the hot, sweet liquid. It hurt to swallow but the tea warmed me, and gradually I shook less and less, until I sat almost still. I wanted to scream and beat the table with my fists, yet I already knew that there was no point in noise. Jack's marriage, Jack's child could not be undone. They were there in black and white and they could never be undone.

'Nell, we should go.' Sherlock was next to me, and when I turned to him he looked utterly stricken.

'Back to Somerset House? Back to Baker Street? Where should I be? Where can I go now?'

'It won't do you any good to stay here. Poskitt, can you order the carriage again for Somerset House, or shall we get a cab?'

'I shall order a carriage.' Mr Poskitt stood up and fumbled in his pocket. 'Here is the key. Make sure you follow the back route to Mr Holmes's office.'

'Aren't you coming?' I burst out.

'I shall walk back later, madam. Mr Holmes is right; it is best for you to return to Somerset House, at least for now. I will spend a little more time with these papers.' His lip curled as he looked at the bound volumes. 'I fancy there is a little more to learn about Mr John Smith.' He strode out of the room and the door closed behind him.

Sherlock turned back to me and took my hand. 'Nell, I am so sorry.'

'Don't be. It isn't your fault. I set out to learn the truth about Jack, and now I have.' I pulled my hand away and stood up. 'I need to wash my face.'

Mr Ransome was standing outside like a sentry. 'Could you direct me to a bathroom, please?' I asked.

'Of course, madam.' He looked relieved that it was nothing more. 'Follow me.' We passed through more little book-lined rooms into a short corridor. Neither of us spoke until he indicated a door marked *W.C.* 'I shall wait over there,' he said, and retreated.

The plumbing creaked and the water was cold, but it was better than nothing. I dried my face on the thin towel and automatically looked in the mirror to tidy my hair. A couple of strands were working loose, and I pinned them tight again. Then the rest of my hair was too loose, so I took it all down and redid it, jamming the pins in so that tears sprang to my eyes. They didn't fall, though; they were gone a moment later, burned away. My eyes stared out of the mirror as though I would fight myself. I was brimful of rage, ready to spill over at the slightest provocation.

I brooded as I followed Mr Ransome. I remembered the guilt which had consumed me for shrinking from widow's weeds, and at being glad to take them off. I had been blanketed under guilt and ignorance for the last three years. Even when it had begun to lift, when I had caught a glimpse of something that might be a new life, I had reproached myself for reaching towards it. I had agonised over my feelings for Sherlock, telling myself how inappropriate they were. And meanwhile Jack had been making a new life without me on the other side of the world.

We reached the anteroom and Mr Ransome stood aside for me. Sherlock and Mr Poskitt were talking over a volume of the newspaper, but broke off when I entered the room.

'Have you found something?' The question was unnecessary. The answer was in their faces.

Mr Poskitt drew the open book towards him as though shielding it. 'I have found the marriage,' he said.

'Show me.' I walked round the table and looked over his shoulder. There was but one entry in the Marriages section of the paper. *SMITH-WILDING. On June 7th, at Home Farm, the residence of the bride's parents, by the Rev. T.C. Stewart, John, son of the late E. Smith of London, to Mary Wilding, only daughter of Mr F. Wilding, Hobart Town, Tasmania.*

'A June wedding, and a baby a year later. He didn't lose much time, did he? And she's an only daughter too – how convenient.' I laughed. 'Jack has fallen on his feet.'

'Nell, the carriage will be—'

'I hope you've written it all down, Mr Poskitt. Do you happen to recall what the prison sentence is for bigamy?'

Mr Poskitt looked down and did not answer.

Sherlock's chair scraped back and my arm was in his grip in an instant. 'It is time to go, Nell.' I tried to shake him off but his grip tightened just enough to let me know I could not. 'Come, now. Goodbye, Poskitt,' he called over his shoulder.

'Goodbye, Mr Holmes,' came the measured reply.

'Can you take us to the back entrance, Ransome? The

carriage will be here shortly.'

Mr Ransome set out at a trot. 'He wants to get rid of us,' I said, laughing.

Sherlock said nothing.

'You don't have to hold my arm; I can walk by myself.' He let go, and I rubbed my arm pointedly.

Soon we were at the vestibule. The bolts slid back and I breathed in the fresh air with pleasure; but then Sherlock took my arm again and hurried me to the waiting carriage. I took my seat, and this time he sat beside me. I pulled down the blind on my side and he did the same, as I had hoped that he would. A tiny chink of light came through the bottom of the window, just enough to show his profile against the blind. We set off, slower this time, and I took off my glove and touched his hand. When he turned towards me, I kissed him. He kissed me back, but not as he had done before we went to the museum. I worked on a shirt button, then slid my hand onto warm skin.

He pulled away from me. 'Not here.'

'I don't mind.' I reached for him again.

Sherlock caught my hand and held it. 'Not like this, Nell.' He pulled the blind up and looked out, then thumped on the roof and shouted 'Stop at Red Lion Square, please.' The carriage took a sharp right turn and stopped.

Sherlock opened the door, jumped out, and held it for me, but I folded my arms and stayed put. 'Where are we going?'

'Into the gardens. It's quiet at this time of day.'

'The gardens?'

'Yes. I need to talk to you, and you're distracting me.'

I pulled up the blind on my side of the carriage and stared at the leafless trees in the square.

'Five minutes, Nell. Please. It's important.'

I thought about staying where I was. I didn't want to be

lectured. But I did want to be outside, with him.

Sherlock took my arm, more gently this time, and we sat on a bench in the cheerless, deserted gardens. I stared at the yellowed grass. 'Talk to me, then. Since you won't do anything else.'

'Not now, Nell. Not because you want to get back at your husband.'

'It isn't that,' I muttered.

'Really?'

I looked at him, and he was smiling. 'Not entirely.'

'You should thank me for protecting your honour.' He laid his hand over mine.

I looked up into his twinkling eyes. I turned his hand over and touched the tip of his middle finger with my own, then traced down the palm to where his pulse throbbed at the wrist. 'I shall try harder next time.'

He swallowed, hard. 'Minx,' he breathed, and when I looked up the twinkle was gone, and desire burned in its place. He shook his head. 'This is not the conversation I stopped the carriage for.'

'Are you disappointed, Sherlock?' I suspected I would not like the conversation we were about to have.

'Less than a year, Nell.'

'What?'

'That's the answer to your question for Poskitt.' He shrugged. 'If Jack were convicted of bigamy, that's how long he would spend in prison. It could be less than a month, even.'

My mouth dropped open. 'Really?'

'Yes.' He squeezed my hand. 'Before all the hullabaloo starts, I wanted to give you a chance to think things over. If you do have Jack arrested for bigamy, and he is tried and convicted, then a woman and a child in Tasmania have no husband and no father, and you are still married to him.'

217

I shuddered. 'I would divorce him.'

'If you were allowed. Certainly you could plead adultery, but you would need more than that; you would need to argue cruelty, or to prove the bigamy was intentional. It is expensive, too.'

'What should I do, then?'

He touched my cheek with his finger. 'Don't get so caught up in punishing Jack that you punish yourself as well.'

'I don't want him back.' My voice came out low and shaky, and didn't sound like mine. 'I want to know what made Jack leave, but I never want to see him again.' Before I could say another word Sherlock's arms were around me. He kissed the top of my head, and held me as I cried.

CHAPTER 42

Somerset House, 17th February 1881

'I expected you back before now.' Mycroft's voice rang out from the flight of stairs above us, where he was leaning on the banister. I was so startled that I missed my footing and clutched Sherlock's arm for support.

'We stopped for a little chat, Mycroft.'

Mycroft snorted. 'Indeed.' As we reached the landing he turned and went back into the corridor leading to his office. 'Shut the door behind you, won't you.'

When we reached Mycroft's office he was seated behind his desk as if he had never left it. 'Poskitt wired me.' His eyes rested on me for a moment, then he looked over to Sherlock. 'I assume we drag Mr Villiers back, threaten him with prison, get a confession and clear up this mess.'

'No.' The word was out before I knew it. Mycroft raised an eyebrow at me. 'This must remain unofficial. Jack cannot be publicly found.'

'You are sure it is he?' He was looking at Sherlock as he asked the question.

'Quite sure. The age and physical description are a good

match, the boat sailed on the day of his disappearance, and he has given his child the name of his best friend.'

Mycroft looked pained. 'I would like my office and my secretary back before the end of the year, you know.' He sighed. 'Very well. What next?'

'We need to work out who is behind it all.' Sherlock leaned his elbows on the desk. 'Inspector Lestrade, Napper Jenkins, or the pair of them working together.'

'Can't we just arrest them?' Mycroft slid a piece of paper away from him.

Sherlock spread his hands wide. 'On what grounds, Mycroft? No one has died. False imprisonment on Lestrade's part, perhaps, for shutting Nell away in Baker Street, but he could wriggle out of that, I am certain. If we bring them in without a shred of proof it will get us nowhere. And, Mycroft, you will look like a fool.'

'Thank you for your concern, Sherlock.' Mycroft spun his pen on the desk. 'Do tell me what ideas you have.'

'We must bring them together.' Both men turned to me. 'Their stories contradict each other. It is a chance to get at the truth.'

'You are right, Nell. Separately they have been able to twist and dodge, and keeping you isolated has enabled them to do it. But how do we bring them in, and where?'

'I could write to each of them and ask them to visit me at Baker Street during the evening. If I tell them I have received strange news from abroad, that should be enough.'

'Good.' Mycroft sat back and examined his fingernails. 'Here is the plan, Mrs Villiers. You will remain here tonight, returning to Baker Street mid-morning tomorrow. I have had someone watching the house while you have been away, and nothing seems amiss. However, I shall send a couple of people down early tomorrow to make sure. After you arrive, post your letters nearby. After that you may do as you wish, provided you do not leave the house. Sherlock, you will accompany Mrs Villiers tomorrow morning. I shall call round to Baker Street for half past six; I suggest you propose seven to your visitors.' He consulted his watch. 'I have tickets for the theatre tonight; I must go home and dress. I will send a note to Poskitt to get things started.' He strolled to the cupboard and retrieved his hat and coat. 'Any questions?'

I shook my head, feeling rather overwhelmed.

Mycroft put on his hat. 'I do not believe in letting the grass grow under my feet.' He shrugged on his overcoat. 'Sherlock, do you have anything to say?'

'I am just thinking it over,' Sherlock pushed his hair back from his forehead. 'I might make a call or two tomorrow.'

Mycroft inclined his head. 'As you wish. Do you have a gun?'

'Of course. I have it with me.'

'Mm. Make sure it is in good order.' He walked to the main door, buttoning his coat as he went. When he turned at the door his expression was unusually stern. 'There is a cold supper on the sideboard; I assume I can trust you both. Goodnight.'

I hadn't realised that I had been holding my breath, and let it out with a sigh.

'Are you all right, Nell?'

'Yes.' I yawned. 'Just a little tired. So much has happened today.'

Sherlock picked up the case notes from the sideboard and took them to the armchair. 'Come and sit with me a little while, Nell. There are just a couple of papers I want to look at again.' He poked the fire into life again, then patted the chair beside him.

I took off my shoes, curled up in the armchair, and

watched him riffle through the papers. 'What are you looking for?'

'The papers about the opium den. There was something I couldn't put my finger on, then we were looking at your report, and the shipping file came... Ah, here they are.'

I reached out a hand and Sherlock looked over the top of the file at me. 'One of the papers is your friend Napper's medical report. It is quite strong stuff.'

I moved my chair closer. 'I have probably read worse.'

He passed me the sheets of paper and I found myself shaking my head as I read. A fractured skull, suspected bleeding on the brain, a broken collarbone, the right leg broken in two places, severe bruising all over the body. The head wound had required thirty stitches. 'It's just so – so much.' I remembered watching for Napper at St John's Arch, and the slight halt in his gait.

'It was a brutal attack. And yet no one saw a thing.'

'Surely there were people working at the den?'

'Not by the time he was found; the only people left in the building apart from Napper were opium fiends, and their testimony is so vague that it is worthless.' Sherlock held up another page. 'The only thing we have is a transcript of an interview with the owner of the building, and that is practically useless. He let the building six months before to a man named Matthew Edwards who paid cash in advance. The description he gives of Mr Edwards is laughable: black beard, thick black eyebrows, heavily muffled, hat pulled low, wearing large tinted spectacles. I imagine all those things disappeared the moment he found a place to take them off.' He snorted. 'He is playing a game with us.'

'Is there anything else about the man? His height, his build?'

'Medium height, medium build, medium complexion,

medium everything.' Sherlock stared into the fire. 'Paid cash in advance...' He scrabbled through the papers again, and pulled one out, wrinkling his brow. 'Nell, do you know anyone called Thomas Jones?'

'No, I don't.' I craned to see the paper. 'That's the person who paid Jack's passage, isn't it?'

'Yes, and if you have never heard of him it is bound to be a false name. People don't pay ten pounds out of charity.' He read through the list again. 'The others are all assisted passengers. They would have had to fill out a form, supply testimonials, and hold passports. As a paid-for passenger, all Jack Villiers had to do was walk on the ship.' He looked at me. 'I am sorry, Nell; I am going too deeply into this.'

'Sherlock, it is what you do; none of this is your fault.' I leaned my head against the chair back. 'Do you think that Thomas Jones and Matthew Edwards are the same person?'

'Quite possibly. I shall go to the shipping office tomorrow.'

'You'll tell me, won't you?'

'Of course I will.'

I uncurled myself from the chair and sat on the arm of Sherlock's. I read Napper's short statement: *Sergeant Villiers and I approached the den at half past eight in the morning. An attendant opened the door to us at once. We entered the building together, showed our badges and asked to speak to the owner. I followed Sergeant Villiers upstairs and as I did, I felt a huge blow to my head. I remember nothing more until I woke up in hospital.* I imagined the attendants slipping the hood over his head, dragging him up the stairs and beating him – but what had Jack been doing? He was big and strong. 'I don't understand,' I said. 'Jack would never let Napper get hurt. He was his oldest friend.'

Sherlock looked up at me, and as I looked back his face changed. His eyes were on me, but his mind was somewhere else.

I touched his arm. 'What is it?'

His eyes refocused on me. 'It is a hunch at the moment: an inkling, an intuition. I will sleep on it. Tomorrow I shall know either way.' He closed the file, stood up, and bent to kiss me. 'Let's have supper, and then I suppose I had better retire to the attic for the night if I am to behave myself.'

I sighed. It was the sensible thing to do, the right and honourable thing, and I loved him for it – but how I wished we could have shut the whole world out for that one night.

CHAPTER 43

221B Baker Street, 18th February 1881

Dear Inspector Lestrade,

Would you be able to call tonight, about seven? I received strange news yesterday from overseas and I would welcome your advice. I have been unable to sleep for thinking about it.

Yours sincerely,

H. Hudson (Mrs)

Dear Napper,

Forgive me writing to you at work, but I received strange news yesterday, from abroad. Would you be able to visit me tonight? I will send my servant out on an errand and we shall have the house to ourselves between seven and eight. I will wait by the back door for you. Please come, I am half-sick with worry.

Nell

PS I shall be able to appear as myself this time.

Sherlock read the letters while I addressed the envelopes. 'Very nice,' he said, putting a hand on my shoulder. 'I particularly like the damsel in distress touch.'

'Thank you.' I blew on the envelopes to dry the ink faster.

'Are you all packed?'

'Of course.' I had woken early, and after repeated tossing and turning I had decided that getting up was the only option. I had been packed and ready to go since half past six. I put the letters into my bag and looked round Mycroft's office to check that I had missed nothing. I had stacked the case notes on the desk, put the breakfast tray on the sideboard, and stripped the camp bed.

'Time to go.' Sherlock opened the door and Mr Poskitt came forward to shake hands.

'Thank you, Mr Poskitt, for all your help,' I said.

'Oh, it is not over yet, madam,' he said, smiling. 'I shall be in attendance tonight.'

'That is kind of you.'

'A break in routine is healthy from time to time,' he said. 'Besides, I want to find out what happens.' We walked back into Mycroft's office, and he held the closet door open for us. 'Until tonight.'

'Until tonight,' we echoed, and stepped through. Even now I still started at each creak of the stair, but we reached the back door unchallenged.

An ordinary hansom cab waited at the kerb. 'No private carriage, then,' I said. 'We have gone down in the world.'

'Not at all.' Sherlock whistled to the driver, who turned and grinned at us, and I recognised the footman from Mycroft's house.

We kept the blinds up and watched London rattle by, going about its daily business. People laughed and joked and shouted their wares, and it was all jolly, all open, with no sign of the depths beneath. It made my heart lift, despite my anxieties about what might come later. Sherlock was looking out of the window too. He had been quiet all morning, and I assumed that he was working through things in his head, ready for tonight.

'It will be odd,' he said, thoughtfully. 'Rooming with Watson again, when I am so used to spending the day with you.'

I squeezed his hand. 'I am sure Dr Watson will be glad to have you back. I imagine he and Billy have been lonely.'

'Possibly. Well, we shall see.' He turned back to the window and I looked out of mine, smiling at that *We shall see.*

We came to streets I knew well and Sherlock knocked on the roof. 'Round the back, Dawkins.'

'Sir.' We turned left into a back street, and right, and there was the alley which led to our back door. So familiar, and yet so strange.

'Thank you, Dawkins.' Sherlock jumped down and helped me out, and the cab clattered away. 'Let us go and meet the welcome party.'

We heard whispers in response to our knock, and the door creaked open with Billy's eye in the gap. Suspicion changed to delight and he opened the door wide, revealing a pair of plain-clothes men in the background.

'I thought I had better knock, rather than risk an ambush,' said Sherlock. 'Gentlemen.' He nodded to the plain-clothes men. 'Dr Watson is at work, I take it.'

'Yessir.' Billy pulled out chairs for us at the table. 'He knows you're back today, though; he was here when the gentlemen came. He said he'll be pleased to see you both.'

'Thank you, Billy. I'm sorry I tied you up.'

'That's all right, sir.' Billy grinned. 'I'd rather it didn't become a habit, though.'

I opened my bag. 'I had better post these letters.'

Billy got up. 'I'll take them, ma'am.'

'It's all right, Billy; I would rather do it myself. You can come too, if you like.'

Billy shook his head. 'That'd look odd. I'll watch you down the road, though.' He opened the front door for me, sliding back the big bolts and turning the key. I had looked at that door in utter despair so many times during that first year, and perhaps soon I would be able to come and go as I pleased.

The postbox was just down the road. I strolled along, enjoying the crispness of the air. The policeman on his beat smiled at me as we approached each other, and I smiled back. We were still in winter; my breath was mist in the air. I blew out a plume and laughed, and a delivery man hastening by looked at me in surprise. I looked at the envelopes once more, held them in the mouth of the post-box for a moment, then let go. They would be on the recipients' desks by mid-afternoon at the latest. I imagined the men ripping them open, staring at what I had written.

It was done.

The front door opened as I climbed the steps. 'I must start dinner, Billy. We shall dine early, and there are extra mouths to feed.' I moved towards the kitchen, but Billy touched my arm.

'I'll cook the beef joint we had in for Sunday, ma'am.'

'Do you need any help?'

'No, ma'am.' He went downstairs, then a moment later reappeared with my bag. 'I'll take this up.'

I held my hand out for it. 'I can manage, Billy.'

'Is there anything else, ma'am?'

I thought of the clean linen waiting in the chest of drawers in my bedroom. 'Yes, Billy.' I said. 'I should like to take a bath.'

'I'll see to it, ma'am.'

When I was halfway up the stairs a door opened and a tall

man appeared, dressed in a business suit and carrying a briefcase. His brown hair was brushed back and he had a neat Vandyke beard. I could imagine him greeting Mr Poskitt in the corridors of Somerset House.

He waited for me at the top of the stairs and I straightened his tie a fraction. 'Where are you going?' I whispered. 'Is it the shipping office?'

'Yes. It is a long shot, but worth a try. I should be back by mid-afternoon; it is a fair trip to the docks.'

'Be careful,' I muttered.

'I shall.' I watched him down the stairs. He did not use the front door, but continued down the kitchen steps. *He is using the back way. He thinks the house is watched.*

My rooms were as I remembered them; all was in its place, books neat in the bookcase, a fire laid ready in the grate. If I had left anything awry in my hasty flight a few days ago, it had been tidied away. I locked the bedroom door and pulled the curtains closed, then undressed and put on my dressing gown.

Billy had left the water cans by the bath, and a fresh bar of soap, a sponge and a large towel stood ready. I poured half the hot water in then added some cold, trying to get the water to the just-bearable stage. By the time I did so there was about six inches of water in the tub. I scrubbed myself, washed my hair, and held my breath as I poured the remaining water over my head. The bath was already cooling. I scrambled out and wrapped myself in the towel, my toes curling in the thick-piled mat. I wondered how much it would cost to fit a bath with taps, and a hot-water system.

Downstairs, I lit the fire in the bedroom and combed out my hair. My wet fringe touched my eyelashes. I caught sight of myself in the mirror, sitting in my dressing gown with my hair spread over my shoulders, and then I did something I had not done since my arrival at Baker Street. I took off the dressing gown and faced myself.

It was not too bad. My bosom did not sag; my stomach did not stick out. But my waist had thickened a little, and when I ran my hands down the backs of my thighs, the skin dimpled. I put my dressing gown back on and walked up to the mirror. I pulled out a few grey hairs and watched how, when I frowned, the wrinkle between my brows remained for a while after I stopped. One day it would not go away at all.

I remembered the moment in the carriage, and Sherlock's lean body beneath his shirt. Twenty-six: two years younger than me. I reached for my chemise. If all went to plan, the mystery would be solved later and everything would be brought to light. It would be over. Would that be the end of Sherlock's interest in me, too?

CHAPTER 44

221B Baker Street, 18th February 1881

I had been pretending to read for perhaps half an hour when the kitchen door slammed. Leaning over the banister, I was rewarded by a head of well-brushed brown hair. 'How did it go?'

Sherlock grinned through his beard. 'Five minutes, and I shall tell you.'

It seemed an age until he opened the door as himself and beckoned me in. He flung himself into the armchair, laughing. 'It is amazing how money can make people talk. And at half a sovereign the information was underpriced.'

'What did you find out?'

'The clerk was more than happy to talk generally. I imagine working in a shipping office is rather dull, and he has been there for five years. He clammed up the moment I said I was looking for someone, but when I spun that coin in the air he became very chatty.' Sherlock leaned towards me, and lowered his voice. 'Jack Villiers nearly didn't sail on that ship.'

I gasped. 'Why?'

'The application was made two days before the ship sailed. The clerk remembered it for several reasons. Most people's passages are paid from Australia and arranged in a block weeks before the departure date. And the address of the applicant, Thomas Jones, was not a street address, but care of a London post office. Mr Jones had sent a cheque with the application, but as there was no guarantee that the money would clear in time, the clerk wrote to advise that the fee must be paid in cash. The next day, around lunch time, a man rushed in, heavily bearded and muffled up – in September – and wearing dark-tinted spectacles. He asked if the clerk was the man dealing with the papers for John Smith to sail to Tasmania. When the clerk confirmed it, he slammed down a handful of sovereigns on the desk. The clerk offered him a receipt, but he shook his head and left without another word.'

'The same man,' I said. 'Or the same disguise.'

'Indeed. Would you care to know which post office Thomas Jones used?'

'I would,' I murmured.

'Charing Cross.'

'Charing Cross,' I repeated. 'In the centre of London, just round the corner from Scotland Yard.'

'I knew you would see it.' Sherlock said quietly. 'What intrigues me is that it was all such a scramble. I don't imagine the person behind this planned to use the same disguise for two different identities; he wanted to carry the business out entirely by post. I asked the clerk if he could remember anything else about the man, and he said no. He was unremarkable except for the fact of being so obviously disguised, which suggests that he was not particularly tall or short or stout. Medium everything, again.'

'Why didn't he report it?'

'I suspect Mr Jones left an extra sovereign or two behind to ensure that he did not.' Sherlock rattled the change in his own pocket. 'But it shows that this was a last-minute arrangement. Jack Villiers had to be got out of the way, post-haste.'

'But who is behind it all?' I sighed and sat back. 'We are going round in circles.'

'We are getting closer. Much closer. And tonight will end it.' He smacked his hand down on the arm of the chair so hard that I jumped. 'Which room shall we use to receive our visitors?'

'I hadn't thought.' I looked around his sitting room. 'This seems too informal. We could open the parlour downstairs.'

'What is it like?'

'I don't know. It's locked and everything's under dust sheets. Billy will have the key.'

'Let's go and see it.' He sprang up and we went downstairs together.

'You haven't had lunch yet, sir.' Billy looked reproachful. 'I could—'

'There's something else to be done first, Billy. Could you open up the parlour? We could use it tonight.'

Billy unhooked a large key from the rack and we followed him into the hall. 'It'll need to air through,' he said. 'The room was in sheets when I came.' He unlocked the door and pushed it wide open.

It was like the ghost of a room. All was muffled in white; even the chandelier was draped in muslin. Billy pulled the dust sheets from what turned out to be an upright piano. Then he uncovered a sofa.

Sherlock flung the curtains open. 'What a waste of a good room,' he said, opening a window.

I stepped onto the richly patterned Turkey carpet and tugged at the nearest dust sheet. It slid easily away, revealing an occasional table. A white ghost on the wall became a

233

landscape painting. Sherlock uncovered a straight-backed chair, climbed onto it, and unwound the muslin from the chandelier. Within ten minutes the room was a parlour again: over-furnished, old-fashioned, chilly, and no different from any parlour I had ever sat in, save for the lack of photographs and trinkets. The parlour in Clerkenwell had had photographs: my parents, Jack's parents, me and my siblings in a group portrait, and Jack and me on our wedding day, smiling out at the world. Whose house was this, and where were they now? Then I shook myself. It had probably been let furnished, that was all. I was letting my imagination run away with me.

Once the furniture was uncovered, Sherlock moved it around until the seating formed a square, two seats on each side. 'That should be enough.'

'Where do you want us?' The taller of the two gentlemen looked at Sherlock.

'By the window, please.'

They walked to the chairs and sat down.

'Wonderful,' said Sherlock. 'That will do for now. Billy, can you lay a fire in here, please?' Billy nodded and hurried away. 'Mrs Villiers, could I speak to you upstairs? It is about tonight.'

'Of course.' I followed him into the gentlemen's sitting room, but once we had sat down he fidgeted with a loose thread on his shirt. I moved to the settee and patted the place beside me. 'What is it, Sherlock?'

He looked up, but did not join me. 'The easy bit first. The lilac dress you have, the one with the pearl buttons – can you change into that this evening?'

'I can.' I looked down at the navy dress I was wearing. 'Why?'

'It suits you admirably, and it is your least widow-like dress. How did you wear your hair before – before all this happened?'

'Like this, more or less.' I touched the bun on top of my head. 'Except for the fringe.'

'Could you pin the fringe back?'

I had not trimmed it yet, and I swept it up with one hand. 'Yes, but why?'

He laughed. 'I have not gone mad, I promise you. I would like you to be friendly with our guests when we receive them, and Napper Jenkins in particular. Not over-friendly, not *Annie*-friendly' – I shuddered at that – 'but a little more girlish, a little more flustered than usual.'

I could feel the heat creeping up my face. 'Why?'

'I plan to disconcert them a little. Having you there looking, even seeming as you did before the disappearance – I think it will give us an advantage. You can be as cool as you like on the inside.'

'All right. I will try.' I twisted my hands in my lap. 'You said that was the easy bit. What is the hard bit?'

He sighed. 'I won't be the same in that room as I am to you. I might say things about your husband that I don't believe. I might even say things about you that I don't believe. You must understand that I am saying them to get at the truth.'

I swallowed. 'What might you say?'

'I don't know; it depends on them.' He looked up at me, and his expression was grave. 'But you must react as though we haven't had this conversation.' He sighed. 'Normally the client is in the dark, but I can't do that to you. Perhaps I shouldn't have done it to the other people I've worked for.' He stood up, and opened the door. 'Till dinner.'

I shook out the lilac dress and laid it on the bed. I had worn it on the day I had cut my fringe, the day when he first noticed me. I took up a comb and some hairpins from the dressing table, and as I did so music floated up: a slow, melancholy air. Sherlock's violin. I pinned my fringe back and held the dress against myself, and all the while the slow, sad music went on. In the mirror I did not look so different from the woman I had been three years before, but I could barely remember what it was like to be her.

CHAPTER 45

221B Baker Street, 18th February 1881

When the kitchen clock chimed seven, everyone but me was upstairs, waiting. Mr Poskitt had arrived punctually at half past six, shaken hands all round, and made a few discreet enquiries. He was now sitting primly on the edge of the parlour sofa, facing the two plain-clothes gentlemen. Mycroft had swept in five minutes later, cross-examined Sherlock about the arrangements, and draped himself across the other half of the sofa as though he were relaxing at his club.

Two policemen were outside: one at the front of the house, one at the back. Billy was in the hallway with Dr Watson. And I knew exactly where Sherlock was: pacing in the hallway, wound up as tight as a spring.

The doorbell rang. The snick of bolts drawing back, then the creak of the door. Inspector Lestrade's low, gruff voice, and Billy's 'This way, sir.'

Then a cry, running feet, a sharp 'Hey!' The inspector's voice again: higher, angry. Sherlock's above it, cutting him off. Then silence.

The clock ticked. Five minutes past seven. Where was

Napper? I recalled what I had written in the note: between seven and eight. My heartbeat sounded louder than the clock. I tried to breathe deeply, to slow myself down.

A rap on the glass made me cry out. I sprang to the door and opened it a crack. 'Is it safe?' whispered Napper.

'It is,' I said. When I locked the door behind him, he tested the handle. Only then did he turn to me.

'Nell.' He took my hand and his eyes drank me in. 'You look just as I remember.'

'Thank you.' My voice wobbled, and it was not an act. Now that the moment had come, I was thoroughly flustered. 'Shall we go upstairs?'

'Why not? Then you can tell me your news.' His tone was low, intimate. I hoped he could not hear my heart thumping, for it filled my ears. I turned to go upstairs feeling as if I had turned my back on a tiger. *Bold as brass,* he had said. I felt as bold as a mouse. I walked quickly, but he was right behind me. At the top I turned the corner and kept walking, and—

'Good evening, Sergeant Jenkins.' Napper was struggling between Sherlock and Dr Watson, his face contorted.

One of the plain-clothes gentlemen appeared and removed Napper's hat. 'Take his coat off.' Sherlock pulled at it, but Napper shrugged it off and it fell to the floor. Underneath was a holster, which the plain-clothes man unbuckled and laid on the hall table. He took out a revolver and emptied the chambers, putting the cartridges in his pocket. Then he ran his hands up and down Napper's body. 'All right.'

'You can have it back later,' said Sherlock. 'This way.'

The policeman held the parlour door open for them, and there was a gasp from inside as Inspector Lestrade spied Napper. 'What are you doing here?' His voice was pure fury. *You will not contact your friends, family or associates.* I did not want to face him. But Sherlock closed the parlour door and walked towards me.

'Well done, Nell,' he whispered. 'Come in with me, and finish it. I have what I needed.' The corners of his mouth, his dear mouth, turned up just a little.

'I am ready,' I whispered. He took my arm, and we went in together.

'What is this, Nell?' Napper glared at me from his seat beside the inspector. 'You lied to me!'

My face flushed hot, and I began to stammer I knew not what.

'Don't blame her,' Sherlock remarked. 'She acted on my instructions.'

'And who might you be?' Napper pushed his hair back from his forehead, and for the first time I saw the faint, faded scar running from his temple into his hairline.

'My name is Sherlock Holmes, and I am a consulting detective.' Sherlock's voice was level, calm.

'Really. And who are the rest of these people?' Napper's eyes travelled around the circle of faces, sizing them up. He did not look at me, though.

'Inspector Lestrade you know. The others have helped me to organise this.'

Inspector Lestrade leaned forward. 'Suppose you tell us why we have been lured here under false pretences, Mr Holmes. I am in no mood for games.'

'They are not false pretences, Inspector. Mrs Villiers has had strange news from overseas.' He glanced at me.

'I have.' My throat was dry and scratchy. 'Jack is alive, and in one of the Australian colonies.'

'What?' The inspector half-jumped out of his seat, then sat back hurriedly as one of the plain-clothes men reached towards his pocket. 'How do you know? How did you find him?'

'Yes, how did you find him?' Napper echoed. 'Are you sure it is him?'

'We are certain,' said Sherlock.

Napper's eyes narrowed. 'I've seen you before.' He looked Sherlock up and down. 'That night, at the Rising Sun – you were at the bar, weren't you? Done up as a rough.'

'That's right.' Sherlock smiled. 'I could hardly let Nell go there alone.'

'No.' Napper's mouth curled up. 'Certainly not dressed as she was.' He shot a glance at me and I looked away. 'When she pranced over, I thought she was a—'

'She was dressed no differently from several other women there.' Sherlock said. 'And besides, I was watching out for her.'

'Oh, I'm sure you were.' Napper's voice was like a fist under velvet. 'Is it a game you often play, when you play detective?'

'I don't 'play' detective.' I could hear the slight shake in Sherlock's voice. I hoped that no one else could.

'Then what are you playing at?' Inspector Lestrade cried. 'Mrs Villiers is supposed to be living quietly under police protection. If I had thought you would encourage her to run round dressed as God knows what, meeting people she has been forbidden to contact, I would never have put these lodgings in your way!'

'I don't suppose you would,' said Sherlock. 'Particularly as together we have done your job for you, Inspector, and found a man you have failed to find despite over two years of looking. And yet there is more to it than that. Isn't there, Inspector? Because Jack Villiers sailed for Australia the very day that he "disappeared"; the very day that Sergeant Jenkins was so badly beaten. We were meant to believe he had drowned, weren't we?'

240

'I don't know what you mean,' the inspector said. 'I searched hospitals, we dragged the river—'

'Of course you did. You did what any by-the-book police officer would do.' Sherlock leaned forward, his hands on his knees. 'And all the time you were doing it, you congratulated yourself that you had got rid of your protege, a man who had, with his wife, got uncomfortably close to the truth.'

'What truth? What are you talking about?' Inspector Lestrade shouted. 'This is utter rubbish. You are completely mistaken, Mr Holmes. One more word, and—'

'You will be quiet, Inspector.' The words came from the doorway, from behind the gun that Dr Watson was pointing at the inspector. 'And you will listen.'

'You have all gone mad!' Inspector Lestrade folded his arms and sat back. 'I listen to this rubbish under duress. You have not a shred of proof.'

'So why did you kidnap Mrs Villiers and shut her away from her friends and family when she needed them most?'

'If whoever did this to Jack and – and Sergeant Jenkins knew that she was working for the police too—' Inspector Lestrade's voice was high and indignant. 'I was acting for the best. Mrs Villiers was terribly ill.' He turned to me. 'I had to protect you; I couldn't let you come back to police work. You have to believe me.' He swallowed and looked at the floor.

Sherlock turned to Napper. 'You're enjoying this, aren't you?'

Napper shook his head, but the gleam in his eye betrayed him.

'Oh, but it must be rather satisfying. The man who has kept you slaving at the desk all these years, taking the credit for it all, taking everyone's credit – oh, I've read the praise in the newspapers, I've found the recopied reports in the files – finally he'll get what's coming to him.'

Napper stared straight ahead.

'After all, he got you beaten up, didn't he? You were the real victim, not Jack. Jack got away...'

Napper shifted in his chair. 'If you're going to arrest him, I suggest you get on with it.'

'Yes, Jack's done well for himself. He's got a big farm now. He'll be a wealthy man.' Sherlock leaned forward, elbows to knees, man to man, confidential. 'It hurts, doesn't it?'

'What?' Napper sat back. 'I don't follow.'

'It hurts when your best friend takes all the things you want. He would never have thought of being a policeman if it wasn't for your ambition. There you are, side by side in the force, but he's the favoured one. The girl in the library you've got your eye on – he's the one who saves the day and gets the girl before you have the chance to make your move. You try to get over it, to rise above him, because you know he can't make sergeant without your help. But now he can, because his girl in the library will coach him. Even your little slip to Lestrade here, that Sergeant Villiers's wife was writing his reports for him – even that didn't work, because Lestrade hired Mrs Villiers, and together, the husband and wife were a better policeman than you.'

'This is all speculation.' Napper crossed his legs and brushed a speck off his knee. 'I've only ever taken a friendly interest in Nell. There's nothing for me to be jealous of.'

'You were a good friend to Jack, weren't you? All those nights you brought him home when he'd been out drinking...'

'I didn't want him to be led astray.'

'No, of course not. You were his best friend, and if anyone were to lead him astray, it would be you. He was Lestrade's favourite, and he got the pick of the assignments while you got the boring stuff. But there's more to you than meets the eye. Isn't there, Napper?'

Napper rolled his eyes at the ceiling. 'Get to the point, will you, then we can all go home.'

'You won't be going home.' Sherlock's eyes were like gimlets. 'When you worked out that you would never be the hero, you decided to become one of the villains. Nothing major, not at first. Turning a blind eye, perhaps. But you got a taste for it, didn't you? You found some associates who welcomed having a bent copper on their side. Gradually you built yourself a nook in the underworld and you planned to move into a little extortion, because there's good money in that.'

Napper huffed in disgust, and shook his head.

'But oh dear, sharp-eyed Nell Villiers spotted the signature your gang left to frighten and intimidate people into paying for protection – smashing kitchen windows, then smashing kneecaps. You only found out how close she was to catching you when you took Jack out drinking and pumped him for information – and then you had to stop them before they tracked you down. So you got your crony Richard Sampson to take the blame – in exchange for what, hm? – fed Lestrade here another of your hints, and hey presto, you were off scot-free. But for how long? You were running scared, but a clever plan came to you: one where you could be the hero at last. You booked a passage to the other side of the world, using a false name. Then you arranged to meet Jack early one morning, just the two of you in plain clothes, near an opium den in Limehouse which you were investigating.' Inspector Lestrade made a sudden movement. 'A useful little place you rented, where you could dodge in and out and the owner didn't care what you got up to – not that he knew it was you, of course. That would be the scene of the crime.'

'What crime is that, then?' asked Napper, 'I was the victim, remember.'

243

'I'm coming to that,' said Sherlock, leaning in closer. 'You told Jack you had bad news for him. I do not know what: possibly gambling debts or an illegitimate child – ah, that twitch tells me it was the latter. So you confront Jack, I expect with a heavily pregnant accomplice you have paid to swear the child is his.'

I swallowed the bile in my throat and choked back a sob. Sherlock's eyes flicked towards me; but he continued to speak.

'Thanks to you, Napper, Jack has been blind drunk too many times to remember what he may or may not have done; he can't deny it. He is utterly ashamed of himself, but this mess cannot be covered up; the woman says she will find Nell and tell her, and she won't be paid off. She exits stage left leaving Jack distraught, and good old Napper steps in with a hastily devised plan. Jack can make a fresh start in another country, and you will look after the rest. You will hatch a plan to make it appear that Jack has been killed in the line of duty, and then Nell can start again too. You may even have promised to look after her – indeed, I am sure that you did. You go to the docks, it is all arranged, and he boards the boat while he is still too dazed to think it over. Then you return to the opium den and ask one of your staff to knock you out, as your alibi.'

'Hah!' Napper pointed to the scar on his temple. 'So your theory is that I asked for this?'

Sherlock nodded. 'It is. Unfortunately your associate takes you at your word – perhaps he took a tip from Sampson? He gives you the thrashing you deserve, and you wake up in hospital several weeks later to find that the trial of the Mile End Gang has collapsed, your associates have flown, Jack is declared not dead but missing, and Nell is in hiding where you cannot get at her. Lestrade is keeping you at arm's length – perhaps through guilt over what has happened to you, perhaps because he is worried you will be attacked again. So back to desk work you go, under Lestrade's protection: back to the safe, dull desk work that you hate, with no opportunity of rebuilding your criminal career.

Then two years later, a miracle. Nell comes to you out of the blue. You are Jack's oldest friend, a policeman, a fellow-victim: someone she can trust. She tells you what she has gone through under Lestrade's protection, and you take the opportunity to twist her account until she is scared half to death that she is mad, and your evil genius is that it is all hearsay in Lestrade's name. At a stroke you have made her ashamed of herself, terrified that she will be caught, suspicious of Lestrade, and dependent on you not to give her away – and you have learnt her address. A good evening's work, all in all. You write and arrange to meet, and you feed Mrs Villiers more lies about Lestrade and her husband. Sadly your plan to frighten Nell into your arms at the Rising Sun backfires, since you were separated in the crowd and I managed to spirit her away. But she will come again, of course she will, because who can she trust more than poor faithful Napper? Then you can feed her more tit-bits until she will eat out of your hand, and you will dry her tears, won't you? Except that it is not to be.'

Napper's gaze did not falter. 'This theorising is all very well, but you have nothing to back it up. Say that Jack is alive and you bring him back from Tasmania – it's my word against his, isn't it? It's my word against Lestrade's too. All you have are words.'

'The owner of the opium den remembers you from when you paid the rent as Matthew Edwards. And the shipping clerk remembers you, from when you paid Jack Villiers's passage as Thomas Jones.' Sherlock's voice was low and firm. 'You looked the same both times.'

'Really,' Napper snorted. 'What did I look like?'

'A man in disguise, as you were meant to. A hat pulled low, a beard, a muffler, and a pair of dark glasses. And that was what convinced me the moment I saw you in the light today. Before then I had not been able to get past the beating you received. I could not stop seeing you as a victim, although so much of the evidence pointed to you. You and Lestrade could both have been the disguised man, as you are of medium height and build, but the dark glasses were a step too far; they would stick in the memory as an unnecessary detail. Unless, of course, your eyes are an unusual enough colour for the dark glasses to be necessary.'

'Unbelievable,' murmured Inspector Lestrade.

'It is all talk, and you know it.' Napper scratched the ankle that was crossed over. 'The man you describe could have been Lestrade, or anyone. It could have been two men in the same disguise. Your case is full of holes.'

Sherlock sighed, drew a pistol, and pointed it at Napper. 'You confirmed your guilt when you mentioned Tasmania. None of us have referred to it once tonight.'

Napper licked his lips. 'What of it? I didn't force him to go. He got on the boat of his own free will. A practical joke that went wrong.'

'I daresay we could find some old associates from your former career to identify you.' Sherlock's hand was steady. 'But that is not the worst of it. Richard Sampson was shot dead in 1879, the year after the Mile End trial collapsed. They found his body in a disused warehouse. I remember the newspaper report. He was killed with one shot from a pocket revolver, at close range.' Sherlock flicked the safety-catch off his gun. 'And I would lay money that the bullet on file is an exact match for the gun you are about to draw from your boot.'

I screamed as Napper's hand flew down and there was a flash of silver; but the plain-clothes men both had their guns pointed and cocked, and Mycroft and Mr Poskitt were not far behind. Napper's gaze fastened on me. He was holding the little knuckle-duster revolver on his lap, pointing to the floor. 'I did it for you, Nell. I didn't mean it to turn out—'

'You did it for yourself, Napper.' I spat. 'You disgust me. And you could never have replaced Jack, no matter what you did.'

Inspector Lestrade opened his mouth to speak, but before he could say a word Napper raised the gun, placed the muzzle against the scar on his temple, and pulled the trigger.

CHAPTER 46

221B Baker Street, 18th February 1881

For some time afterwards I saw the scene whenever I closed my eyes: Napper's body slumping sideways; Dr Watson hurrying towards it; Sherlock trying to shield me from it.

Sherlock helped me up, keeping me turned away, and when my legs buckled under me he picked me up as easily as if I were made of feathers, carried me up to my sitting room and laid me on the settee.

'If he hadn't killed himself, it would have gone to trial.' He was talking to himself, not to me. 'Even if one of the men had shot him, if it had been self-defence, there could have been an enquiry, and then it would all be out in the open.'

I could hear movements downstairs. The front door opened and a pair of heavy feet entered: probably the policeman who had been watching. Voices buzzed, Billy ran through the hall, and the front door opened and shut again. I reached for Sherlock's hand, and squeezed it. 'You did the right thing.' I did not know if he had or not, but it was done now. Napper was dead, and it was finished. It was over.

Feet came upstairs, their owners talking low. They paused

at the sitting room below, then continued up. I called 'Come in' to the timid tap on the door.

Inspector Lestrade and Dr Watson filed in. If the inspector had been wearing a hat, he would have taken it off.

'Is it all in hand?' Sherlock asked.

'Billy's telegraphing Scotland Yard.' Inspector Lestrade wiped his forehead with a handkerchief. 'There's a team – not that I've used it before – who specialise in this sort of thing.'

'Suicide, or misadventure,' said Dr Watson. 'I heard a shot, I found him in the alley. If that would be useful.'

'That would help a great deal.' The inspector put his handkerchief back in his pocket. 'You gave me quite a scare, Mr Holmes. For a moment I was almost worried.' The relief in his eyes was plain. I remembered how he had pleaded with me not half an hour before: *You have to believe me.*

'You gave Mrs Villiers quite a scare, Inspector.' Sherlock looked Inspector Lestrade straight in the eye, and his gaze fell. 'I appreciate that you acted for what you thought was the best, but you could have handled it better.'

The inspector sighed. 'Perhaps I could. I'm sorry, Mrs Villiers, if I was heavy-handed.'

'You were.' He looked at me, surprised. 'I understand why, though.' I hesitated before asking the next question. I was not sure I wanted to know the answer. 'What did you tell my family, and Jack's?'

The inspector bit his bottom lip. 'I am afraid I spun them a yarn that Jack had been chosen for an important undercover mission, and that you had accompanied him.'

'I suppose you were half right.' I couldn't imagine how the conversation would go when we did meet again.

A faint tap at the door and Mycroft ambled in, followed by Mr Poskitt. 'Just seeing how you are, dear boy. That was quite a show you put on.' He extended a hand to Sherlock.

'Glad you enjoyed it, Mycroft.' They shook hands firmly. 'Sorry I had to pull you in.'

'Ah, what are brothers for…' Mycroft shook his head. 'Anyway, if we are no longer needed, Poskitt and I shall be getting off. As you know, I am extremely busy.' He looked down his nose at me. 'I daresay we shall meet again before too long, Mrs Villiers.'

'I hope so, Mr Holmes.'

Mr Poskitt shook hands with us all. 'Wonderful to meet you. If you are ever in the vicinity of Somerset House, do call.' He twinkled at me. 'You could even use the front door.' The inspector stared at me, but refrained from speaking.

When the two men had gone, Dr Watson turned to me. 'Are you quite well, Mrs Villiers? No shock, or—'

I shook my head. 'A little shaken, perhaps. Nothing more.' I looked over at Sherlock, who was staring into the fire. 'Perhaps you should ask Mr Holmes. He has borne the brunt of it.'

Dr Watson touched Sherlock on the shoulder then took his pulse, watching his face as he did so. 'I'll pass you as fit,' he said. 'Just about.' They continued to confer in low voices.

'So how did you find Jack?' Inspector Lestrade asked.

'In the end it came down to shipping lists and newspapers. And Mr Holmes's skills,' I replied.

'I never even considered that he might have gone abroad.' The inspector rubbed his chin. 'I was led astray completely.'

'Jack has married again.' I looked up at him. 'He has a son. That is how we found him, through the announcement.'

Inspector Lestrade's eyes widened, then he looked away. 'I am sorry,' he murmured.

'Thank you,' I said, for lack of anything better. I did not feel sorry now that Jack had gone. Being Jack, he had fallen on his feet in Tasmania, just as he always had in London until

Napper had set his plan in motion.

'What should I call you now?' the inspector asked. 'Do you still answer to Mrs Villiers?'

'I hadn't thought.' I had, of course. 'Mrs Villiers' had jarred on my ear ever since I had learned of Jack's betrayal. 'Where did the name Hudson come from, Inspector?'

The inspector flushed. 'It is the name of my bootmaker. When you collapsed I took you to hospital and they asked me for your name. I panicked, looked around for inspiration, and, well, that was it.'

'So I have been named for your bootmaker?' I laughed. 'Perhaps I should keep it in his honour.'

Inspector Lestrade grinned. 'I can arrange official documentation, if you like.'

'Helen Hudson. It has a certain ring to it.'

'I have something else to confess.' The inspector fiddled with his watch chain before continuing. 'I had to let your house go. I couldn't find the money to keep it, because of this place.'

I remembered the little house in Clerkenwell which I had loved so much. But it was firmly in the past. Jack would be in every room, everything I touched. 'What happened to – the personal things?'

'They are all safe in storage. You can have them back whenever you like.'

'I shall visit when I am ready. There is no hurry.'

'No, not at all.' The inspector glanced at me sidelong. 'Can I ask what your plans are?'

'What do you mean, Inspector?'

'Well, you could carry on here. You could still let the rooms – I can transfer the lease to you – and you could do some work for me…?'

It was the offer I would have jumped at a few weeks

251

before, but so much had changed. 'I would like to stay at Baker Street and let the rooms. The rest I will think over.' But even as I said it, I knew I would not write reports for Inspector Lestrade again. That belonged to my old life, and to the pipe-dream I had had of returning to it and finding Jack along the way.

'Good, good.' The inspector rubbed his hands. 'I had better go down and wait for the team. Goodbye, Mrs Hudson.' He raised a hand to the others, and clattered downstairs.

Dr Watson looked at the open doorway. 'I should probably go as well. They may need a medic.' He stood up and brushed down his trousers. 'You too, Holmes.'

Sherlock straightened his cuff. 'I shall follow you down shortly, Watson.'

'Yes.' Dr Watson looked at him, then at me, and I couldn't quite make out his expression. 'Goodnight, Mrs Hudson.'

Sherlock came to sit by me. 'What are you doing?' I had put my right hand over my left, but he had caught a glimpse. Carefully, tenderly, he moved it away and touched the indentation where my wedding ring had been.

'I cannot wear it,' I said. 'I have been wanting to take it off, ever since—'

'Your hand looks bare without it.' He looked away. 'I should go downstairs and help.'

He stood up, and so did I. I longed to catch hold of his hand and never let him go. But he wanted to be downstairs tying up the loose ends. Perhaps I was the biggest loose end of all. And yet— I couldn't help it. I caught his hand as I had told myself I should not, and looked into his eyes. 'Is it over?'

He smiled as he looked down at me, and shook his head. 'It isn't over.' He took off his signet ring and held it to the tip of my ring finger. I nodded, and he slid the ring into place. 'It has only just begun.'

CHAPTER 47

The Times, *22nd February 1881*

WANTED: MAID-OF-ALL-WORK, for a household of three adults near Regent's Park. Duties to be shared with the existing manservant. Some knowledge of cookery preferred; willingness a must. Liberal wages for the right candidate. Apply in writing to the office of this paper, quoting '221B'.

CHAPTER 48

221B Baker Street, 22nd February 1881

I watched my hand rise and fall with his chest, outlined in the dim light from the fire. 'When did you first—'

'First what, Nell?' he whispered back.

'Don't tease me, Sherlock.'

'First fall in love with you? Let me think... Oh, it was when you were dressed as that delightful old woman.' I punched him on the shoulder. 'Ow!' he whispered, laughing. Then he sat up in bed and I snuggled against him. 'I am not sure. I knew that I cared about you quite early on.'

'Was it when you caught me with your wig and I confessed to you?'

'No, although it was all I could do to keep from laughing at first. Your face when I jumped out of the wardrobe . . . don't hit me...' He took hold of my wrist to make sure. 'It was before that.'

'Was it the day I changed my hair and wore the lilac dress?'

'Before that.' He let go of my wrist and stroked my hair. 'You weren't even in the room. It was when you went downstairs, just after I had made some stupid remark about busybodying and Watson had called you a childless widow, and I knew from the sound of your footsteps that you had heard us. I was thoroughly ashamed, and then that same day you caught me got up as a clergyman. You could easily have got your own back or even given me notice, but after your initial surprise you were entirely professional. Before that day I had thought of you as the landlady, the person who brought up my breakfast tray and made light conversation. And the day after, when you appeared with a new hairstyle and a light dress – oh, my heart went out to you, and I would have done anything to take my words back. But I had already decided that you were interesting. I started to learn your little ways, and of course that was how I came to jump out of the wardrobe at you, and how we got here.' He ran his hand down my back and pulled me closer.

'I am glad you did. If you had not...' I shivered at the memory of Napper twisting his lies around me, that night in the police station, and what might have happened next.

'Don't think about that. It didn't happen, and it will never happen now.' He kissed the top of my head. 'Your turn. When did you first fall in love with me?'

'Oh, that would have to be when you pushed me up against the alley wall and kissed me. How could I resist such a charmer?' He grinned, and tickled me. 'Stop it!' I whispered. 'You'll wake the whole house!' He laughed, and pinned me down, and kissed me over and over.

Afterwards, while he slept, I remembered how I had sat by the sitting-room window trying to spot the man I had been told would call about the rooms. My eye had flitted from person to person until it was caught by a tall, thin young man, carrying his hat. He was striding from the direction of the park with a spring in his step, looking about him. He pulled a slip of paper from his pocket, glanced at it, and stopped. He looked up at the house and I moved away from the window; I did not want him to catch me out. I risked a peep; he was on the front step now, and I watched him push back his hair, put his hat on, and button his coat. I watched him hide. And though I knew no more than his name, though to me he was no more than a useful cover for my plans, something about him touched my heart.

I kissed Sherlock on the forehead, and lay down beside him.

CHAPTER 49

221B Baker Street, 13th September 1882

I fastened my earring and turned towards him. 'How do I look?'

'Beautiful, of course.' Sherlock handed me my fan.

'And you look most distinguished. I like you in tails.'

'Thank you.' He half-bowed. 'We had better go; Billy is outside with the carriage.'

I looked at the pair of us in the mirror. Sherlock was immaculate in evening dress, with a neatly trimmed beard which made him look about ten years older. I wore a deep-red velvet gown, one of Angel's finest, and full-length gloves, and my dark hair was piled high. 'I shall enjoy this.'

'So shall I. I wish every suspect had such good taste in music.' He gave me his arm and we went downstairs, stopping on the way to say goodbye to Dr Watson, who was writing away at his desk.

Dr Watson looked us up and down. 'Very nice.' He smiled. 'Make sure you tell me all about it later.'

'Well, don't wait up; we'll probably be late home.'

'All right. Look after each other, won't you.' He picked up

his pen again.

Billy touched his hat from the box as we opened the front door, and Sherlock helped me into the carriage. 'Ready, Billy?'

'Course. Royal Opera House, here we come.' Sherlock took his seat beside me, and rapped his cane on the window.

He sat back and we watched London roll past. 'Do you know what day it is?' he said, his voice light.

'Yes.' I looked at him and his face was carefully blank. 'It's four years today since Jack left.' Sometimes I thought of Jack and wondered how he was, and whether he ever thought of me: when I came across our face-down wedding photograph at the back of my desk drawer, or when the atlas in the bookcase caught my eye. I imagined him lifting a child up into the air, or looking across a field in the sun. Then I shook my head, and he dissolved again.

'I prefer to think of it as three years to go. A sort of anniversary, but in reverse.'

'I like that.' Through my glove I touched the plain gold ring, almost a wedding band, that he had given me. 'Though it seems a long time to wait.'

He looked out of the window. 'But we should.'

'Yes, we should.' I put my hand on his. 'Does that mean that I get a reverse anniversary present?'

'Of course! A night at the opera.' He grinned at me. 'I'd buy you a diamond necklace, dear, but my landlady takes all my money.'

'Yes, but she is very accommodating.' I leaned forward and gave him my brightest smile.

'And rather distracting.' He folded his arms. 'We're at work, remember.'

'With excellent tickets. A box, no less.'

'Well, it is a present. And it will be much easier to spy

from. You have your glasses?' I showed the opera glasses in my evening bag, and he patted his pocket. 'It is time.' The carriage rolled to a stop.

Sherlock jumped down and held out a hand for me. I descended the steps, he tucked my arm through his, and we walked towards the dazzling lights and the crowds, just one more couple going out for the evening. And I knew that under his sober evening suit his heart thumped as loudly as mine, as we walked towards another adventure.

ACKNOWLEDGEMENTS

First of all, thank you to everyone who read and commented on the manuscript of A *House Of Mirrors*: Chloe Garner, Liz Hill, Thérèse Markham, Tamara Rogers, Gaynor Seymour and Alaura Shouse. Apologies to those of you who lost sleep because you had to find out the ending!

Thanks as always to John Croall, whose indefatigable proofreading skills rooted out cabin fever and some highly unseasonal asparagus! Any errors which remain are entirely down to me.

I would also like to thank (again) Nickianne Moody of Liverpool John Moores University for allowing me access to the Liddell Hart Collection of Costume, where I researched late-Victorian fashion. I have no idea how Victorian women managed to do anything at all, given the outfits they had to wear! You can find out more about the archives at https:// eccentricarchive.wordpress.com.

I should also thank the internet in general, as I've spent so much time delving into Victorian plumbing, emigration policy, the history of mealtimes, late nineteenth-century mourning dress . . . the list could go on for ever! I found Tasmanian Archives Online absolutely invaluable for browsing digitised nineteenth-century immigration registers (at http://search.archives.tas.gov.au/Default.aspx), and I also read digitised copies of *The Mercury* newspaper at the National Library of Australia's website: http://trove.nla.gov.au/newspaper/. My characters are indebted to *Beeton's Book of Household Management* (facsimile edition, Chancellor Press, 1994). Without it, they would have been eating all sorts of unseasonal food (we'll leave the asparagus out of this), and the menu plans saved them from a diet of chops and cutlets.

Huge thanks to the late Sir Arthur Conan Doyle for creating the great detective, and I hope he wouldn't mind the liberties I've taken.

But as ever, the biggest thanks are to my husband Stephen Lenhardt. He is always my first beta-reader, and as this was my first novel-length work to be published, I was even more than usually paranoid. Did it make sense? Would the villain be obvious? Most importantly, did Nell fiddle with her hair too much? To my great relief, he enjoyed it, and we've gone through the whole process a few times since...

Finally, thank you for reading *A House of Mirrors* and I hope you enjoyed it. If you did, a short review or a rating on Amazon or Goodreads would be very much appreciated. Ratings and reviews, however short, help readers to discover books.

FONT CREDIT

Title page and chapter heading font: Libre Baskerville by Impallari Type: https://www.fontsquirrel.com/fonts/libre-baskerville License: SIL Open Font License v. 1.10.

ABOUT THE AUTHOR

Liz Hedgecock grew up in London, England, did an English degree, then took forever to start writing. After several years working in the National Health Service, some short stories crept into the world. A few even won prizes. Then the stories started to grow longer…

Now Liz travels between the nineteenth and twenty-first centuries, murdering people. To be fair, she does usually clean up after herself.

Liz's reimaginings of Sherlock Holmes, the Pippa Parker cozy mystery series, the Caster & Fleet Victorian mystery series (written with Paula Harmon), the Magical Bookshop series and the Maisie Frobisher Mysteries are available in ebook and paperback.

Liz lives in Cheshire with her husband and two sons, and when she's not writing or child-wrangling you can usually find her reading, messing about on Twitter, or exploring museums and art galleries. That's her story, anyway, and she's sticking to it.

Website/blog: http://lizhedgecock.wordpress.com
Facebook: http://www.facebook.com/lizhedgecockwrites

Twitter: http://twitter.com/lizhedgecock
Goodreads: https://www.goodreads.com/lizhedgecock
Amazon author page: http://author.to/LizH

BOOKS BY LIZ HEDGECOCK

Mrs Hudson & Sherlock Holmes series (novels)
A House Of Mirrors
In Sherlock's Shadow
A Spider's Web

Maisie Frobisher Mysteries (novels)
All At Sea
Off The Map
Gone To Ground
In Plain Sight

Caster & Fleet Mysteries (with Paula Harmon)
The Case of the Black Tulips
The Case of the Runaway Client
The Case of the Deceased Clerk
The Case of the Masquerade Mob
The Case of the Fateful Legacy
The Case of the Crystal Kisses

Pippa Parker Mysteries (novels)
Murder At The Playgroup
Murder In The Choir
A Fete Worse Than Death

Murder in the Meadow
The QWERTY Murders
Past Tense

The Magical Bookshop (novels)
Every Trick in the Book
Brought to Book
Double Booked
By the Book

Sherlock & Jack series (novellas)
A Jar Of Thursday
Something Blue
A Phoenix Rises

Halloween Sherlock series (novelettes)
The Case of the Snow-White Lady
Sherlock Holmes and the Deathly Fog
The Case of the Curious Cabinet

Short stories
The Secret Notebook of Sherlock Holmes
Bitesize
The Adventure of the Scarlet Rosebud
The Case of the Peculiar Pantomime (a Caster & Fleet short mystery)
Christmas Presence (collection)

For children (with Zoe Harmon)
A Christmas Carrot

WHITE
RHINO
BOOKS

265

Printed in Poland
by Amazon Fulfillment
Poland Sp. z o.o., Wrocław
12 February 2023

1c7c75ee-260a-4828-83ee-fbe2d826a4d0R01